A Secret
for the
LIFEBOAT
SISTERS

BOOKS BY TILLY TENNANT

TILLY TENNANT

A Secret
for the
LIFEBOAT
SISTERS

bookouture

Published by Bookouture in 2023

An imprint of Storyfire Ltd.
Carmelite House
50 Victoria Embankment
London EC4Y 0DZ

www.bookouture.com

ISBN: 978-1-83790-759-5
eBook ISBN: 978-1-83790-758-8

To the people who keep us safe, thank you.

CHAPTER ONE

It should have been a perfect August bank holiday. For most it was a well-earned day off and valued time with loved ones. For Gaby Smith, oldest daughter of Jill and Jack Morrow and who would always consider herself a Morrow, it was also the culmination of a year's worth of meticulous planning. A year where she'd battled to juggle a tempestuous family life with the demands of running a home, working as a maths tutor and fundraising for the local lifeboat station. This Flag Day was supposed to be the triumphant pay-off.

The annual event was the most important in the lifeboat service's fundraising calendar. The lifeboat station would throw open its doors to visitors, and the town would come alive, all in the name of getting the donations they needed to continue their vital lifesaving work for another year. In the past, Gaby's mother, Jill, had always taken charge, but after losing her husband – Gaby's dad – at sea, Gaby had seen that someone needed to take that burden from her, and she'd been more than happy to do just that. Nobody loved organising quite like Gaby did, and for a cause so close to her heart, she'd give her all.

But as everyone else soaked up the sun on the beach or

explored the lifeboat station and marvelled at the boats, ate ice cream perched lazily on walls and benches or drank cider, tried their hand at hooking the duck and naming the donkey or guessing how many sweets were in the jar, or any of the other myriad activities Gaby had organised, she wasn't enjoying it as she ought to have been. She was out of sight, quietly seething.

In a secluded spot on the beach, in the shadow of the walls that separated it from the promenade above, Gaby stood with Killian, wife and husband glaring at one another. This man, who she'd vowed to love and cherish, the man she'd had children with, the man she'd given so much for – she didn't even know who he was anymore. She thought, as she looked at him now, that she might even hate him.

'I've done nothing wrong.' There wasn't a flicker of remorse, not a single note of empathy in his voice, no sign that he even understood what he'd done. His dark eyes were defiant, his chin jutting out in a gesture of stubbornness that Gaby knew only too well. 'I'm not going to apologise. I'd do the same again, every time.'

'You really don't get it, do you?'

'No,' he said, his voice so irritatingly level that she itched to slap him. 'I don't get it. I did the right thing, and I'm not the one who got caught out with—'

'I didn't get caught out doing anything!'

'And neither did I. If anyone ought to be apologising, it's you.'

'I have – a million times.'

'I didn't put our marriage in danger, so I don't see why I'm the bad guy.'

'How can you stand there in front of me and say that? Of course you did! The minute you decided to keep secrets, you put our marriage in danger! If you can't share something like that with me, then how can we even say we have one?'

'Gab, you're overreacting—'

'How dare you! How can you not understand how huge this is?'

'You're the one who pushed it that way,' Killian said coldly. 'At least I didn't—'

'Nothing happened!'

'I only have your word for that.'

'Then I don't know where we go from here,' Gaby said quietly.

'Me neither,' Killian said. 'So what now?'

'I don't know.'

Silence fell between them for the briefest time, and a word swam around in Gaby's head. She was terrified that it would come from Killian's mouth, but there was a part of her that could see no other way out of this corner their marriage had been forced into.

'Do you want a divorce?' she asked.

'No. Do you?'

'No, of course not! But we can't keep going on like this. I don't think I can get past you keeping such a huge secret from me. How can I ever trust a thing you say again? And how does that help us carry on if I can never believe you?'

'We've been over this a thousand times. I didn't tell you because I didn't see the point in complicating things.'

'Complicating things?' Gaby let out a mirthless laugh. 'Jesus, Killian! How much more complicated would things have got? It wasn't exactly plain sailing before. And the way this year has gone...'

'You've been to blame as much as me for how this year's gone.'

'Maybe.' Gaby was forced to acknowledge that much. 'Maybe you're right. In which case, I'm amazed it's taken so long to have this conversation at all.'

'You certainly picked the day for it,' Killian said with a wry glance around. The beach was bathed in golden summer sunshine, children racing up and down the sand and leaping over the foam-topped waves as they rolled gently in, gulls circling overhead and tinkling music carried on the air from the travelling fair. 'There's enough going on today; we should talk about this later.'

'I don't think I can even look at you, let alone talk to you. You kept the biggest secret from me, and yet I'm the one being unreasonable; I'm the one who doesn't deserve trust? I never lied to you about anything—'

'No, you didn't lie,' he cut in. 'You just kept things from me. Which is what I did too, but somehow it's OK when you do it, but not when I do.'

'What you did was so much bigger.'

'Was it? Are you sure about that?'

'I don't want to hear it.' She paused, the next sentence forming almost against her will. 'I think we're done.'

'Good, because I'm needed at the station—'

'No, Killian, *we're done*. I don't see a way out of this. You don't trust me and I don't trust you. It's gone too far. The only way this can end is with divorce.'

'So you *do* want a divorce? Is that what this has been about from the start?'

'Maybe... yes, I think I do.'

For a second there was such anger, such pain in his eyes, she was afraid he'd lash out. But his expression cleared into something so cold she could barely believe they'd ever been in love.

'Fine,' he said. 'Whatever.'

Gaby watched him walk away without another word. She drew in a breath and put a hand to the wall to steady herself. This was her day. Flag Day, the fundraising event she'd worked like mad to make happen, and her arrogant, lying husband wasn't going to ruin it for her.

She took a compact from her bag, opened it and checked her reflection in the tiny mirror, rubbing away a smudge of mascara before snapping it closed again. The raffle was due to be drawn; she had to get over to the lifeboat station to do it and announce the winning numbers. Killian would be there, and it would hurt to see him after what had just happened, but this was about raising vital funds for the lifeboat service and it was bigger than both of them – even she could see that.

As she climbed the steps from the beach and emerged onto the busy promenade, people she knew greeted her from every angle.

'Brilliant day! Well done!'

'Cracking Flag Day!'

'It's the best we've ever had; your dad would have been proud!'

She acknowledged everyone with gracious nods and the odd word, every inch the cool, graceful, unflappable woman that Port Promise believed her to be. But inside, she felt desperately broken. She wanted to fall to the pavement and sob. She wanted to tell them all how her life was a sham, a hologram of success she'd always projected without ever really knowing why she felt the need to. Her sisters – Clara and Ava – were open and honest, and in return they received sympathy and love. Gaby had never been like them – she'd never been able to expose her vulnerabilities in that way. Perhaps that was why nobody ever offered her support, and why, as the years went by, she'd felt as if she'd been slowly drowning with nobody to save her.

It wasn't just the lies – perhaps she could have forgiven Killian those – it was all the other things too. Suspicion, jealousy, irrational behaviour, double standards... And it was the not being there for her. It was the always putting other things first. She loved Killian, despite it all, but she was sick and tired of him. Love alone wasn't enough, and she had nothing else left to give.

As she reached the lifeboat station, she became aware of a sudden flurry of excitement, of electricity in the air, and a crowd forming rapidly at the launch ramp. If there had been an alarm, she hadn't noticed it, but perhaps she ought not be surprised; she'd been busy, and her mind had been cluttered with thoughts of what her life might be from this day forward, the echoes of Killian's words in her ears, the sight of his stubborn anger still in front of her eyes when she closed them.

'They're going out!'

'It's a rescue; a real one!'

In all the years she'd been connected to the lifeboat service, it never failed to amaze her how excited people became at the thought of a launch. It was strange really, because somewhere out of sight was someone in distress, and when all was said and done, that wasn't a cause for excitement at all. But she also understood it. People were thrilled and awed by the men and women who went out to sea to bring those poor souls back. It was like watching a real-life movie, rooting for the protagonist, hoping for that Hollywood happy ending.

Then Gaby noticed her sister Clara watching the station from the safer distance of the promenade, rocking baby William in her arms.

She went over. 'Hey...'

Clara nodded towards the lifeboat crew as they ran to the station. Killian was amongst them, as was their youngest sister Ava, Ava's boyfriend Harry and Clara's partner Cormac. 'They don't even get Flag Day off, do they?'

Gaby shielded her eyes to scan the horizon.

'Doesn't look like it. What's the shout for?'

'Not sure,' Clara replied, her eyes on the horizon now too. 'At least the sea's calm, isn't it? That's something. Hopefully it'll be a quick one.'

In the August sunshine, the beach was almost tropical today. The sea was a turquoise millpond, calm and bright, flecked with darker patches where rocks and reefs lay beneath, lazy currents tracking the surface where the sun glinted from the crests of waves.

Gaby nodded. It was beautiful, and it was hard to believe anyone was in any danger from it today, though she knew better than to trust the ocean, no matter how benign it looked. She continued to look for the source of the Mayday and then caught sight of the shape of a boat – perhaps a cargo vessel – near the rocks of the headland and wondered if that might be it. 'I'll go and see what I can find out,' she decided out loud.

Clara pulled a silk scarf around William's face to keep the sun from it and nodded. 'I'm going to find some shade – I think he's overheating. Let me know, will you?'

Crossing from the fierce sunlight into the cool of the station, Gaby went to the radio room and found Maxine, one of the shore crew operatives, running through preparations to launch.

'What is it?'

Maxine didn't look up, but her answer was terse. It wasn't her usual manner, and Gaby understood that at work things were different. 'Nothing to worry about. Stranded vessel, anchor stuck on something.'

'Does that need a lifeboat?'

'Casualty on board, so...'

So the lifeboat was going to pick up the casualty? That made more sense than simply helping them to haul anchor, although she supposed they might do that too if they could. It sounded fairly straightforward in any event.

Gaby left Maxine and slipped outside quietly, doing her best not to get in the way of the launch. By now she could hear the crew in the locker room getting their kit on. It didn't sound tense, but they would be focused on their task and she didn't want to distract anyone. They were against the clock after all, even during shouts that didn't seem dangerous.

When she found Clara again, her mum, Jill, and their old family friend, Marina, were with her. Both Jill and Marina had lived their whole lives in Port Promise and, like everyone born and raised there, the lifeboat service was at the centre of everything they did. It meant they were always on edge when it was called out. Their lives were linked with everyone who served at the station.

'Where are the kids?' Gaby asked her mum, looking around for her two children.

'Bob's got them,' Marina said. 'He took them to the carousel... ah, here they are now.'

Gaby watched Elijah and Fern race over. At ten and eight, they were both old enough to understand the gravity of a lifeboat shout. Fern, in particular, worried every time her father went out – even though she was proud of him – since she'd lost her grandfather on a rescue. Elijah was more thrilled by it. If Gaby knew anything, she knew he was destined for a life of adventure in one form or another and would very likely end up serving on the lifeboat himself, despite her opposition to it. Perhaps even because of her opposition, if he was anything like his father.

Gaby was pricked with guilt at the sight of them. Was she really about to break up their family? Were she and Killian really going to do this? It would turn their worlds inside out, and yet they couldn't carry on as they were.

'Did the boat get called out?' Elijah panted.

Gaby nodded. 'Yes, but I've seen Max and it's nothing to worry about.'

'So Dad went?' he demanded.

'Yes, your dad's gone.'

'Dad always goes,' Elijah said, and the way his chin jutted now, dark hair and dark eyes full of steel, for a startling moment he looked exactly as Killian had done only moments before as Gaby had tried, and perhaps failed, to save their marriage.

Fern turned her gaze to the sea. 'Hope he's all right.'

'It's a routine thing.' Gaby put an arm around her, trying to sound bright, even though inside she was dying. Fern was like her sister Clara had always been – gentler than either Gaby or Killian, eager for harmony, wanting always to see everyone safe and happy no matter what that meant for her. She worried far too much for such a young girl. 'And look at the sea – calm as anything today. He'll be fine.'

She'd barely finished her sentence when the all-weather boat emerged, flying down the launch ramp to cheers and applause from the beach, a spray of seawater in its wake. Then they watched as it stabilised from the impact on the water and then throttled up, racing across the waves and making good time. Gaby wondered why they hadn't taken the smaller boat out if they were simply picking up a casualty, but perhaps they were planning to free the stuck vessel, and if it was the cargo ship she'd seen, the anchor would be big.

After a couple of minutes, they'd reached the stricken vessel. As Gaby had suspected, it was the one she'd seen close to the headland of Promise Rocks. The lifeboat manoeuvred alongside it, and then Gaby looked down at Fern.

'See, what did I tell you? Nothing to worry—'

Her words were stolen by a sudden, searing explosion. It rocked the bay, echoing from the cliffs and the harbour walls, sending gulls screeching into the air. And then the abrupt cacophony of sound receded, and an eerie, shocked silence descended on the crowds of the beach.

Where the lifeboat had last been sighted, the sea had blasted into the air and then rained back down, obscuring both vessels from view. Then a wave radiated outwards, sending a swell so big crashing onto the headland that they could see it from the promenade, miles away. Thick black smoke started to pour from one of the vessels, though it was difficult to tell which one. It was like a film, as if Gaby wasn't watching a real thing happen. She only came back to reality when Fern began to cry.

'It's the boat,' Clara breathed. 'Gaby, it's the lifeboat!'

'Are they dead?' Fern sobbed. 'Mum, are they dead?'

Gaby gave her head the tiniest shake. For the first time since her children had been born, she didn't have the right words to soothe them. Looking up for help, she could see that her mum, Clara and Marina had nothing either. They were in shock, just as she was. And they were in fear, just like her. She had to look strong for Elijah and Fern, but inside she was already falling apart. Since the night her dad had been lost at sea on a rescue, she'd dreaded it happening again. Worry had characterised every call-out as she waited for news, but she'd hoped never to have to grieve anyone from the boats ever again. Now this. Had a new nightmare come to turn her life upside down once more?

She desperately loved every single person aboard that boat, even the husband she'd just decided to divorce. Were they really all gone?

CHAPTER TWO

EIGHT MONTHS EARLIER

Gaby stretched out a leg and nudged Killian with her foot. It was mid-January, but an onlooker could be forgiven for being confused by the smell of a turkey dinner on the air and the sight of Christmas bunting adorning the walls of the sitting room of Thistledown Cottage. It was all part of a late, alternative celebration for Cormac – local hero and owner of the fish shack on the beach – who'd been in hospital during the actual festive season and had missed out.

'Oi!'

'Leave him alone, poor lad,' Jill said with a low chuckle. 'Must be worn out.'

'Nope.' Gaby kicked him playfully again. 'He's been asleep for long enough – it's boring. All those people in the village who think he's this handsome hero wouldn't be quite so sure if they could see him now.'

Gaby was about to nudge Killian again when Cormac and Clara walked into the living room. She could smell the cold of the night air on them – had they been out in the garden together? Gaby couldn't fail to notice how they were suddenly standing close to one another too. There was an air of... something seemed different. Now she thought about it, they'd both been missing for quite a while.

'You two look happy,' she said.

'We are.' Clara grabbed Cormac's arm and gave it an excited squeeze. He shifted on his crutches and smiled down at her. 'There's something we want to tell you – right, Cormac?'

'Hang on,' Gaby said, sitting up straight on the sofa and slapping Killian on the thigh. 'Wake up!'

Killian snorted one final snore and then opened his eyes, pushing off the paper crown that had fallen to one side. 'What? Is there a shout? Shit... where's my pager?'

'No,' Gaby said. 'Calm down; you didn't miss anything. We just decided you were being antisocial and it was high time you got up. And Clara and Cormac want to tell us something.'

'Ignore her,' Jill said. 'We all thought you'd earned a Christmas Day nap.'

'It's not Christmas Day,' Gaby reminded her. 'This is our alternative Christmas. And as it's for Cormac, because he spent the proper one in hospital, he's the only person allowed to snore in front of the telly.'

'Don't be mean,' Jill replied with a laugh.

'Actually...' Cormac glanced at Clara, and she smiled and nodded encouragement. But then he leaned closer to her and lowered his voice. 'Did you want to wait for Ava and Harry to come back?'

'Bloody hell, just tell us!' Gaby said. 'We know you've got something to say, and we can probably guess what it is.'

Clara smiled at her. 'Might have known you'd figure it out.'

'It wasn't exactly hard.'

'Sorry...' Cormac's mum, Sinead, cut in, her gaze going from Cormac to Clara and back again. 'I seem to be missing something here.'

Cormac's smile grew. 'I got her, Ma. Clara's the one I told you about all those months ago, and here we are!'

'I knew it!' Gaby said smugly. 'I knew you two would get together. We were definitely rooting for it – weren't we, Kill?'

'Don't get me involved!' He grinned. 'But well done, you two,' he added. 'Thank God you've finally sorted it out – we thought we might have to get involved like we did with Harry and Ava.'

'We're all thrilled for you.' Gaby looked around and everyone nodded. 'In fact, I think this calls for another drink!'

'Cormac will be the most amazing dad.' Gaby slipped her hand into Killian's as they walked back to Thistledown Cottage. Elijah and Fern had begged to stay with their grandma overnight, so Gaby and Killian had walked them all back to Jill's and ended up staying for a couple of drinks before heading back home. It was gone two in the morning, and Port Promise was silent and dark, save for the orange of the streetlamps and the sea breathing in and out.

'But he's not the dad, is he?'

'What difference does that make?'

'None to him, I expect. He's a good guy, and he'll do his best for Clara and the baby. It's not him who might be the issue.'

'Logan?'

'Who else? When he gets wind of this, he's going to be pissed off. Most men would be – especially when you consider Clara ended it with him, so he probably still wants to be with her. In fact, we saw that first-hand tonight when he called her, didn't we? He hasn't really left her alone since they split up.'

'But he wouldn't try to come between them, would he?'

'That spoiled brat? I wouldn't put it past him. Even if he didn't still love Clara, it's the sort of thing he'd do out of spite.'

'He wasn't that bad. You never did like him much though, did you?'

'He was all right. Might have even got along eventually,

except he never gave us much of a reason to like him – even you have to admit that.'

'At least we took a more straightforward route.'

Killian gave her a sideways look. 'Your dad hated me when he first met me.'

'He did not! He was being a dad... they're always protective of daughters – you'll be exactly the same with Fern.'

'Oh, Fern's not going anywhere with any man. I know too much about what makes them tick to trust a single one.'

'Do you lump yourself with that untrustworthy brigade?'

He laughed. 'God yes!'

'Then my dad was right to be wary, wasn't he?'

'Oh, he was...' Killian halted on the path and pulled her into his arms. 'He was very right, because I'm a very bad one...'

The wind lifted her auburn hair as he kissed her hard.

'How far away is the house again?' she asked breathlessly as he pulled away to stare at her with such intensity, there was no mistaking what he wanted. She wanted it too, so badly it was like a sudden burning fever.

'It might be too far,' he said, leading her by the hand, down the steps of the promenade and down to the beach, where he pushed her up against the wall and kissed her again.

'Not here!' she said, half laughing but half breathless with desire.

'Who's going to see? Nobody is out now.' He lowered his voice, his breath on her neck as he whispered, 'You want to live dangerously, right? How often do we get to be spontaneous these days?'

'Your pager might go off,' she sighed as he kissed her neck.

'It might...' He pulled her coat aside for his lips to explore her collarbone, and waves of desire pulsed through her. 'Then again... it might not.'

Thoughts of family and lifeboats and the world at large left her mind as his hands travelled her body beneath her coat. She couldn't remember the last time she'd wanted him this badly, and so she gave in.

The next morning, Gaby woke as the sun came into the bedroom and smiled at the sight of Killian sleeping beside her. His dark hair was tousled from sleep, his toned chest gently rising and falling, and his firm jaw seemed to advertise the strength of character he possessed. It wasn't often they had a night that was free of the lifeboats or the children or a million other demands on their time, and it was like they were newly married again.

Close to twelve years on, he was still as handsome as the day she'd met him, when he was out on a cycling trip from a neighbouring village. He'd stopped at the cafe for a drink, and Gaby had been there with Clara, chatting to Betty, who'd only been a Saturday girl back then. He'd always been sporty and well built, though these days he put even more effort into it to stay fit for his lifeboat duties, and so his muscles were even more defined than they'd been back then, despite him heading towards thirty-seven.

Memories of the day they'd met were as fresh now as they had always been. It was strange, but Gaby almost divided her life into two halves – before Killian and afterwards – because the impact of meeting him had been so great. It had changed everything. She'd had boyfriends, but she'd never known that love could be so consuming, that a person could entirely lose themselves in the soul of another until she'd met Killian. All three women had ogled him as he'd sat down with his orange juice. Clara had dared Gaby to go over and say hello, and even though Gaby had been nervous at the prospect, she'd never been one to back away from a challenge, so she'd strode over to his table.

'You want my number, right?' she'd said.

He'd looked up in surprise but with some amusement. Then he'd noticed Clara and Betty giggling behind their hands, and, perhaps to teach Gaby a lesson, thinking she was jerking him around, he'd grabbed a napkin from the table and handed it to her.

'Go ahead – write it down. Maybe I'll call you.'

Gaby was in too deep at this point. She'd written it down and then swaggered back to Clara and Betty, trying to look as cool as possible but fairly certain the stupidly handsome man she'd just tried to chat up thought she was a silly little girl not worth his time. Shortly after that, he'd drunk the rest of his orange juice and gone on his way with a casual nod.

But a day later he'd called her. She hadn't even got his name at the cafe, but as soon as she'd heard his voice, she'd known it was him. Just as the first time they'd slept together, she'd known he was the one.

The early months had been tempestuous, incredibly physical and very intense. They laughed at the same jokes and liked the same movies, but they had firm opinions that didn't always align and their arguments were spectacular – almost as spectacular as the making up. They were soon obsessed with one another, and Gaby understood now that perhaps it had scared her parents a little. But Killian had only two gears – everything or nothing – and it was one of the sexiest things about him. Gaby fell for his passion, his drive, his determination to get what he wanted and his refusal to compromise.

They'd mellowed over the years – having children had necessitated that – but sometimes she'd still see a spark of that man. Sometimes it was infuriating, and sometimes it reminded her of what she fell in love with. It was why they'd clashed like the lava from an erupting volcano hitting the sea when he'd first told her he was joining the lifeboat crew.

She'd spent her life watching the sea during every storm, praying for her dad to be safe when he got called out, and her grandfather before that, and now the man she loved wanted to go out there to do the same. She wasn't sure she could bear watching and praying for another person who meant everything to her. There'd been no consultation, and although she'd always known he was exactly that man, she'd been angry at that too.

He'd acted as if her view didn't matter, not because he didn't care about her or her feelings, but because he was the sort of man who couldn't turn away from a path once he'd set his mind to it. And in his mind, once it was made up, nothing was more important than his duty to save others. Neither had wanted to give in, and the fallout had been seismic. It had taken her dad to step in and smooth things over in the end.

Once Jack had got used to Killian and realised he was serious about Gaby, he'd come to like and respect him. They'd become close, and Jack had looked on him as a son even before he'd been a son-in-law. When they'd got married, Jack had been happy to welcome him officially to the family, where Jill had been more cautious, and so he'd been behind Killian's application for the lifeboats every step of the way.

Gaby leaned across now and pressed her lips to his bare chest.

He opened his eyes and grinned. 'Again?'

'We have a few hours until the kids are due back – wouldn't want to waste them, would we?'

He looped his hands around her waist and slid her across the bed towards him. 'Even with morning breath?'

'I'll hold my nose.'

'I meant yours.'

'Bastard!' She giggled.

As they melted into a kiss, a bleeping sound came from the floor next to the bed.

'You're joking!' Gaby looked up as Killian leaped off the bed to look at his pager.

He shrugged. 'Better go – sorry.'

'Not as sorry as you will be!' she said, flopping onto her back as he pulled on his clothes.

'Promises, promises,' he said, laughing as he ran out of the bedroom, shoes in his hand.

She listened to him clatter down the stairs and then out of the front door, leaving the house in sudden silence.

'And this is my life,' she said to herself.

She could have gone back to sleep, but she knew from experience that she'd never be able to rest while Killian was out on a rescue. So she got up to make some coffee and wait for his return.

CHAPTER THREE

Two months later, the sound of the post dropping onto the mat accompanied Gaby signing off from the first pupil of the day. She loved her new job working as an online maths tutor. She'd been uncertain at first but had been encouraged by Killian to make use of her talent for numbers. While the kids had been young, she'd dedicated her time to the family – especially as Killian was often working or at the lifeboat station and couldn't share the parental duties as much as some other husbands might. But as Elijah and Fern were growing up and needing her less and less, she'd felt increasingly redundant. It was Killian who'd suggested she set up as a private tutor, after a chance conversation with a colleague who'd been looking for one. It fitted in with her life, meant she could work remotely so she didn't have to travel out of Port Promise and, most importantly, she felt useful and valued again.

With half an hour until the next session was due to start, she got up and went to collect the post while the kettle boiled. It was the usual assortment of unwanted advertising, a postcard from the school to celebrate Fern's exemplary behaviour and an innocuous but official-looking envelope. Gaby took it all to the table to go through while her tea brewed. The postcard she put to one side so she could congratulate Fern when she got back from school, the advertising she mostly binned, and then she turned her attention to the mysterious envelope. With a growing frown, she read through the information.

'Brilliant,' she muttered as she tossed it on the table and went to take the teabag out of her mug. 'Just perfect.'

One thing she was certain of, it wasn't her who'd been speeding in the car that was registered in her name – she barely used it, and she never went as far as the motorway out of Cornwall. She stared out of the window, watching the March winds rattle the branches of trees. Though it must have been Killian driving her car, it was odd for him to be that far from home too. Occasionally he needed to drive out to see a client, but he'd deliberately requested to cover a territory in the immediate vicinity of Port Promise in case he needed to rush back for a lifeboat call-out.

She went to get her phone and googled the location where the car had been caught on camera and her frown deepened. The road into Bristol? Why would Killian need to go to Bristol? He'd never mentioned knowing anyone there.

She went back to the table and read the letter again. Killian was at the station doing some routine stuff and was unlikely to answer his phone, though she wanted very much to talk to him about what she was looking at. Aside from being irked that the speeding fine and points were in her name, which meant another thing to sort out, she just couldn't see why he'd be driving to Bristol. It was a city with no obvious connection to him, it was on a weekday and he'd never mentioned he was going to be so far from home.

Her musings were interrupted by the sound of a call coming through on her laptop. Her next pupil was waiting, and this mystery would have to wait too.

. . .

As they'd arranged that morning, Killian had picked up the kids from school and had taken them straight over to the lifeboat station so that Gaby could do her last tutoring session of the day in peace. Not only that, but Elijah had been bugging to go over for weeks. Gaby hated the idea of course, because she worried that the more contact Elijah had with the station, the more likely he was to end up joining the service, but Killian had argued that denying him these opportunities would only make him want them more. And so Gaby had been forced to relent.

She was peeling potatoes for supper when she heard them come in. Elijah and Fern were full of excitement and tales of what they'd done at the station with their dad. He'd set them both tasks, such as polishing the ornamental bell that hung at the door of the locker room and straightening the photos and certificates of commendation and cleaning the glass, and though they were silly jobs that hadn't really needed doing, and jobs that usually no child would want to do, it had clearly instilled a sense of purpose and importance in both children. She'd never known them to be so excited about cleaning, and she said so.

'But it wasn't cleaning,' Elijah said indignantly. 'That bell is important – they used to ring it so everyone could run to the ship!'

'Yes, I know,' Gaby soothed.

'They both did a brilliant job,' Killian said.

'Can we go next time, Dad?' Fern asked.

'We'll see.'

'Right...' Gaby looked at them both in turn. 'Baths, supper, bed. Any homework you're trying to hide from me thinking I won't know if you don't do it?'

'No,' they said in unison.

Gaby frowned.

'Oh, I have some,' Fern said, as if she'd only just remembered it, which was clearly not true at all.

'Then you go upstairs and do that while Eli has a bath.

Then Elijah can do the homework he's not telling me about while you're in the bath, and then you can both have some supper. Right?'

'OK...'

Both children sloped off, and the living room was suddenly a lot quieter, the atmosphere suddenly tenser too. Or was that in Gaby's imagination?

In the future, she might pinpoint this event as the moment her troubles began, but right now, she only saw it as an opportune moment to get some answers.

'I'm starving,' Killian said. 'Don't suppose there are any leftovers in the fridge I can heat up?'

'Seriously?' Gaby asked. 'I'm cooking. You can wait another half hour surely?'

Killian went to the fridge, grabbed a handful of blueberries from an open punnet and shoved them into his mouth as he searched for something more substantial. When he closed the door again, he had a tub of leftovers in his hand. Gaby took the speeding fine from her pocket and smoothed it out on the table. She folded her arms and aimed a silent question at him as he caught sight of it.

'What's that?' he asked, his mouth full of cold rice.

'It's a speeding fine. In my name, but I wasn't driving, so thanks for that.'

Killian put down the tub and picked up the letter. 'I don't recall speeding.'

'Well you must have done. The photo is there, it's our car and it looks like you in it.'

'Bugger.'

'Yes, bugger! Those points are going on my licence, not yours, so thanks, Kill.'

He handed it to her. 'I'll sort it. It'll only take an email to tell them I was driving.'

'Make sure you do. Where were you going?'

'How should I know? It could be anywhere. I drive a lot; I can't remember where I was driving to every single day.'

'You'd remember this,' Gaby said carefully. 'It's, like, three weeks ago. And I checked where the road is... it's on the approach to Bristol. Is that ringing any bells?'

'Is it?' He shrugged with irritating nonchalance. 'I must have been going somewhere for work.'

'You don't ever go that far for work. You never go that far full stop unless you really have to because you never want to be far from the station, so don't tell me the fact you're hundreds of miles away isn't significant.'

'It's not hundreds of miles.'

'It's far enough!'

'What is this? Are you a private detective now? I have to report my every movement to you? So what if I went a bit further than usual for work – what does it matter?'

'It matters because I feel as if you're not being honest with me.'

'If you don't trust me, then isn't that a failing in you and not me?'

'Jesus, Killian!' Gaby cried, then checked her volume for fear of alerting the children to an argument. They weren't quite there yet, but it was coming. 'Why do you have to be so bloody facetious? I'm not being paranoid here – this is a long way from home and you didn't think to mention that you were going this far? You just hopped into the car one day and drove a six-hour round trip and didn't think that was worthy of note? What did you go to Bristol for?'

'I told you – it was work.'

'OK...' Gaby folded her arms. 'Which client?'

'You wouldn't know them.'

'I might.'

'Bakers.'

She was silent for a moment. She'd never heard of them and

it irked her that he'd been right. She also hated where her mind was going, because his evasiveness had triggered other suspicions, ones that she pushed out. Surely Killian wasn't doing something else in Bristol? Whatever the reason he'd been going there, it felt very much like he didn't want her to know what it was. If it was work-related, there would have been no reason not to tell her he was travelling that far at the time. So why didn't he? 'And you had to go?' she asked instead. 'All the way to Bristol? Didn't they have anyone closer?'

'Not in this instance. It was a rush job, some security breach. They needed someone on site ASAP, and I happened to be free.'

'I still don't get why it had to be you,' she grumbled. 'You're seriously telling me there wasn't a single engineer closer?'

'That's what I'm telling you.'

'But what about the station?'

'They know we have to earn a living and sometimes we can't get to a shout.'

Gaby pursed her lips. 'Now I know there's something fishy in it. You'd never deliberately miss a shout.'

'Sometimes even *I* have to.'

Gaby opened her mouth to reply. She didn't even know what was going to come out of it, and it was perhaps just as well that in the end she didn't get to say anything.

Fern's voice came from the top of the stairs. 'Mum! Can you help with this sum? It's too hard!'

Killian went through to the living room and switched on the television. Gaby went to the stairs, turning over their conversation in her mind, unconvinced and unable to shake her annoyance at his obstructive attitude to her perfectly reasonable questions. This wasn't over; not at all, but it would have to wait.

CHAPTER FOUR

It was early spring, not yet the balmy days that would mean tea on the beach with the kids after school, but darkness arrived a little later in the evening and there was less of a frost on the air when it did. Out in the garden of Thistledown Cottage, a row of daffodils had erupted in the borders beneath the kitchen window, while the glossy leaves of their annual lily of the valley poked through in another.

As more of the garden awoke, Jill would want to come over and tame it, as she did every year. At first, Gaby had thought it a chore for her and had felt guilty about her mum doing all their gardening, especially as it was such a busman's holiday. Jill had enough gardening to do, tending to the allotment where she grew the plants she sold to make her living, but then Killian had pointed out that she loved being outdoors with her hands in soil so much that she almost certainly wanted to do it.

Gaby stood in her bathrobe and stared into the open wardrobe, wondering what to wear. In a strange way, it was a welcome distraction from the fact that Killian had been on top form in the irritating stakes again. When she'd told Elijah he couldn't go to Betty's party in his stained old sweatshirt, Killian had undermined her by telling him that nobody would care what he was wearing. When Gaby had insisted that she didn't want to be late, he'd decided to go outside and chop some firewood and then had come back in so mucked up that he'd had to have another shower and had totally thrown out her schedule. And then she'd found a tear in the dress she'd planned to put on, and though it was another spanner in the works, she was quite glad she couldn't blame this one on Killian, because it was only a matter of time before he annoyed her so much she'd end up throwing something at him.

'We're not going to Buckingham Palace,' Killian said as he combed his wet hair. 'Betty won't care what you wear.'

'But I will,' Gaby said.

'Whatever it is, you'll look great,' he said absently as he put down the comb and checked a new text message.

'I thought I might dress as a Teletubby,' Gaby said.

'Huh...?' Killian continued to read something on his phone.

'Yes,' she continued, 'Tinky Winky. What do you think?'

'Sounds fine...'

Gaby huffed as she yanked out her claret maxi dress. It wasn't what she'd intended to wear, but at this point it would have to do, and it certainly didn't look as if Killian would care anyway.

'Just got to email a guy about some quotes,' he said, getting up.

'Can't it wait? We're getting ready to go out and it's not work time. It's bad enough you're always at the lifeboat station without your day job taking over as well.'

'But I don't want to lose the contract... I won't be a minute.'

'But, Killian—'

'I said I'd be a minute!' Killian shook his head before stomping out of the room.

So much for the schedule. But if Killian was going to make himself late, that didn't mean Gaby had to be. She stepped into her dress and twisted to zip it up. If he wasn't ready, then tough, she'd go on without him and he'd have to follow. It wasn't like she was desperate for his company right now. In fact, the way they were lately, it might be better for everyone if one of them stayed away from the party, and Gaby was damned if it was going to be her.

Since the speeding fine had dropped onto their mat the week before, he'd stuck to his line about going to Bristol for work, and though she kept on explaining why she couldn't get her head around it and asking him for more detail – to feel reassured more than anything else – he refused to elaborate. It was the usual Killian, digging his heels in. Gaby was well aware that was how their marriage had always worked, but even though they could both be stubborn, unwilling to back down in an argument, she'd never felt as uncertain of him as she did right now. She loved him and she trusted that he loved her, but she couldn't shake the notion he was hiding something and she couldn't rest not knowing what it was.

As far as she could see, his reluctance to give her the information she badly needed made things worse, not better, and so, if his intention was for her to forget all about it, he'd failed. Not getting an answer left her with unsavoury explanations to fill the gaps. She didn't want to believe that her husband, the man for whom her love was like fire, could be unfaithful to her, but the notion kept stealing into her thoughts. Bristol was a long way to go for a bit on the side, and yet the idea wouldn't leave her.

But to say it out loud, to ask Killian straight... usually, neither of them would baulk at getting things out in the open, but there had never been a thing this dangerous to air before. And so, Gaby had skirted around the issue, asking leading questions, hoping he'd get the subtext enough to address it without her needing to say it straight, but it had made no impact on his policy of silence. If he'd understood what she was really asking him, he hadn't given her any kind of answer, and in the end he'd lost his temper in front of the kids and so Gaby had dropped it – for now at least. But that didn't mean it had gone from her thoughts.

Approaching the open door of Betty's cafe was a bittersweet experience that evening. Gaby had been coming to this cafe for as long as she could recall, and some of her fondest memories were from afternoons spent there. Her parents would bring her in for ice cream or a milkshake back when Betty's mum ran it, and the idea of it not existing in its current form was a strange one. But Betty's great new adventure was something long overdue – at least, as far as Betty herself was concerned – and how could her friends be anything but pleased and excited for a woman who was as dear to the Morrow girls as they were to each other?

They'd all been through school together – admittedly in different year groups, but at a school as small as theirs, even different year groups became close. They'd attended all the same village celebrations, and they'd grieved together when they'd lost one of their own. They'd cheered on each other's triumphs and consoled each other in darker moments. Port Promise without Betty and her cafe was going to be a strange new place, but it was going to happen regardless.

Aside from the sold sign outside, there was no other clue of Betty's impending departure. She'd continued to open right to the last moment, only closing for good the day before so she could ready the space for her leaving party. She'd been excited about that, explaining in breathless detail to anyone who'd listen exactly what she had planned.

As Gaby went inside, she saw bunting hanging everywhere. There was often bunting, but it was always made from a subtle, pastel fabric. This was glittery and metallic and there was a lot more than there usually was. From the ceiling hung a large glitterball that wasn't usually there either, and a metallic ribbon curtain ran along one wall. There was a sound system erected in front of it and a DJ sitting next to it, not yet on duty and eating a sausage roll. Clearly, the details were part of the school disco theme Betty had been so enthusiastically planning. This early, things were relatively sedate, but Betty had promised a party to end all parties, and Gaby could only imagine what that meant.

Betty raced over to greet them. 'You look amazing as always, Gaby.' She beamed. 'You all do. You're all looking very smart.'

Gaby glanced to her side. Killian did look good in his midnight-blue shirt and jeans, but her observation was tainted by how she felt about him these days.

'You look incredible too, Betty,' Gaby said. 'Is this new?' She ran a hand over Betty's sleeve. 'It's gorgeous... What colour is that?'

'It's sort of an iridescent thing – you know, not really a colour at all. Unless you can call disco a colour, because it's sort of just disco-y.'

'Well it looks amazing on you. You really pushed the boat out with the disco theme then?' she added, gesturing to the cafe's decor.

'It looks like that film,' Fern said.

Betty frowned slightly. 'What film is that?'

'Mum watched it with us. That boy who goes back in time and there's a school disco and he plays guitar at the end...'

Betty clapped her hands together and grinned. '*Back to the Future* – has to be!'

'Yes!' Fern nodded eagerly. 'It was so good.'

'Only the best bloody film there ever was! Glad to see your mum's educating you in the right way!'

'We were struggling to find something we could all watch that day,' Killian said.

'Well it was a good shout...' Betty's gaze was diverted to the doors. 'Sorry, more people! I'll catch you later!'

As Betty went to greet her next guest, Gaby, Killian and the kids went to get drinks. On a counter there was a punch bowl which Gaby sniffed at and decided was definitely not for the children, an iced bucket filled with bottles of soft drinks, another filled with beers and one with bottles of sparkling wine. Betty also had various spirits and mixers lined up, along with bowls of sliced lemon and more buckets of ice.

'She's thought of everything,' Killian said, inspecting the beers. 'Not that I'll be able to have much.'

'I'm sure you could have a couple.'

'I could, but you can bet there'll be a shout if I get tempted to have more than I should.'

Gaby took a beer for herself and Killian did the same. Fern made her way over to the punch bowl and Gaby shook her head.

'I don't think so. Cola over there for you.'

'But I want to try the juice.'

'That's not juice,' Killian said with a laugh. 'One sniff of that and we'll have to carry you home.'

'Oh...' Fern looked confused. Killian pointed her in the direction of the soft drinks.

He seemed relaxed, and somehow that riled Gaby even more. How could he be relaxed when there was such constant tension between them these days? It was like he didn't even recognise it – or maybe he simply refused to. Gaby couldn't decide which of those two scenarios annoyed her more.

As their children went to inspect the drinks on offer, Gaby and Killian stood side by side in silence, both gazes sent out across the room. One by one, couples and families Gaby knew and loved arrived at the cafe. It wasn't the last time they'd be in here but almost certainly the last time in its current form. The identity of the new owner still wasn't public knowledge, and even Betty still knew little about them. Gaby suspected she didn't really care; she'd never felt attached to the cafe in the same way as the rest of the village did, as far as Gaby could tell. It had been a legacy foisted on her, and she seemed very glad to be rid of it. And apart from the fact that it had been sold as a venue geared up to serve food, nobody knew what type of business it would become. It might continue as a cafe, but it might become something else entirely.

Cormac had borne the disappointment of missing out on the sale with remarkable cheeriness, but Gaby had felt sorry for him and Clara. Of course, she and everyone else in Port Promise had wanted to see them take ownership. Although the opportunity had been perfect, the timing had been far from it. Cormac was still recovering from the accident that had almost killed him only a few months before, and Clara got a bit more pregnant every day; neither of them were in a place where they could take on such a commitment. For now at least, Cormac would carry on running his shack on the beach.

Ten minutes later, Jill arrived with Ava, Harry, Harry's dad, Sandy, and Harry's mum, Cynthia. The new arrivals hadn't yet noticed Gaby and Killian, having gone straight over to greet Betty, who was now with her mum, who'd come over from Truro with Betty's stepfather. Her grandmother, the woman who'd opened the cafe all those years ago and had handed it down to two generations of Bell women, was conspicuously absent. Betty said it was because she wasn't well enough to come, but most people suspected it was really because she was furious that the cafe was leaving the family and even more furious that there was nothing she could do about it.

But it was just another sign of the times, Jill had said,

another way in which Port Promise was changing. It had always changed of course, over the hundreds of years it had existed, but those changes suddenly seemed so much faster and bigger than they had before.

While Jill, Ava, Harry and his parents were chatting to Betty, Marina and her husband Bob arrived, followed immediately by Clara and Cormac, then Tanika who worked at the caravan park, and then Maxine and Shari from the lifeboat crew, with their partners, so that quite a queue was forming to say hello to Betty. Gaby watched as they waited, Clara catching her eye and gesturing that she'd be over shortly to chat. Nigel, the octogenarian owner of Salty's Chips came in, walked to the front of the crowd, handed Betty a card and then left again, but that was more than anyone had expected because he rarely left his shop. As Clara kissed Betty and handed her a gift bag, Robin, who owned the trawler that went out to catch a good deal of Cormac's fish, arrived with his two sons, which was remarkable in itself as Robin preferred his own company and rarely attended parties.

'Vas is here,' Killian said into Gaby's thoughts. 'Just going to get a word with him.'

Gaby watched as Killian strode over to where Vas and his husband were talking to Maxine and Shari. By this time, Elijah and Fern had gone off with some of the local kids and were racing around perilously close to the DJ's console. He glowered at them over the top of a plate of sandwiches he'd been given but clearly didn't think he had any authority to do much about it, because he said nothing.

While Harry got sidetracked by the arrival an old school friend, Ava and Clara came over to where Gaby was standing.

'This is so weird, isn't it?' Ava inspected the drinks table.

'Tonight?' Gaby asked.

Ava nodded. 'Saying goodbye to Betty, knowing this won't be Betty's cafe anymore. I've never known it as anything else.'

'That goes for all of us,' Clara said. 'I think it probably goes for Mum too. There's been a Betty here for years, even before our Betty, hasn't there?'

'We'll all miss her, that's for sure,' Ava said.

Gaby nodded. 'So where's this odyssey beginning?'

'What?' Clara grabbed a bottle of cloudy lemonade and twisted it open.

'You know,' Gaby said, 'Betty's big adventure? Where's she starting out? Has she decided now that it's almost time to go?'

'New Zealand,' Clara said. 'She's got family there, and I think she's planning to be there a while... maybe even until her visa runs out. Then she says she'll decide what she's doing next, but she's quite chilled about it really. Money won't be an issue with the proceeds of this place in the bank. It's all very exciting, I expect. Makes me feel a bit dull.'

Gaby shot her a sideways look. 'I think you've got enough excitement in your life right now.'

'True.' Clara turned to her with a smile, a hand going to her belly. 'But of all the people living in the village, I'd have never said Betty would be the one to do any of this. I suppose it just goes to show people are never exactly how you think they are.'

'Well, as Mum would say, she's a dark horse,' Ava said.

'I'm so glad for her though.' Clara sipped at her lemonade. 'She never really liked running the cafe, and I think she only ever did it because she felt there was nothing else for her here.'

'And because her grandma was determined she would take it on when her mum moved away,' Ava put in. 'Should have told her to stick it, you can't live your life a certain way just because it's expected of you.'

'Says the girl who joined the lifeboats because her dad did,' Gaby said, arching her brow.

Ava's expression darkened. She and Gaby had never seen eye to eye on Ava's decision to join the lifeboats, and while they'd both learned to live with it, Gaby sometimes found it hard to hide the fact that she hadn't wanted her sister to follow in the footsteps of her father and Killian. If anyone knew how dangerous the service could be, it was Gaby.

'You know that's different,' Ava said.

'Anyway...' Clara stepped forward, as if to disrupt the space between her sisters so she could block an impending disagreement. 'In the end, she realised what she wanted out of life and she took the step, and that's brilliant. I hope it's everything she wants. I have to envy her a little bit.'

'Me too,' Ava said, her expression clearing as the moment of danger with Gaby passed. 'I haven't ever done anything like that, and I always thought I might like to travel.'

'God, don't say you're thinking of leaving!' Clara turned to her with a faint look of horror.

'After the trouble I've gone to getting on the lifeboat crew? Not likely. And I have Harry to think about too now. His mum and dad need him here and I'd only want to go if he came with me. As much as I envy Betty, it's not right for us – at least, not at this moment in time.'

The lights of the space suddenly dimmed, the glitterball began to throw diamonds across the walls, and the DJ announced the start of more lively entertainment. Gaby smiled as she watched Elijah and Fern race to the dancefloor with a gaggle of schoolfriends. As some chart hit kicked in, something that made Gaby feel instantly ancient for not knowing it, Elijah and his friends broke into some bizarre robot dance, which they all seemed to take so seriously it was comical. The girls tried to copy, but they clearly thought it was a lot funnier than the boys did. Then some of the older girls must have decided they were way cooler and more sophisticated than that, and started to sway to the music instead. Once the younger girls caught sight of the change in tack, they began to do the same.

Harry came across and put an arm around Ava. 'OK there?'

She nodded and he turned to Gaby and Clara. 'Weird, isn't it? Saying goodbye to Betty.'

'We've just been saying the same thing,' Gaby replied.

Harry gave an amiable smile and turned his gaze on the room.

'Harry!'

They all turned to see Cormac wave him over.

Harry sent him a thumbs up and then turned to Ava. 'Sorry, just got to...'

'Go on!' Ava grinned. 'Go and play with your mate!'

Harry looked sheepish as he kissed her and went to see Cormac.

'Thick as thieves these days, those two,' Clara said as they watched him go.

'Especially since you and Cormac got together,' Ava said. 'I think Harry might feel a bit safer now,' she added with a mischievous look. 'Not sure he ever quite believed that I didn't have the hots for Cormac, even though I told him a million times.'

'We definitely did all right for ourselves, didn't we?' Clara said. 'All the Morrow girls got fine men.'

Ava started to laugh. 'But all on the lifeboat crew – what does that say about us?'

'It's hardly surprising when you think about it.'

'I suppose not. Anyone would think the only thing that goes on around here is the lifeboats though.'

'They would,' Gaby agreed, and perhaps her tone was a little too heartfelt because Ava could barely disguise her grimace of sympathy. They all knew Gaby's views on the amount of time Killian spent at the station for one thing or another; she'd made no secret of them. While Ava and Cormac did their share, to Gaby they at least seemed to maintain some sort of balance. It might have been her imagination, or down to the fact they weren't exactly getting along, but these days Killian seemed to think of little else.

'You all right?' Clara asked.

Gaby turned to her and forced a smile. 'Of course! I'm just tired, got a lot on, you know, with the kids and Killian working so hard and this new tutoring job.'

'How is the teaching going?' Ava asked.

'Brilliant! I love it. There's such a sense of satisfaction when you help someone figure out a complicated maths problem. And I love it when people say they're crap at maths and then realise they're actually not.'

'Of course you would love that.' Ava laughed lightly. 'You always were the only person I knew who liked maths at school.'

'I can't help that my brain works that way. I don't get poetry or philosophy, but give me an equation; I can deal with that.'

'I can't believe it took you this long to figure out this was the job for you,' Clara said.

'Honestly, me neither!' Gaby smiled. 'Then again, I've had my hands full for the past few years so I couldn't even think about it.'

'You've got your hands full now,' Ava said. 'How is the Flag Day stuff going?'

'Good. Busy, of course. I don't know how Mum did it for all those years when she had us and her allotment to worry about too.'

'Again,' Clara said, 'that's kind of exactly what you're doing. Kids, Killian, your new job…'

'I suppose so. At least Flag Day is only once a year, and I'm happy it's making life a bit easier for Mum.'

'You know we'll help with whatever you need,' Ava said. 'I know what you're like – you'll think you have to do it all yourself and you won't ask.'

'I'll ask,' Gaby said.

Ava gave a sceptical look and she laughed. 'Eventually.'

Clara frowned. 'But you are looking after yourself?'

'Of course.' Gaby smiled. 'Honest, I would say if it was too much.'

'No you wouldn't,' Ava said. 'You'd keep going, and you'd never admit to needing help. But like I keep saying, if you do need help you only have to ask.'

For a fleeting moment, Gaby's fears burned to be spoken. She loved Killian and she wanted to trust him, so why wouldn't her doubts leave her? She hated feeling this way about him. Surely she gave him enough? Surely he felt as she did about their marriage. He wouldn't stray – she had to believe that despite what the nagging doubts told her. It would be good to air her worries though, to get her sisters' opinions. And even if they had no opinion to offer, at least a worry shared would be that much easier to bear. But she only shook her head. 'I think you give me too much credit there. Killian would say I complain like anyone when I've got a lot on.'

Ava sipped at her beer. 'That's Killian for you – typical man. They don't know the half of what we have to do.'

'You can say that again,' Gaby said, forcing a smile and deciding she wasn't going to ruin her night by giving her doubts another thought.

They had a brief chat with Jill and Marina, and then Betty's mum stole the two women away. The three of them had grown up in Port Promise together, and now that Betty senior had moved away, they clearly had a lot to catch up on. That left Gaby with Clara and Ava again. She felt they ought to mingle a bit more and was just going to suggest it when Ava nodded at someone standing by the counter.

'Who's that?'

Gaby turned to follow her gaze. It was obvious who Ava meant, because Gaby didn't recognise him and Ava mustn't have done either.

'I don't know,' Clara said. She looked at Gaby.

'Me neither,' Gaby replied with a vague frown as she took a second look. The man was perhaps in his mid to late forties, though clearly no stranger to a fitness regime; dark hair, cheek-bones and a jawline that men twenty years younger would give a lot for. Despite being there alone, he seemed perfectly at ease, leaning on the counter with a drink in his hand, watching with some amusement as everyone else partied. 'I've never seen him before.'

'Do you think Betty knows him?' Clara asked doubtfully. 'I suppose she must do if he's here.'

'Or,' Ava said, 'he's seen there's a party on and decided to come in and help himself to some freebies while nobody's looking.'

'Hardly looks to be sneaking around,' Gaby said. 'You'd think he'd be a bit discreet if he was doing that.'

'I've never understood why people do that,' Clara said. 'Why would you want to hang out at a party where you know nobody?'

'It's more fun when you gatecrash with a mate,' Ava said.

Gaby gave her a sideways glance. 'I won't ask.'

Ava simply grinned and put her beer bottle to her lips.

'Does it look like he's with anyone here?' Gaby asked, more of herself than her sisters as she studied the man. 'I'm going to ask Betty if she knows who he is.'

'I'll go and ask the crew, see if they know anything,' Ava said.

'Why would the crew know who he is?' Clara asked.

Ava shrugged. 'Just trying to be useful. We can't all ask Betty who he is.'

'Can't bear to be apart from Harry is more like,' Gaby said with a faint smile. 'Off you go then.'

'I'll go with you.' Clara put her empty lemonade bottle in a recycling bin.

As they parted, Gaby scanned the room for Betty, every so

often taking a peek at the stranger leaning against the counter with his drink like he owned the place. He was wearing jeans and a casual shirt, but Gaby could tell these were no supermarket own-brand clothing lines. This stuff screamed money, from the tiny logo on the breast pocket of the shirt to the embossed label at the waistband of the denim. He wasn't bad-looking either, and perhaps if she'd been single, he might even have been Gaby's type. If he was a party crasher, she had to admire his cool – he wasn't making an effort to stay under the radar at all.

Unable to see Betty from her current vantage point, she decided to walk the room for a better look. Along the way she was stopped by people she knew, and though she asked all of them as discreetly as she could if they could identify the stranger, nobody could. But they all assumed that Betty must know him or he wouldn't be there.

Others might have been happy to let it slide, but Gaby didn't like the thought of her friend's hospitality being taken advantage of by some passing chancer, especially on such a big night for her. And so she resolved to get to the bottom of it.

Eventually she found Betty in the toilets. She definitely looked a lot drunker than she had an hour before.

'Gaby!' she cried, throwing herself across her. 'Are you having a good time?'

Gaby laughed. 'Not as good as you apparently.'

'I'm having... it's brilliant! I almost don't want to leave after all. I mean, look how many friends I have!'

'You do, but you might feel a bit differently about it tomorrow. And you've spent so much money on a leaving bash, the very least you can do is actually leave for a bit.'

'So true...' Betty gave a comically sage nod, as if really thinking about what Gaby had said. 'S'pose I ought to get out there then.'

'Come on then...'

'After Clara's baby is born,' Betty began as Gaby led her out of the toilet, 'I'll come back and get drunk with her. It's boring she can't get drunk tonight, and drunk Clara is the best.'

'Oh, she is,' Gaby said.

Back in the main room, she halted and pointed as discreetly as she could to the stranger. 'Do you know who that guy is at your counter?'

'Who?'

'Him... leaning on the counter on his own.'

Betty wobbled slightly as she leaned forward to get a closer look. 'Oooh... He's the man of my dreams, he is!'

'So you know him?'

'No, but I'd like to. Do you know him? Never mind...' She hiccupped and then shouted over the music. 'You're a bit late, mate! I've already booked my plane tickets!'

'Nobody seems to know who he is. Should I go and have a word?'

'Why?'

'To ask what he's doing here.'

'He's having a beer.'

'Yes, I can see that.'

'Ask Killian to go.'

'Why would I ask Killian?'

'Because he's your man and he ought to do it.' At this point Betty started to sway on the spot, then sat heavily on the nearest chair, which was fortunately empty, because she didn't look as if she'd had much input in the whole sitting-down decision.

'I'll be back in a minute,' Gaby said and made her way to the counter.

He noticed her before she'd even got there, and watched her with a look that she couldn't quite decipher and definitely didn't like.

'Must be my lucky night,' he said before she had the chance to open the conversation. 'Yes I'm single, and yes I'm interested.'

'Who are you?' Gaby demanded, her hackles rising at his obvious and immediate arrogance.

'Lloyd Turner.' He held out a hand, but Gaby simply stared at it for a moment before continuing.

'I don't mean your name, I mean *who are you*? This is my friend's party and she doesn't know you. Nobody else seems to know you either. So could you explain why you're here?'

He paused as he studied his beer for a second then looked up and met her gaze with that maddening arrogance again. 'I was passing, thought I'd check the neighbourhood out...' He gave her a very deliberate once-over. 'And I'm glad I did. I like what I've seen so far.'

'You were passing? Like, what? On holiday?'

'Sort of. At least, I am right now.'

'Then you don't know anyone here.'

'We're talking, so I know you. And if you tell me your name, I'll know you even better.'

Gaby clamped her hands on her hips and glared at him. 'Oh my God! Does that ever work on anyone, ever?'

'I'd say I have a ninety per cent hit rate. The thing is, it's always worth the gamble. I always say if you see something you like and want, you only have yourself to blame if you don't get it.'

'Well I always say people who don't belong at parties ought to leave when they're caught out.'

'Quite right. I'll leave if you come with me.'

'Are you drunk?'

'No. I'm a lot less choosy when I'm drunk.'

'OK, *Lloyd*... I really think you ought to leave now.'

'Ah, so I did make an impression...'

'I'm sure it's not the impression you think you're making.' Gaby glanced towards where Cormac, Harry and Killian were in conversation. Despite telling Betty she didn't need Killian to deal with this, perhaps it was an occasion that called for a man after all.

'Are they your minders?' the stranger asked into the gap.

'No.'

'If I had you, I'd hire a minder. So tell me, which of that bunch of grunts is yours then?'

If there had been a bottle in reach, Gaby might have been sorely tempted to grab hold and slam it over his head. Instead, she turned on her heel and marched over to Killian.

'All right?' he asked, clearly reading her face without much effort.

'There's a guy at the counter; nobody knows him and quite frankly he's a total prick. I've asked him to leave – he's admitted he doesn't belong here – but he won't go.'

Killian suddenly looked tense. He rose to his full height. 'We'll see about that.'

'Want me to come?' Harry asked.

Gaby shook her head. 'It might come across as overly aggressive if two of you go. The type of bloke he seems to be I think that might make things worse. I don't think he cares about pissing people off.'

But as the four of them turned to look again, the man was watching them. Perhaps seeing that there were plans afoot to eject him, he downed the rest of his drink, aimed a nonchalant wave at them and strolled to the exit.

'That was easier than expected,' Cormac said.

Killian grunted. 'Probably realised he was out of his depth.'

'I wonder who he was,' Harry mused.

'Some out of towner, I expect,' Killian replied.

'Well,' Cormac said cheerily, 'no trouble in the end at least.'

'It would have ruined Betty's party,' Gaby said, relieved the incident was over but still seething from the man's brazen arrogance. She turned to Killian. 'Thanks,' she said stiffly.

'I didn't do anything. You dealt with it, like you always do.'

'So how are the plans for the Flag Day going?' Cormac asked Gaby.

'Good,' she said vaguely, still distracted by the man they'd just thrown out. Lloyd, he'd said his name was. Perhaps she'd ask around tomorrow, find out if he was staying at any of the holiday cottages in the village. The caravan park wasn't yet open for the holiday season, but he didn't strike her as a caravan kind of guy. Maybe he'd bought a second home nearby. She sincerely hoped not, because if she was going to see him around a lot, she'd find it very difficult to be civil.

The incident was eventually forgotten and Gaby recovered some of her good humour. After a few more drinks, she didn't think about it at all. The disco got louder and more raucous, Betty was practically legless at this point and had to be escorted to the toilet by Clara because she could barely get her underwear down, and by the time the night was coming to an end, nobody wanted it to. The DJ played the last song and then the lights came up, and everything suddenly seemed so final that a melancholy sort of hush fell over the room.

As people lined up to hug Betty and wish her luck before they left, she was sobbing.

'Goodbye... Oh, I can't believe this is it! I love you all so much, you know... I'll be visiting before you know it...'

Gaby held her tight. Clara had always been closest to Betty, but that didn't mean Gaby wasn't desperately sorry to see her leave. She was going to miss her – they all were. 'You'd better keep in touch. We want to hear every detail of every step of your journey.'

'Oh you will!' Betty sniffed. 'And I want all the news from here. I want to know everything that happens. Just because I'll be far away doesn't mean I'll forget you all.'

There was a bit more toing and froing, of Betty telling Gaby how much she loved her and Gaby reassuring her she was doing the right thing, and then a hug for Killian where Betty told him she loved him too but then had to explain that it wasn't in a sexy way, which made Killian and Gaby laugh, and then they left her to start on Marina and Bob, and made their way into the chilly night to walk home.

Jill had taken Elijah and Fern to Seaspray Cottage with her a few hours earlier. She'd said she was tired and recognised that things might get rowdy, and as lots of the other children had been taken home by then, it seemed sensible for them to go with her. They'd protested, of course, but had been swayed by the promise of a sleepover and a trip to an adventure playground the following day.

So that left Gaby and Killian to walk the promenade alone. Alone apart from others leaving the party of course. The air was cold but the sky clear, swathes of stars sweeping across it and a moon with a frosty halo. There were lights out at sea: a lighthouse on a distant shore, buoys and ships anchored for the night. The gentle rush of waves breaking on the sand and slapping against the harbour walls, and the low murmur of voices going in different directions to theirs were the soundtrack as they walked in lockstep.

'It was a good night in the end,' Killian said, reaching for her hand.

She closed her eyes for a second, relishing the contact. There had been so little of that in the past few weeks, ever since the letter containing the speeding fine had dropped onto their mat, along with the understanding and patience they seemed to have lost with each other. Her reaction to his touch might have been fuelled by drink – because Gaby had downed more than enough – but she'd take it, because she realised now, despite her new doubts and anxieties about him, how much she'd missed it.

'It was,' she said. 'Weird at times, but good. I keep thinking about Betty's mum. I mean, it must be hard for her to see Betty taking off halfway around the world.'

'Betty's a grown woman, though.'

'I know, but I bet it doesn't get any easier. Don't you think so? How would you feel if it was Fern?'

'I can't say I've given it much thought. I suppose Fern will do whatever she wants and we'll have to deal with it, just like Eli will. We can't keep them by our sides forever.'

'No, but we'd miss them if either of them left Port Promise. I mean, both of them might go.'

'That's years away – no point in stressing over it now.'

'I'm not stressing; I'm just discussing it.'

'I don't see any point in discussing it either. Like I said, years in the future. Let's just enjoy them now and worry about all that when the time comes.'

There was a sudden peal of laughter, loud enough to echo across the beach. Gaby turned back to Betty's, still lit up, the last of the guests filtering out.

'Do you think Harry and Ava will have kids?' she asked, turning back to Killian.

He gave a bemused shrug. 'How should I know? That's a bit of a random question, isn't it?'

'Not really – we were just talking about ours and it made me think. They just don't seem like they will. Both too wrapped up in the lifeboats. If they had kids, one of them might have to quit.'

'Why?'

'Because it's not so easy to raise kids with one parent in the service, let alone two.'

His hand left hers. 'Here we go. This is the part where you tell me I don't do enough.'

'That's not what I mean at all. I was just saying, I can't imagine how they'll manage to have kids if they both stay on the lifeboats.'

'I really couldn't say. That's a question for them, isn't it? I think you're getting a bit ahead of yourself anyway. Kids seem a long way off for them. They're not even living together yet.'

'That's never stopped anyone having children.'

'I'm just saying it doesn't seem a priority for them right now.'

Gaby wanted to feel his hand in hers again, but somehow she wasn't able to make the move. So she walked by his side, close by and yet suddenly feeling as if there were miles between them.

'That was weird, wasn't it?' she began, more for something to say than because it bothered her now. 'The guy who crashed the party.'

'He was just seeing what he could get – people do that.'

'It's quite a specific place to be, though.'

'How do you mean?'

'Port Promise. It's not like it's a huge place, not the sort of place where lots of people would be randomly passing by and be like, ooh, party, I'll see if I can get in.'

'I thought you said he was on holiday here.'

'I'm not sure. He said so, but he was... well, he was a bit of a dick. Seemed like the sort of man who'd enjoy telling porkies to wind people up.'

'I wouldn't waste another thought on it. He went and we didn't see him again.'

'Yes, but what if he's on holiday here?'

'What about it?'

'Then we'll see him again.'

'And?'

'I didn't like him.'

'Hmm. You seem very preoccupied by a man you don't like. Forget him. If we do see him again I doubt he'd dare start anything else. Not with you, that's for sure – not if he has any sense.'

'What does that mean?'

'It means you had the measure of him and I'm sure he must have realised that. Probably why he cleared off in the end.'

'He cleared off because I came to get you.'

'Well I know that, but I was trying to flatter your feminist principles.'

Gaby couldn't help but grin, and she slapped his arm playfully. 'Git! I'm going to ask around tomorrow, see if he is staying here.'

'What on earth for? If you fancy him, Gab, just say so.'

'Don't be stupid!'

'I'm not the one wasting my time worrying about some dickhead who just happened to be passing through and thought he could get a free beer.'

'I just didn't like it.'

'I know you didn't, and I love your sense of fair play, but he really isn't worth your effort.'

'You're probably right.'

'There's no probably about it.'

'Did all the crew stay sober tonight?'

'Fairly, yeah.'

'It'd almost be a shame if there was no shout after all that.'

Killian shot her a sideways glance. She could just make out a look of disbelief in the gloom. 'Are you saying you want us to get called out?'

'No, of course not. But it's a shame you couldn't have a drink.'

'Some of us could have, but we all decided not to. Didn't seem right for some to be ready to go and some not. But there are other advantages to being sober.'

'What are those?'

He stopped dead and pulled her into his arms. 'What do you think?'

'Ah!' She reached to kiss him, and for one glorious moment

all the doubts, all the misunderstanding, all the resentment was forgotten.

'No kids at home,' he whispered, his breath on her neck sending thrills of desire through her. 'You can make as much noise as you like.'

'Maybe you'll be the one making the noise.'

He grinned as he dipped to kiss her again. 'I'm kind of banking on it.'

CHAPTER FIVE

'Morning, my love!' Marina looked up from the newspaper she had spread across the shop counter with a bright smile as Gaby walked in.

'Hi, Marina. Good day so far?'

'Better for seeing you. Have you come for anything in particular or just saying hello?'

'A bit of both. I thought I'd pop in, but I could do with some candles while I'm here.'

'No worries, my love. Any particular sort?'

'Big ones for the storm lanterns.'

'Right you are.' Marina pulled a set of ladders open and began to climb for a shelf.

'I also wanted to ask if you could spare any raffle donations for Flag Day.'

Marina returned to the counter with three different coloured candles. 'Raffle prizes, you say? I expect so. So your mum's handed all the organising to you this year...' She held up the candles. 'Any of these do you?'

'I'll take three of the white ones.'

'No problem.'

'I thought it was time someone took the Flag Day prep off Mum. She's done it for years, and it's hard work. And I know it reminds her of dad too much now – last year's was really tough on her.'

'Yes, he did always do a lot of it with her. Needs a whole committee if you ask me – you ought to think about getting some more hands on deck. There's so much to organise... unless you're scaling it back this year?'

'God no!' Gaby said. 'I'm determined to raise more for the station than we've ever raised before. Killian told me last year's total was the highest they've ever had and said that I couldn't possibly top it, so...'

Marina chuckled. 'Oh, that would do it all right. Even I know not to throw the gauntlet down when you're involved in something. You might want to consider that Killian said it on purpose.'

'A bit of reverse psychology to get more money in for the station?' Gaby grinned. 'I'd like to agree with you, but he's not smart enough for that.'

Marina wrapped the candles in some brown paper. 'How are your sisters? Haven't seen much of Ava – expect she's busy with so much on. Seems happy with Harry – is she? And Clara's showing nicely now, ain't she? She got lucky with that Cormac – not many would take on someone else's baby as their own. And who was that man you were talking to at Betty's party? Haven't seen him around before; I'm certain of that, because I wouldn't forget a face like his in a hurry.'

'Clara and Ava are both fine. I don't know who that man was. He might have been good-looking but, trust me, he wasn't nice at all.'

'Oh. Pity that – packaging all nice and the inside rotten – that's how it goes sometimes.'

'So how much for the candles?'

'Oh, hang on... need to get my blasted glasses...'

'I can read the price for you.'

'Don't think it's on there; just looked as we were chatting. But I got a wholesale list so won't take me long to work out...' Marina got a notebook out and put on her glasses. She started to mutter as she went down a handwritten list that looked like a stock inventory of some kind. 'So if wholesale was three, then mark-up...' She looked up. 'Twenty-one for the three. Sounds a lot, but they're the good wax and a good burn time, so you won't have to buy any more for a while.'

'No, that's fine – I'll take them.'

'And it would cost you as much in petrol to drive out to the discount store anyway. And their candles... the smoke! You buy cheap, you get soot all over your walls.'

'Probably,' Gaby said as she handed over the exact money. Marina had never taken payment cards and everyone in Port Promise was fine with that. If there was a need to go into her hardware store for anything, they made certain to have enough money with them. And if they didn't, Marina would usually work something out anyway.

'So you'll have a think about raffle prizes and let me know?'

'I will, my love. You got a bag for these?'

'Yes, thanks, Marina. Whatever you can spare for the raffle, don't worry about how much – everything's gratefully received.'

'You been to see Sandy yet? I expect he'll do something on the ciders for you – usually does.'

'Oh, not yet, but Mum did say he usually sets up a stall on the day and gives us some of the profits. I'll probably see him in the next couple of weeks about it.'

'And are you auctioning afternoons with the men this year?'

'Hmm... I don't know.'

'Folks did like that.'

'I know, but it got a bit... well... a bit creepy last time,' Gaby said warily. 'I'm not sure we ought to do it again.'

'Oh yes.' Marina chuckled. 'Now I remember! That woman

from Truro who won your Killian... what she said she wanted him for made even him blush, and I don't think I've ever seen him blush before or since. And I don't think she was joking one bit.'

'That's hardly surprising. The winners are supposed to get an afternoon of gardening or DIY or cleaning the car or something. But if a man had suggested that to a woman crew member, nobody would have been laughing.'

'Poor Killian.' Marina was still grinning and didn't seem bothered by Gaby's comparison. 'If that woman turns up this year and she was taken with your Killian, we might have to get an ambulance on standby once she clocks Cormac!'

'Anyway...' Gaby put the candles into her tote bag. 'Least said about all that the better.'

'But it does raise a lot of money, so I'd think about it.'

'I'll see what Mum says.'

'Remember me to her when you see her, won't you? We're overdue a lunch date, tell her. And she's been missed at the ramblers these past few weeks.'

'She's had a lot on, but I'll tell her,' Gaby said, certain that Marina had already sent her mum a text to say all this.

'Doesn't do her good to forget who her friends are.'

'Don't worry, she'd never do that. I'd better get back. Don't forget—'

'Raffle – I got it on my to-do list.'

Gaby stepped out of Marina's shop and into a light drizzle. From here she could just about make out a strip of sea partially hidden by a row of cottages and the curve of the road, but what she could see looked like the washed-out greys of a hazy watercolour.

A sudden flash of orange whizzed across the scene – the inshore lifeboat on manoeuvres, she supposed. At least, she hadn't heard an alarm coming from the station to say there was a shout. She racked her brain to recall Killian mentioning a practice launch, but she had so much going on right now that she couldn't remember.

Her steps took her to the beach. She'd decided to wait for the boat to come back in. Perhaps she could walk home with Killian.

'Hey...' Ava was standing on the sand in her waterproofs, waiting for the boat as well. She wasn't yet qualified to go out as seagoing crew, but she'd still have plenty to do on shore. It looked to Gaby as though she was keeping an eye on the conditions at sea, as she had a radio in her hand and her eye fixed firmly on the horizon. 'What brings you here? It's not exactly the weather for a stroll.'

'I went to see Marina about raffle prizes.'

'Right.'

'And I saw the launch so I thought I'd say hello.'

'Cool. Killian's on the boat.'

'I guessed as much.'

'Not to pry, but... are you two all right?'

Gaby looked sharply at her. 'What makes you think we might not be?'

'Nothing in particular. Call it my Spidey-sense.'

'We're fine.'

'Hmm... that's good then. Are you waiting for him?'

'I thought I might. Thought we could walk back together after he's done.'

'Looks like they're on their way back now, actually.'

Gaby watched as the boat turned and headed back to the station. Ava climbed onto the tractor that would bring it back onto the beach and started the engine. A few minutes later, Vas had steered the boat into the cage attached to the tractor, and then Ava had skilfully picked it up, driven it back and dropped it onto the sand. Killian was the first out – Gaby would know his frame anywhere, even with his face obscured by his safety equipment. He pulled off his helmet and gave her a brief wave as she walked over. It was a practice run, and so more relaxed than usual – she'd have never bothered him at this point if it had been a real shout.

She smiled. 'Hello, sexy.'

'Hey...' He shook out his dark hair. 'What brings you down here?'

'Oh, Flag Day stuff. But I could be persuaded to drop that if you wanted to come home and spend some time with your wife.'

He gave her the slightest grin. 'I'd love to, but I have stuff to finish here – we haven't been through our fire drills for ages.'

'Oh. Ava didn't say anything about fire drills.'

'Me and Vas only decided as we came back in that they needed doing.'

'So you'll be here a bit longer yet?'

'Yeah... not sure what time I'll be back. Eat without me if it's late; I'll grab something myself when I get in.'

Without another word, without even a brief kiss, he strode back to the station. Gaby tried not to frown as she walked back across the beach alone. She'd made an effort to wait for him, but she wished now she hadn't bothered.

CHAPTER SIX

'Hey!' Ava waved at Elijah and Fern as they ran along the sand to her. Gaby followed with Killian. She'd told him not to bother coming out this morning with them, to have a lie-in after a busy week, but he'd insisted. They'd bickered incessantly – at least it felt that way – in the weeks since Gaby's discovery of the speeding ticket, but it had been about unconnected things, as if they'd both been skirting around what she felt was the real issue, as if to deflect from it in any way they could.

Ava waved a hand at a perfect iris-coloured sky. 'Told you the weather would settle by the weekend. Perfect for a kayaking lesson.'

'The kids have been so excited about this you'd have had to take them whatever the weather was doing,' Killian said. 'That's what you get for planting ideas in their heads.'

'Where's your gear?' Ava gave him a once-over. 'You're not coming out with us?'

'Didn't realise I was invited.'

'You're always invited, crewmate!'

He smiled, but Gaby could see how hollow it was. 'If you

can handle these two, I'll make myself comfy on the sand and watch.'

'Lazy sod. I thought you were meant to be Mr Sporty.'

'Not when there's a danger my sister-in-law is likely to show me up.'

'Oh yeah, that's right,' Ava said with a grin. 'You only like games you can win.'

'That's not true. I'm married to your sister, and that's a game no man can win.'

Gaby gave him a sharp look, but she didn't comment and he didn't elaborate. Instead, he went to sit where the sand was dryer. When Gaby turned back to Ava, she could see something like pity in her eyes.

'There are life jackets over by the kayaks.' Ava gestured for Elijah and Fern to go over and get them on. 'You know what to do. I'll be over in a minute and we'll get started.'

As they raced over to follow her instructions, Ava lowered her voice. 'Gab... tell me to mind my own business, but is everything really all right? I know you said so last week when I asked you, but...'

'It's fine. He's in one of his moods – you know what he's like.'

'Are you sure, because—'

'I'm sure,' Gaby said firmly. She sent her gaze out to where the sun glinted like silverfish on the dancing waves. The weather was warming, winter becoming spring, and the sun today had stained the sea cobalt and turquoise. 'You're bang on with the forecast, of course. I don't know what we'd have done if those two hadn't been able to come today – they've talked about nothing else all week. You're sure it's no bother teaching them? I mean, you teach all week as it is without doing it in your free time.'

'God no. These two will be a doddle compared to some of the cocky you-know-whats I get at the swim academy. And who doesn't need an excuse to get out on the waves today? You ought to have come out with us – it would have been fun.'

'I haven't been out in a kayak for years; not sure I'd even remember where to start.'

'Like a lot of things people say is like riding a bike, it's like riding a bike,' Ava said.

'Only on the sea with the definite prospect of falling in.'

'Ah, you'd have picked it up again in no time. It's not too late – I can get some gear for you.'

Gaby looked over to where Elijah was trying to tell Fern she had her life vest on incorrectly and she was having none of it. 'And cramp their style? I don't think they'd thank me for going out with you.'

'So you're just watching today then? Fair enough. I'd fetch a blanket or something. It looks pleasant enough, but if you're sitting in one spot you might get cold.'

'Thanks, Mum.'

Ava laughed. 'You know what I mean.'

'A few weeks ago I'd have wandered down to Betty's for a breakfast or something. I guess that's out now.'

'Yeah.' Ava looked to where Betty's cafe sat in darkness on the promenade. 'It's still weird, isn't it?'

'Heard anything from her?'

'Clara has. Says she's loving New Zealand. She was in Christchurch last she heard from her. No news on the new owner yet?'

'Nope, not as far as I know.'

'Hey, I bet you could get a drink at Cormac's when he opens up.'

'I had thought that. I'll walk along in a bit. I can leave Killian here in case you need him for backup.'

'I'm sure once we're out on the water we'll be fine. Why don't you take him for a coffee?'

'No, you can have him.'

Ava gave her that look again. Pity, sympathy... whatever it was, Gaby couldn't stand it. Wasn't she the one who had the good marriage? Wasn't she the one the others looked up to?

'That bad?' Ava asked.

If only Gaby could open up. She wanted to – desperately. Either of her sisters would understand. They'd listen and perhaps they wouldn't judge, but Gaby couldn't be sure. She could tell them things were rocky with Killian, but they'd want to know why, and she couldn't bring herself to tell them the secret suspicions that she could barely admit to herself.

Ava went over to Elijah and Fern, while Gaby settled on the sand next to Killian. They watched in silence as Ava showed her niece and nephew around the kayaks, how to hold the oars and how to move their bodies to steer and steady.

'She's brilliant with kids,' Gaby said after a while.

'She is,' Killian said.

They were silent once more. Killian pulled out his phone and began to scroll through his messages. The breeze lifted Gaby's hair. She smoothed it down again and kept her hand in place, bringing her knees up to rest her chin on them.

'It's nice this,' she said.

'Hmm.'

'Peaceful. Makes a change not to be charging around doing something or other.'

'Hmm.'

'I'll probably get a coffee at Cormac's when it opens.'

'OK.'

'Want to come?'

'I'm good here.'

Gaby watched as Elijah and Fern took to the water. Then she stood up. Having any kind of conversation with Killian these days was like trying to pull out her own fingernails. What was the point? They'd never been like this before – what was happening to them? Something, but right now Gaby couldn't tell what it was or how to stop it. The notion scared her.

'I think I'll go see if they're setting up.'

'OK.' Killian didn't even look up.

Gaby walked away, across the sand, towards the fish shack. When she looked back, Killian was still staring out to sea. There was a time he'd have watched her go. She'd have turned to look back, and their eyes would have met and they'd have both smiled, that spark of excitement zipping around in Gaby's belly. Was this normal? she wondered. Did all marriages go this way eventually, or was it just theirs?

But as she caught a snatch of squealing and laughter on the wind, she turned back to see Fern roll her kayak and then emerge, spluttering but laughing, and Elijah and Ava laughing too, and she suddenly understood that whatever else happened, she had to fight for this marriage. If not for her and Killian, she was going to do it for them. Whatever it took, she was going to keep her family together.

CHAPTER SEVEN

Gaby saw the helicopter through her kitchen window as she chopped onions for the lasagne she was planning to make. She recognised it instantly as the one that often accompanied the lifeboat when it required an airlift. It meant someone was seriously hurt or trapped in such a way that the boat couldn't get them out.

Killian had been gone for an hour now. He hadn't said what the emergency was, but then that wasn't unusual. Often he didn't have the full picture until he got there – it was far quicker just to answer the pager and expect anything.

Putting the onions in the fridge and washing her hands, Gaby pulled on a coat and headed out to the lifeboat station.

A crowd had gathered on the beach nearby. It was mid-spring, not quite at the point where tourist season really kicked in, but visitor numbers were growing rapidly as the weather warmed. Today there were far more strangers than locals staring out to sea, watching the lifeboat bob on the waves where it had stopped, the helicopter hovering above, and another vessel which looked, from a distance, to be capsized.

'Gaby...'

She turned to see Clara behind her. Clara's movements were slower now, but that was hardly surprising given how pregnant she was.

Clara shielded her eyes and peered out to sea. 'What's going on? We saw the helicopter from the shack. Cormac wanted to come down to help, but I convinced him there was no point. He's not back on duty yet and might cause more problems than he solves.'

'I bet he's not happy missing this.'

'No. Looks like the sort of situation where they need everyone they can get – he guessed as much. I take it Killian's gone.'

Gaby nodded. 'As he always does.'

They watched together as the helicopter lowered something. It was hard to make out, but Gaby supposed it was the stretcher they used to airlift patients who'd been immobilised.

'It doesn't look good,' Clara said quietly.

'No. Poor soul, whoever they are. Want to go down to the station to see what we can find out?'

'They'll be busy. We'll know soon enough.'

'But if Ava's there, she'll fill us in.'

'I suppose we could walk down there anyway so we're close when the boat comes back in.' Clara took her phone from her pocket and typed a message. 'Just telling Cormac I might be a few more minutes.'

When she was done they started off for the station. As they drew closer, Gaby could see that the waves were bigger and more unpredictable than they'd first appeared. They sucked and crashed against the harbour walls. As the two women pushed their way through the crowds, the helicopter pulled away and flew towards the land. Then there was a collective murmur and arms pointing to a second one that had appeared and headed for the same spot.

'Shit.' Gaby exchanged a desperate look with her sister. 'This is not good.'

Their progress halted, they watched as a second stretcher was lowered, a patient placed on it and then winched up again. And then that helicopter set the same course towards land as the first, and the lifeboat turned for the station.

'Looks like they're done,' Clara said.

'But the boat's still capsized.'

'Maybe they're waiting for better conditions before they try to right it.'

They stood on the beach with all the tourists for another forty minutes. By the time Ava finally emerged from the station, most of them had got bored and moved away.

Clara gasped at the sight of her younger sister and rushed over, Gaby close behind.

'Ava! What happened?'

Gaby couldn't recall the last time she'd seen Ava so distraught. Or maybe she could now that she thought about it – it was the night their dad had died. Seemingly oblivious to anything else that was going on, Ava was sobbing. Gaby reached for her hand.

'What happened?'

Ava shook her head but didn't seem able to speak. A moment later Harry appeared, looking ashen and sombre. He strode right over and took Ava into his arms.

'Hey, hey... you did good,' he whispered, stroking her hair. 'We did our best. We can't save everyone, no matter how much we want to, but we tried.'

'They were...' Ava stuttered. 'They were...'

'I know,' Harry murmured, pulling her closer. 'I know.'

'Harry,' Gaby said.

He looked up, Ava still held tight in his arms, and shook his head. 'I'm going to take her home.'

Gaby immediately understood, and she was overcome by a

hollow, sick feeling. They'd lost someone. Not a crew member, and she felt guilty for being glad of that, but they'd lost someone they'd gone out to save. How many had died? Ava had said 'they', not him or her. Perhaps, in the end, it didn't matter if it was one person or ten.

Everyone at the station would take it badly, including Killian. Gaby felt guilty for thinking of her own situation in this moment, but she couldn't help it. The others might be able to talk to each other about today – indeed, Ava and Harry had each other to help them through – but Killian didn't talk about these things like everyone else did. Killian would pull up the drawbridge and shut out the world and make it impossible for anyone to reach him. Gaby had seen it before, and she didn't relish the prospect of going through it now. But then she had to remind herself again that this was bigger than her and Killian. Someone had died today. A family would be grieving, a hole in their midst that would never close.

'Shall we come over later?' Clara asked Harry.

'That might be good,' he said. 'But let me text you first.'

Clara nodded and sent a worried glance Gaby's way. 'What are you going to do?' she asked as Harry and Ava left them.

Gaby looked towards the station. Killian hadn't come out yet. Gaby wondered whether he'd decided to stay on site to do some routine post-mission stuff or perhaps to wait and be ready to go out when the conditions improved enough to allow them to pick up the capsized vessel.

'I don't know.' Gaby dug her hands into her coat pockets. 'I'd wait for Killian, but I don't know how long he'll be. I bet he's decided to stay on and do whatever... especially if Ava and Harry have left.'

She wanted to go in and talk to him. She wanted to know what had happened and what she might be facing later, but she couldn't go barging into the station now. It looked as if Harry might have taken Ava home at Vas's request – did that mean he'd come straight back to help with the salvage operation? In which case, could she get more information from him, so she'd be ready for whatever was coming?

Then her phone began to ring.

'Mum,' she said, looking at the screen but aware of Clara's eyes on her. 'Hi, Mum.'

Jill's voice was tense. 'Did you see the helicopters?'

'Yes, we're down here now, me and Clara.'

'Do you know why they were called out?'

'Not exactly but... well, I don't think the rescue went great. I know...' Gaby glanced around and lowered her voice. You never knew who was listening, and she didn't want to spread false rumours by saying things when she didn't have all the facts. 'We know at least one person didn't make it – possibly more.'

'Oh dear Lord!' Jill squeaked. 'Is Ava OK? Have you seen her?'

'Yes. She's upset, as you can imagine. This is her first time dealing with something that's gone so wrong, and she's bound to take it hard. Harry's taken her home – he's been through this stuff, so try not to worry too much, Mum. He'll help her through it.'

'Yes, of course. I'll see if I can speak to her later. Poor Ava. She would have known it would happen sooner or later, but I'm sure that doesn't make it any better. I know how your dad used to get, even after years in the service. He'd be so frustrated and angry at himself, I was always terrified it would make him that much more reckless next time he went out.'

'I suppose it's lucky she's not seagoing then, isn't it?'

'But it won't be long before she is. What about Killian?'

'He's still in the station – the vessel they went to still needs to be salvaged, so I wonder if they're getting ready to go back out.'

'All right, my love. Let me know if you get any more news.'

'I will.'

'And, Gaby... if things get tough for you and you need to talk—'

'I know at least one woman who understands exactly how it is because she's been through it. Thanks, Mum.'

'He's a good man. I don't often say it to you, and I don't always see eye to eye with him, but I do know that much. I know this will hit him hard, as it used to your dad.'

They said their goodbyes, Jill reminding her that she was on standby for her family and all her extended family at the station should they need her. Gaby ended the call and then turned to Clara.

'We might as well walk to the shack and fill Cormac in. I'm guessing Killian will be a while yet.'

Gaby didn't realise Killian had already left until she went back to the station, expecting to find him still there or out at sea. But the salvage operation had been deemed unnecessarily risky and so the boat had been secured to stop it from drifting, and they were planning to go and retrieve it the following day when the forecast was for better conditions.

She rang him as she walked home but got no answer. She tried not to worry – he could have been in the shower or he might have arrived home and fallen asleep. It wouldn't be the first time she'd found him fully clothed, face down on the bed where he'd collapsed from sheer exhaustion after a gruelling rescue.

But when she got home, he wasn't there. She checked the garden and the upstairs rooms and quickly rang round to see if anyone knew where he was, but nobody did. It was strange and unnerving, but she didn't have time to solve the mystery right then because the children needed picking up from school.

As she headed over to the school, she felt more and more frantic. She called Killian for a second, third, fourth time, getting no answer, trying not to allow space for the sickening misgiving that was building inside her. The news from the mission was bad, but Killian had been on rough missions before and he'd coped. He'd been on board the night her dad had been lost at sea and he'd dealt with that too – better, some would say, than he ought to have done. But then Killian's way had always been to bottle up his pain where it couldn't hurt or distract him from future missions.

Jill said she worried Jack would become more reckless after a failed rescue, but Killian became more obsessed, more focused than ever, often to the detriment of everything else in his life. Things would settle eventually, and Gaby was hopeful this time would be the same, even if she was finding that hard to believe right now.

She was at least cut a break when she got to school and Fern ran across the playground to her.

'Mum, can we go and play with Abigail and Simeon?'

'When you say "we", what do you mean? Does Elijah want to go?'

'He told Simeon he would go to his house, and I said I wanted to go too to play with Abigail. Can I?'

'The thing is—'

'Look here's Elijah! Eli!' Fern raced over to him.

There was a brief, lively conversation including some very expressive gestures that led Gaby to believe Elijah didn't want to take Fern to his best friend's house to play with his sister, but Gaby spotted an opportunity. If they were both out of the way for an hour, she could locate Killian and talk to him properly.

A moment later Fern came running back. 'He says I can't come, but it's not up to him, is it?'

'No it isn't.'

'So can we ask Abigail's mum?'

Gaby aimed one of her sternest, most disapproving looks at Elijah as he came over with Simeon. 'Hi, Simeon,' she said, transforming into a gentler smile for his friend. 'Is your mum here yet?'

'She's...' He pointed to a woman with scarlet hair, who had a girl of Fern's age at her side as she chatted to another woman.

Gaby made her way over.

'Sorry to interrupt,' she said, 'but, Jeanette, I just wanted to check these arrangements for Eli to come and play with Simeon.'

'Oh I don't have a clue – I don't get to hear about any arrangements until they're already made; I'm just expected to supply the snacks.' She looked at her son. 'So you've fixed for Elijah to hang out at ours?'

'Is that OK?' Simeon asked.

'Of course.'

'Can I come and play with Abigail?' Fern asked.

'I don't see why not.'

Fern and Abigail squeaked their approval in unison, while Elijah exchanged an unimpressed look with his friend.

'Will you be all right taking them with you?' Gaby asked. 'It's just... well, I could do with speaking to Killian... you know... not sure if you heard about the—'

'I saw the helicopters,' Jeanette said. 'Did something bad happen?'

'I'm not really sure yet, but I think it might have done. I just want to know...' She glanced at the kids, but none of them were listening, too busy making their plans. 'I want to know Killian is OK.'

'I get it. I'll feed them. No rush to pick them up – just drop me a text before you start out so I can find lost shoes and stuff.'

'That's brilliant; I owe you one,' Gaby said with a tight smile.

'Any time you need, you know you only have to ask. Your kids are a pleasure to have around – and you never know, they might rub off on mine and make them actual decent humans.'

'Thanks, Jeanette. I really appreciate it.'

· · ·

Gaby arrived home, this time finding Killian in the bedroom.

'Thank God! I was worried—' she began but then stopped dead, her eyes wide as she took in the scene.

Killian was sitting on the end of the bed, straight-backed, staring at the window, and as he turned at her approach, there was such absolute, soul-sick pain in his eyes, Gaby could scarcely imagine how anyone could endure it.

'Shit, Kill...' She threw her arms around him. 'Talk to me!'

He stood and pushed her off.

'Killian, please!' Gaby stood up and reached for him again. 'Someone died – I know that much. Please tell me. Don't shut me out this time, because I don't think I can take it!'

'The car needs cleaning,' he said in a dull voice, moving her hand from his arm and heading for the door.

But she reached for his wrist and took hold once again, and she held fast this time, halting his progress. 'Stop it! Stop trying to keep this in! You can't control everything all the time, Killian. Sooner or later something's got to give, even for you. Talk to me; I want to listen.'

'Where are the kids?' he asked in a dull voice.

'They went to play with Jeanette's kids.'

He nodded slowly, as if he was taking an age to understand her words.

'Sit down,' she said, leading him back to the bed. 'Do you need anything? Food? A drink?'

He shook his head.

'Then what can I do?'

When he didn't reply, she asked again but got nothing a second time. Rather than keep coaxing him to talk, she pulled him into her arms and held on tight. And suddenly, there was a heaving breath, and she heard the sound of stifled sobs.

'I know...' she soothed. 'I know... when you're ready.'

'The other kid died,' he said into her shoulder.

'There were children?'

'Two boys. One was already gone when we got there and the other... I've just heard he died in hospital.'

'It's not your fault.' Gaby pulled him closer, fighting her own tears.

But he yanked away, and when he looked at her there was a sudden fury in his eyes. 'Then whose fault is it? That's what we were there for! That's what we do! If we can't save anyone what's the point of us?'

'You save people all the time!'

'Not this time!' Killian yelled. 'Not every time!' He stood and went to the window, every muscle tense, every bit of him so angry that the very air around him seemed to hum with barely suppressed rage.

She knew it wasn't aimed at her and she wasn't afraid – not of any physical hurt at least.

Two boys. She didn't dare ask how old, not when he was on the edge like this. Her thoughts went to Ava and Harry. They'd be devastated too. Even Cormac would blame himself, would wonder if they could have been saved with one more pair of hands, whether the outcome would have been different with him on duty.

'I'm sorry,' she whispered. 'I'm so sorry.'

He turned to face her, his voice cracking again. It was so clearly taking every ounce of his strength not to cry again. 'What's the point of us? What's the bloody point?'

She sat with him for another hour. She didn't ask him any more about the mission, and she let him speak when he needed to, though he didn't say much. Eventually, he seemed calmer, getting up and kissing her gently before going to get showered.

She'd never seen him like this before – not this bad – and she didn't know what to do. Not only that, but she'd have to pick up Elijah and Fern soon and she couldn't let them see it. Days like this had featured in her childhood, days where her dad had grieved for people he hadn't even known, for someone he hadn't been able to save. She hadn't understood it fully back then, but the memories had stayed with her. Even now, she could say with clarity what they'd eaten that night, what her mum had been wearing as she'd tried to comfort him, what she and her sisters had watched on the television when they'd been told to stay out of the way, what the garden had smelled like... All such tiny details that had somehow stayed with her, to the point that the smell of a gardenia or a certain flavour of crisp or the music from an old TV game show would make her feel suddenly melancholy. Gaby didn't want those memories for her children – at least, if they had to come, not yet, not while they were still so young.

While Killian was in the shower, Gaby called Jill to see if she could pick them up from Jeanette's house to spend the night with her.

'I thought you might ask,' Jill said. 'Of course I can; it's the least I can do. How's Killian?'

'Hard to say. He's not good at the moment. Must have been a really tough one.'

'They were children. It's bound to be hard.'

'So you know about it?'

'I spoke to Ava.'

'How is she?'

'Upset, as you can imagine. She says she knew a day like this would come, but she'd always assumed it would be much further in her future than this.'

'In the end, knowing Ava, it will make her more determined to make the boat crew.'

'That's just what Clara said about Cormac.'

'So you spoke to her too?'

'Yes. You have to, don't you? You have to see the crew are all right at times like these – your dad would have always done it.'

'He would. So you know what happened?'

'A dad and his two boys out on a yacht. Not local, not sure

where from. I can only guess they might have been staying close by. As far as I can tell, they took the yacht out and somehow capsized it. One of the boys got tangled in the rigging and the dad couldn't free him – he'd drowned before the lifeboat had even got there – though it's no use pointing that out to Harry or Ava; they'd only say they should have got there quicker. But I don't think the distress call came in all that quick, so how could they have launched any faster than they did?'

'The other boy died in hospital later – Killian told me.'

'Yes. Harry said Vas took the call and told them all. I can't even begin to imagine what that family is going through.'

'The dad survived?'

'Yes, he's in hospital, but if he's in any state to know what's going on he must be bereft right now. He was an experienced sailor by all accounts – just goes to show the sea doesn't care about any of that.'

'How old were the boys?'

'That I'm not sure about, but I don't think either of them were yet teenagers.'

'God, Mum. This is going to hit everyone hard.'

'It will. But we'll be there to pick up the pieces, just like we always are.'

'I can't tell you what a favour it is, you getting the kids for me. I could really do with getting Killian to open up, if I can.'

'Take as long as you need; you know they're always welcome to stay here.'

'I'll bring some clean clothes over for school tomorrow when I get a minute,' Gaby said, though, in truth, as much as she wanted to support Killian, she was so desperate to see and hold her children she'd have found any excuse to go over to Seaspray Cottage. Killian might need her, but she was also a mother, and it was at times like this she was grateful to see her kids safe. Elijah had escaped his own close call the previous year, and if anything could bring that into sharper focus, it was a tragedy like this.

Ending the call, she was about to go see how Killian was when she heard a phone ringing downstairs. It was Killian's, still sitting on the kitchen table where he must have left it when he'd arrived home, shattered and wretched, from the disastrous shout. Gaby went to pick it up, noting an unknown caller. If it was a work thing, she'd tell them now wasn't a good time.

'Killian's phone; he's not available right now, but—'

The line went dead. Gaby let out a sigh, dropped the phone to the table and went back upstairs. When she walked into the bedroom, Killian was getting into his uniform.

'There's never another shout?' she asked tensely.

'No, but I'm needed back at the station.'

'They're not salvaging the yacht until tomorrow. Maxine said it had been secured so it won't drift—'

'There are other things to do.'

'Now?'

'Yes. Ava's not up to it and Harry needs to stay with her so we're two down there – with Cormac not yet back it's three.'

'What's so important that you need to do it now?'

'If there's another shout tonight, the boat isn't ready.'

'Vas would have taken care of that. You're in no state to—'

Killian rounded on her, that barely controlled rage in his eyes again. 'If I don't do it, who will?'

'Someone else!'

'Who, Gaby? Someone has to step up to the plate, and if I don't, how can I expect anyone else to?'

'Everyone does, all the time. Right now you all need a breather. For God's sake, stay home, get some sleep, talk to me, drink, whatever... just take a moment.'

He shook his head as he bent to fasten his shoes. 'You don't understand. You never understand.'

'I understand that our kids want to know you're all right,

but you'd rather go down to the station and work than go to see them!'

'You haven't told them—'

'Of course not, but they're not stupid! They might not know exactly what's going on but they'll be able to tell it's something. Trust me, I know from experience.'

'I work to keep the kids safe! We lost two boys today – what if they'd been our two? If I have to be at the station twenty-four-seven to make sure we never lose another, then I will!' He got up and pushed past her.

Gaby could have called him back, she could have chased him, but there was no point. While he was like this she knew there would be no reasoning with him, and she'd been with him long enough to recognise when to back off. With luck, Vas or Maxine would be at the station, perhaps the two calmest members of the team, and they'd be able to talk him down. She hoped so, as she listened to the front door slamming shut, because she sure as hell couldn't.

CHAPTER EIGHT

Over the next few weeks, it felt to Gaby like Killian was never home. Elijah and Fern didn't ask, but Gaby felt they had to have noticed, and though she understood to an extent what was going on in her husband's head, that didn't excuse him neglecting his family. She didn't need to doubt this time that when he was missing he was likely to be found at the lifeboat station – everyone on the crew mentioned it to her every time they saw her, but none of them could persuade him that he didn't need to be there all the time. His pain caused her guilt for ever doubting him before. He was a good man; she knew he was, and she was wrong to have even considered he could hurt her.

It wasn't just the kids who were suffering. Gaby and Killian had always had a healthy sex life, but even that had stopped. Gaby didn't want to force the issue, but she felt that the issue would force itself sooner or later and she was afraid of how that might play out. He didn't want to talk about it and, for now, she couldn't make him, but that didn't stop her feeling unloved, neglected and unwanted.

It was a long shot, but Gaby's hope was that the upcoming spring celebrations would lighten the mood. Port Promise loved a celebration and this was one of their favourites. Some called it Jack-in-the-Green day, some the Green Man celebration, some May Day, and some thought it was all the same thing. Whichever deity or tradition they liked to think it served, one thing everyone agreed on was that it performed one important function, and that was to banish the winter and welcome in the spring, and it always took place around the first weekend of May. Amongst the festivities would be a maypole threaded with bright ribbons, with local folk music and traditional Cornish dancing to accompany the children as they circled around the pole. The school-aged girls would weave flowers in their hair and wear white dresses, and the boys would wear white trousers and a straw hat as part of their maypole uniform.

But Elijah was having none of it this year. They were all in the tiny kitchen at Thistledown Cottage, falling over one another to get ready. Fern was on a stool having her hair braided by Gaby, Killian wasn't quite as productive as he read through the morning paper, and Elijah slumped against the doorframe looking sullen.

'He's too old,' Killian said carelessly. 'Let him be.'

'But its May Day!' Fern said with an almost comical note of outrage in her voice as Gaby wove snow-white gypsophila into her braids.

'I'm not wearing stupid white trousers and a stupid hat,' Elijah shot back.

'He'll have to sit out of the dancing then,' she said impatiently.

Elijah scowled. 'Didn't want to dance anyway.'

'Only because Byron Forster said it was gay,' Fern said.

Gaby's head snapped up. 'Is that true?'

Elijah at least knew he ought to pay attention this time. 'No,' he said in a voice that suggested his answer was a blatant lie.

'Do you even know what that word means?'

'Yes, but—'

'Then you should know not to use it in that way!'

'But I didn't—'

'Did you put Byron right when he said it?'

'No, but—'

'Then I don't want to hear your excuses. If you didn't call him out, then it makes you as bad. Your grandpa Jack would have been so sad to see this kind of behaviour from you. Never an unkind word – that was how he lived. Unkind words turn into unkind deeds.'

Elijah was silent as he fiddled with his shirt buttons, but Gaby noticed how he flushed from his neck up to his cheeks. She'd got through, and he was ashamed.

Killian put his paper down. 'Elijah,' he said, 'if you know what's good for you, you'll go upstairs and put those white trousers on and that hat and dance that maypole and bloody well look like you're enjoying it.'

Elijah sloped off and Gaby shot Killian a grateful smile. A united front before the children meant a lot; it meant they hadn't strayed so far apart that she couldn't still pull him back to her with some effort.

Finishing Fern's hair, she was filled with hope for the day. Perhaps this would mark a turning point where they could get back on track.

'Are you going to put on *your* white trousers and straw hat?' she asked him.

'Don't push it,' he said with a quick grin.

He got up from the breakfast bar, folded up his paper and looked towards the space Elijah had just vacated. 'I'd better go and have a talk to him.'

'Not even a teenager yet,' Gaby said as he went to the door. 'God help us in a couple of years. He gets it from you, you know.'

Killian turned to her. 'You think? I've heard the stories your dad used to tell about you at that age; I wouldn't be so sure about that.'

'What stories?' Fern twisted to look up at Gaby, who simply smiled.

'Never mind. Go and find your shoes; we're running late as it is.'

Before the food, music and maypole dancing, there was always a parade. Not just any parade, but a mad fever-dream of a parade, where the people of the village dressed up as chimney sweeps or milkmaids or smugglers of old or giant fish on bicycles or just about anything else they could think of. Gaby had never been keen on that, but she would stretch to a crown of spring flowers and a long white cotton dress.

'You look gorgeous,' Killian said in her ear as they left the house.

She flushed with pleasure. He was in a better mood today than she'd seen him since the yacht tragedy a month earlier. Perhaps he was finally coming round. He certainly seemed as if he was trying.

The sky was pearl grey as they walked into the village as a family. Although the sun hadn't shown up, it was warm and the forecast promised no rain.

One by one, various characters came into view. Gaby spotted a few mermaids, plenty of milkmaids – which were always a favourite – someone dressed as a daffodil, someone else as a daisy, a blackbird complete with cardboard wings, a couple of old-fashioned farmers wearing smocks, a scarecrow and lots of chimney sweeps. The sweeps and the milkmaids had been the first characters, or so Gaby had been told, back when the parade began, which explained why there were always so many of them, but people had got creative since then, which explained how the other costumes grew madder and madder every year. They were all heading to the promenade, which was the official starting point, and all offered a smile or a nod or a friendly word as they met Gaby and her family.

Every year, the procession was headed up by Jack-in-the-Green – one of the men of the village who wore a headdress of leaves. If it could be called a headdress at all, because it had grown bigger and bigger over the years, and now it was so huge it covered the wearer's entire torso, balanced on his shoulders by a wooden frame. They used real leaves taken from local trees woven into it, often complete with bugs and pollen and just about anything else to make a man itch. It was his job to lead the characters around the village and at the end of the route to meet the spirit of winter dressed in glittering frosted robes, where they would do battle. If Jack-in-the-Green won, then spring would begin. If winter won, it was going to be a miserable summer. But winter, of course, always let Jack-in-the-Green win.

'There he is!' Fern cried, pointing to a figure that was part man but mostly tree. She raced over and threw her arms around his legs.

'Steady on – you'll have me over!'

It was Harry's voice that came from inside the foliage. Ava was standing with him, and she greeted Fern as Gaby, Killian and Elijah caught up.

'Enjoying yourself in there?' Killian asked Harry.

'Doesn't he look sexy?' Ava said with a wink.

'Stop it,' Harry grumbled. 'I feel like a total—'

'Zip it, Harry!' Gaby laughed. 'Young ears listening in!'

'I was going to say tree,' Harry replied.

Killian chuckled. 'I don't know what you're moaning about – you're the star of the show.'

'Thank God no one can see my face,' Harry said.

'I knew it was you,' Fern said. 'They looked like your feet.'

'Well...' Ava grinned at her. 'I have no answer for that!'

Harry turned with a swish and a rustle towards Ava. 'Does that mean everyone will know it's me? You said nobody would be able to tell!'

'Of course they're going to know it's you!' Killian said. 'Everyone already knows it's you without being able to recognise your feet. Have you forgotten where you live?'

'Quit your complaining,' Ava said. 'It was either you or your dad, and you said you didn't want your dad overdoing it since the oyster festival so...'

'Yeah, I know,' Harry said. 'I don't know how he did this every year for so long.'

'Because it's fun, and he's fun,' Ava replied breezily. 'In fact, I have no idea how he managed to produce someone as boring as you.'

'Thanks,' Harry muttered. 'Such a supportive girlfriend... I'm so lucky...'

'Is it Bob doing winter again?' Gaby asked.

'Yes,' Ava said. 'So that's one fight Harry's in with a chance of winning.'

'Ha ha, you don't get any funnier,' Harry said from inside his leaves.

From the promenade, the sound of pipes and fiddles reached them.

'The music's started!' Fern stepped away from Harry and looked up expectantly. 'Is it time to do the parade?'

Ava reached through the shrubbery and put a hand on Harry's back. 'I'd better get Tom's Midnight Garden over to the starting point.'

'You're so dead when this is over,' Harry said as Ava led him away, laughing as she steered him from behind.

Killian looked at Elijah. 'And you thought you had it bad with your trousers and hat.'

The pipes and fiddles were now accompanied by a steady drumbeat.

'Time to go,' Gaby said.

Curious tourists lined the streets to watch. Gaby could feel their eyes on her as she led her family to the starting point of the parade. Some were taking photos, some pointing at characters that caught their eye and marvelling at the technicalities of the costume, some obviously finding it all quite funny. It didn't bother Gaby; she'd seen such curiosity every year. Visitors found it quaint and maybe a little backwards – but it was their tradition, it brought the whole village together and they enjoyed it. So she took her place behind the milkmaids, sweeps, tin miners, sailors, smugglers, shepherds, farmers in smocks with straw in their mouths, fishermen, wood nymphs, mermaids and those in costumes she couldn't quite fathom, with Killian looking handsome beside her in his green shirt and Fern and Elijah in their maypole clothes, and she walked, proud of her place in this community, of her husband and family, of her corner of Cornwall.

The procession was a wondrous whirl of colour and noise. It snaked along a route almost identical to that of the Promise Procession, an event that took place much later in the year where the whole town carried lanterns to commemorate the first Morrow to rescue people from the sea, Gaby's ancestor, Iziah. And as they passed the harbour where a bronze plaque remembered the heroism of her father, she cast a glance at the small square of metal and spared him a fond thought. Looking to her side, she saw Killian do the same and wondered what he was thinking.

Killian had not only looked up to Jack, he'd loved him like his own father – Gaby knew that. He'd have done anything for Jack, though it hadn't always been so. When Gaby had first brought Killian home to meet her parents, Jack had been disapproving and distrustful, in the way most fathers are when meeting a new man in their daughter's life. But once Killian had proved himself, they'd been inseparable. She'd seen that clearly for the first time one night when Killian had gone drinking with his friends in Truro. He and Gaby had only been dating for six months or so, but Killian had already become good friends with Jack. That night he'd got into a fight and he'd been arrested. Jack had been the person Killian called to get him out, and when Killian explained he'd only got into the fight because he'd been standing up for his friend, Jack had believed him without question.

'I know his character,' Jack had said, going to get his car keys to drive out for him, 'and that's good enough for me.'

In the end, there had been no charges and no follow-up, and though Jack sometimes teased a young Killian about it, it was clear he'd never doubted Killian's account and Killian had never forgotten Jack's faith in him. It was more, he'd once told Gaby, than his own dad had ever shown.

The sound of Killian's voice over the music snapped her from the memory.

'He'd have loved seeing Harry at the front there. He'd have ribbed him something rotten.'

'Dad?' Gaby smiled. 'He would.'

'Despite what you think, I still miss him.'

'Despite what I think? Why would I think anything else? I know how much you respected him.'

'It was way more than that.' Killian looked down at Gaby.

His face was giving nothing away and she wished she could tell what he was thinking.

'I wish I could make you understand.'

'I do.'

'Sometimes it doesn't feel that way.'

His words unsettled her. She felt as if he might be talking about more than just his affection for her dad. Did she fail to understand him in other ways? Was it often? If she had, he'd never said so before – at least, not in such stark terms. Was he referring to the recent lifeboat tragedy? Gaby had done her best to be supportive and to comprehend just what he was going through, but at the end of the day, she hadn't been on the boat when those young boys had drowned. The only people who would truly understand it were the other crew members. She could only do so much, though it saddened her to think that he felt she'd somehow failed him when he'd needed her.

She was thinking of her response when she felt a tap on her shoulder. She turned to see Clara and Cormac with Jill and Marina.

'Hello!' she said. 'I wondered where you'd got to!'

'I'm not so quick these days,' Cormac said ruefully. 'Took a bit of catching up.'

'But on your own two feet at least.'

'Aye. No more physio either and back on my exercise programme.'

'That's brilliant!' Gaby smiled.

'It is,' Killian agreed. 'The best news, mate. So you'll be ready for that boat crew in no time.'

'I hope so. Got to pass my last few competencies, get fit again and I'll be raring to go.'

Killian nodded his approval. 'I'll look forward to it – we need everyone we can get.'

'I know,' Cormac said, seeming vaguely troubled. 'I only wish I could be quicker.'

'Whatever you do at the station helps, though,' Gaby said. 'Right, Killian?'

'Exactly.'

They turned back to face the front and continue their march. By now they'd reached the lifeboat station and Betty's empty cafe. Only, when Gaby glanced up, she noticed the lights were on. She nudged Clara and pointed.

'Someone's in Betty's!'

'So they are,' Jill said, following her gaze. 'I wonder if it's the new owner. They picked a good day to arrive.'

'Or a bad one,' Clara said. 'Might think we're a bunch of weirdos.'

'Well if they're going to live here then they'll have to get over that,' Jill said. 'When the parade is over, we'll pop back to see.'

The procession danced on, winding up the steep hill to the Spratt, where everyone was handed a drink by the landlord, and then down again to finish on the beach. When they got there the maypole was staked into the sand. Usually it would have been on a green at the edge of the village, but rain over the previous couple of days had made it too boggy, and nobody had any complaints about moving it to their beloved stretch of golden sand. As the children of the village took their places ready to twist their ribbons around it, Jack-in-the-Green and his adversary, the spirit of winter – otherwise known as Harry and Bob – were handed wooden swords, had a laughable duel in front of the maypole in which Harry pretended to stab Bob and Bob threw himself to the sand in an Oscar-worthy performance, and everyone cheered as winter was vanquished for another year.

Harry finally got to shrug off his leafy headdress and claim his reward – a kiss from Ava – and then the maypole dancing began. As pipers piped and fiddlers fiddled, Fern quickly got into the spirit of the occasion, smiling and skipping, but Elijah looked so mortified by the whole thing that Gaby realised this would probably be the last year she could expect him to do it and that, perhaps, she shouldn't have even pushed him to do this one.

Harry still had leaves in his hair when he and Ava came to join them.

'You make a beautiful tree.' Cormac winked at him.

'Ha ha.' Harry tried to frown but wasn't doing a very good job of hiding his grin. 'Your turn next year.'

'I'd love to,' Cormac said, 'but I'm not a local, am I?'

'Local enough.' Killian aimed a quick grin at Harry. 'Right?'

'Too right,' Harry said.

'Did you see the lights on in Betty's?' Ava asked them all.

Jill nodded. 'We did. We were wondering whether to go up there and say hello.'

'Give them a minute to settle in,' Killian said, and Gaby detected the merest hint of impatience in his tone. 'They've just got here. Send the town inspection party over and you might just have them running for the hills.'

'We're not an *inspection party*!' Gaby sniffed. 'We just want to make them feel welcome.'

'Well I'm not sure the entire town descending on them as soon as they arrive is going to make them feel welcome. We're a tight-knit community and I imagine we can be overwhelming as a pack when you first get here.'

'Oh, I don't know about that...' Cormac smiled at Clara. 'My first visitor made me feel pretty welcome.'

'I think it's all the more reason to say hello,' Jill said. 'So they know they're wanted here. And a handful of us is hardly a pack.'

Killian shrugged and Gaby noted that impatience in it again. She turned to where the children were dancing round the maypole. The coloured ribbons were almost wound tight, so that now they were all laughing helplessly as they were forced to bump into one another, moving around it as they were in two different directions.

'We won't be going anywhere just yet,' Gaby said. 'We've got the may queen to crown first.'

'Who've they picked?' Jill asked.

'Abigail,' Gaby said.

'Oh...' Jill glanced over at the maypole. 'And was Fern happy with that? I know she'd hoped it would be her.'

'She was fine. She loves Abigail and, besides, isn't this just an early lesson in life's disappointments. She can't grow up thinking she'll always get what she wants – best to find that out now. It's not the first disappointment and I'm sure it won't be the last.'

'I smell barbeque!' Harry said, and everyone laughed.

'Of course you do,' Ava said. 'You could smell a hot dog from three miles away.' She turned to Cormac. 'Aren't you opening the shack today?'

'I'll head over in a bit, though most of the action seems to be here. Probably should have set up something mobile like I did for the oyster festival last year, but to be honest I've been a bit...' He glanced at Clara.

'Preoccupied,' Clara finished for him. 'Fussing over me when you really ought to have been more bothered about the fact that you've spent most of this year limping everywhere and with bits of metal in your back.'

He flexed a bicep and grinned. 'That doesn't bother me. If it's good enough for Wolverine, it's good enough for me.'

Clara rolled her eyes. 'Whatever. I'm sure if people want our food, they'll walk the few hundred yards they need to. The stalls here will be gone in a couple of hours once the celebrations are over. We might make some decent trade afterwards.'

'I expect so,' Ava agreed. 'We'll have to head off around then to help Sandy pack up the cider stall, but we'll come down afterwards to grab something to eat.'

'Aren't you having something from the barbeque?' Jill asked Harry.

Ava shook her head wryly. 'Have you actually met this man? Two lunches would still leave room for pudding.'

'I've carried a tree on my back all morning,' Harry said. 'I'm hungry.'

'Yes, Harry...' Ava soothed. 'But what's your excuse every other day?'

.   .   .

As the May Day celebrations wound up, Gaby and Jill made their way back to Betty's to make good on their decision to welcome the new owner. Killian wanted to call at the lifeboat station to do something or other that wasn't at all clear to her, but she was getting so used to him being there that she couldn't be bothered to argue. Ava and Harry were helping Harry's dad pack up the cider stall, while Clara and Cormac had gone to open the fish shack, and Elijah and Fern had gone crabbing with some of their friends and their parents, not ready for their day of fun to end just yet.

As Betty's terrace came into view, they could see a man bent over the wall, his gaze seemingly trained on the beach as he pulled on a cigarette. He seemed to notice them approaching and straightened up, tossing the cigarette to the terrace floor. As they climbed the stone steps leading to it, he came to meet them.

'Hello again. I'm feeling slightly underdressed today. Should I have got the fancy-dress memo?'

Gaby stared at him, recognition hitting her over the head like a clout with a rolling pin. 'You?'

'Yes, I was me last time I checked.'

'I mean... you?' She glanced at Jill and then turned back to stare at the man some more. 'You bought the cafe?'

'Why else do you think I was here the night we met? Although, I like to think it was the hand of fate. Of course, it wasn't...' He mocked a pensive look for a moment. 'Or maybe it was. I'm interested to find out. How was your party today? You people love your parties, don't you? Is life one long party in Port Promise? I'm beginning to think I might like it here after all.'

'Am I missing something?' Jill asked Gaby.

'This... *gentleman* was at Betty's party,' Gaby said.

'Until your village goons turfed me out,' the man said.

'We wouldn't have asked you to leave if you'd explained

who you were,' Gaby said. 'You could have avoided all that by just opening your mouth.'

'I know, but I was interested to see how I'd be treated if you didn't know. And I have to say, I'd expected it to be a bit duelling banjos around here, but I hadn't expected it to be quite so brutal. And from one so lovely too. Face of an angel, heart of stone... just my type.'

'I'm sorry,' Gaby said stiffly. 'You must be able to understand it from our point of view. It was our friend's leaving party and we thought you were crashing it.'

'I suppose I was.'

'I mean, even Betty didn't know who you were, so how could any of us guess?'

'I know – I wanted it that way.'

'Why?'

He gave a careless shrug. 'Come to a new project with knowledge of the prior owner and it makes you soft on it.'

'What does that mean?'

'What I said.'

Jill cut in. 'So you're planning to make big changes here?'

He smiled at her, but it wasn't warm. It was knowing and a bit smug. Gaby didn't like it. 'Why wouldn't I?' He glanced at the building and then back at them. 'Have you seen it?'

'There's nothing wrong with it,' Gaby said sourly, even though she would have been the first to admit that it had needed updating for years. It was serviceable and even rather adorable, but modern it wasn't.

'When will you be open?' Jill asked.

'Not for a few weeks yet,' he said. 'Maybe even months, depending on what horrors I find. There's a lot to be done either way.'

'You'll be taking the flat above?' Gaby asked.

He started to laugh. 'Live here? God no! Why do you ask? Would you like it if I did?'

'No, but Betty used to.'

'I'm not Betty. You people are really having a hard time getting that, aren't you?'

'But you're going to be local?' Jill asked.

'Does that make a difference?'

'No,' Gaby said, offended on Jill's behalf at his mocking tone. 'We're just asking, just trying to be friendly.'

He raised his eyebrows. 'Like you were at the party?'

'I've apologised for that.'

'So you have. Apology accepted then.'

Gaby exchanged a glance with her mum. 'I suppose we'll let you get on then... Lloyd, wasn't it?'

'Well remembered,' he said, taking a fresh cigarette from a pack. 'See, I knew I'd made an impression on you.'

'Lloyd who?' Jill asked.

'Isn't Lloyd enough? Are you planning to research me?'

'No,' Gaby cut in, 'we just think it's courteous to offer more than just Lloyd if you're going to be here a lot.'

'All right then, what's your name?'

'Gabriella.'

'Gabriella...?'

'Isn't Gabriella enough?'

'Touché.' He grinned. 'Was there anything else? Perhaps you want to go and get your menfolk to bring their pitchforks to chase me out of town? Or as this is the twenty-first century and women are equals, perhaps you're planning to do it yourselves?'

'Listen...' Gaby took a breath and gathered her patience. She couldn't remember when she'd met a more infuriating man, but she was damned if she was going to let him get the better of her. 'I apologise again for the way we treated you at the party, but in our defence, we didn't know who you were. You could have told us and avoided all this misunderstanding.'

'I know, but the misunderstanding has been entertaining.'

She bit back another angry retort and smoothed her

features, though inside she was boiling. 'Can we put it behind us? We came here to welcome you. We're not a bad bunch if you give us a chance. If you're fair with us, then we'll be fair with you.'

'Hmm... you're saying I haven't been fair?'

'No, of course not.'

Jill laid a hand on Gaby's arm. 'We've taken up enough of your time,' she said, looking at Lloyd, but her grip on Gaby told her she thought enough was enough. 'It was nice to meet you.'

'Was it?' he asked, looking at Gaby instead of Jill, which made her want to swing for him in a way that nobody, not even Killian in one of his most exasperating moods, had ever done. 'Anyway, this might make you happy or you might miss me – but I won't be around much for a week or two. But my contractors will be here tomorrow to gut this place.'

Gaby caught a troubled look from Jill. They'd all be sad to see the remnants of Betty's go, but they had to be ready for change. Change had always been inevitable once she'd left.

'You're still going to be running it as a cafe?' Jill asked.

'No,' Lloyd said.

'Then what will it be?'

He started to walk past them, down the steps, towards a pickup truck parked on the promenade. 'It'll be a very good seafood restaurant. You should come when we open.'

Gaby and Jill looked at each other as he started his engine and drove away. A seafood restaurant? Direct competition for Cormac and Clara's fish shack. As if things couldn't get any worse.

CHAPTER NINE

'He's just so bloody awful!' Gaby spat.

'You might have said that a few times already,' Killian commented as he pulled off his shirt and tossed it into the laundry basket.

Outside their window, a vast moon hung over the bay. The clouds of the day had cleared, and a spring frost was already forming on the garden below.

'I know, but he's just so chronically vile that I don't even know how to deal with it. I have to keep saying it out loud in the hope it might sink in. I can't express to you, Kill... you'd have to meet him to get it. I mean, why? Why would anyone go to such lengths to be so argumentative? You'd think, being a new venture and a new village for him he'd be less... obnoxious than he is. You'd think he'd try a bit. And poor Cormac... I'm telling you, this Lloyd character strikes me as the type of man who wouldn't want to play nice. He'd take the greatest pleasure in putting Cormac out of business.'

Killian took off his jeans and got into bed, where he sat against the pillows, watching Gaby take off her mascara with a faint smile on his face. 'Cormac's only got the shack; I can't see how they're in competition at all. This guy is offering proper sit-down restaurant meals; he won't care about a wooden shack with a few benches on the beach.'

'I wouldn't be so sure...' Gaby threw a stained cotton pad into the waste bin. 'If we were talking about anyone else I'd agree with you, but this guy... I swear he has a screw loose. It's like he enjoys antagonising people, like he wants people to hate him.'

'His restaurant might not even be any good.'

'I bet it will be. I got the impression he knew what he was doing – maybe he's got others. I'm going to see if I can find out. And I've got a good mind to get people to boycott him.'

'I'm not sure Cormac would thank you for that. And if there's one way to make people curious enough to try it out, that would be it. They'd want to see for themselves just what's riled you to do that. And you can't stop visitors from going there. Even you have to admit it's what Port Promise has been missing for a long time.'

Gaby grabbed a pot of moisturising cream and twisted off the lid. 'Well I hate him and I hope his food is shit, and I hope he has to close down after a week.'

'Wow...' Killian put his arms behind his head and grinned lazily at her. 'Remind me never to get on your bad side again.'

Gaby turned to him. 'You can't be happy about this?'

'Of course I'm not, but what can we do? It's a free country. The guy got his bid in, he got the building and Cormac missed his chance. If this bloke wants to turn it into a seafood restaurant we can hardly stop him. I'm on Cormac's side, but even he'd hold his hands up and say this guy won fair and square.'

'Hmm...' Gaby put the lid back on her pot.

'I'm sure it won't be nearly as bad as you think,' Killian continued. 'In the summer there'll be plenty enough business for them both.'

'And what about when it's not summer?'

'I don't know what you want me to say here. Maybe we should try getting on his good side and see where that gets us. He might have felt cornered and come out fighting – we did try to throw him out of Betty's party. He might not be as bad as you think.'

'You're saying I'm no judge of character? Because if there's one thing—'

'I'm saying what you've seen might not be what he's always like. Who knows, if he settles and starts to get on with people there might even come a time when he and Cormac can join forces. Cormac wanted a partner.'

'Yes, and it would have been Clara!'

'Clara's going to be busy soon with the baby – she'll hardly be thinking about running a restaurant.'

Gaby climbed into bed beside him and settled into her pillow. 'I'm sorry, he's just got to me. Doesn't seem fair that Cormac loses out to someone so... I don't know.'

'Hmm...' Killian moved closer, holding her in a steady gaze. 'Would it help take your mind off it if I tell you how incredible you looked today?'

'Maybe a little,' she said, smiling now.

'And how I kept thinking about how proud I am and how lucky I am that you married me...?'

Gaby gave a smile that was brighter than the sudden doubt she felt. Of course she loved hearing those words from him, loved that he was proud and that he thought himself lucky, but did he really mean any of it? What if it was smoke and mirrors, distractions from a truth he didn't want her to uncover? She wanted to trust him and she wanted things between them to be this good, as they'd always been before, but the secrets he'd kept about his trip to Bristol and his refusal to enter into discussion about it crept back under the door and issued a quiet warning.

But this was Killian, and no matter how they'd clashed

during their time as a couple, he'd never been any less than adoring of her. Surely the possibility of unfaithfulness was paranoia on her part? Surely Killian would never do that to her? And wasn't it good to see him interacting again, almost the old Killian instead of the hollow, wounded version she'd been living with ever since the capsizing tragedy that had shaken everyone on the lifeboat crew badly, but seemingly Killian worst of all?

With those thoughts, she pushed the doubts aside. She loved him and he loved her and she wasn't going to let her stupid, suspicious brain ruin this moment.

'You are lucky – that I won't argue with. Maybe I'm a bit lucky too.'

'All day I just wanted to bring you home.'

'Really? And why would you want to do that?'

'To do this...' He reached across and pulled her into a kiss.

Gaby melted into it, the first breathless explosion leaving her desperate for more. It felt like years since he'd kissed her like this, since he'd wanted her, and knowing that he wanted her now set her on fire. In seconds she was on top of him, holding him by the wrists and kissing him hard.

'Mum!'

With a groan she paused.

'Mum!' It was Fern's voice. 'Mum, I've been sick!'

'Jesus!' Killian gasped. 'Talk about timing.'

Gaby got out of bed with a look of regret. 'Look on the bright side,' she said, putting on her dressing gown, 'at least it's not your pager. Maybe if she's not too bad we can pick up where—'

Her words were stolen by an urgent bleep from the bedside table. For the first time ever, she could have sworn he didn't want to look as he leaned over.

'You know you don't have to go,' she said. 'Vas doesn't expect you to attend every single one.'

'Of course I have to go,' Killian said. 'If we all thought that, nobody would go.' He got out of bed and started to dress. 'See to Fern – hopefully I'll be back shortly.'

Killian was missing for the rest of the night. A tanker had run aground further along the coast and lifeboats from several stations had needed to attend to rescue dozens of its Icelandic crew. By the time he'd arrived home the first light of dawn was colouring the sky. Gaby woke at the sound of the front door opening, Fern asleep in bed beside her.

'How was it?' she asked as she found him in the kitchen with a glass of water.

'All right. We got everyone off.'

'That's good.'

He gave a short nod, drank the last of his water and sidled past her. 'I'm going to get a shower.'

Gaby raised her eyes to the ceiling and counted to ten. So much for getting back to normal.

A few days later, Gaby took the children to school and then went by the cafe – or whatever it was called now— to see if she could start again with Lloyd. Killian was right – it looked as if he wasn't going anywhere soon, and it was better to have him onside than make him an enemy.

He wasn't there, but the contractors who'd arrived and had already set about ripping out Betty's old fixtures and fittings told her he was likely to be over later that day. She walked away, resigned to the fact that she'd have to come back another time because she had marking to do, and that was on top of all the Flag Day stuff, when she noticed a black pickup truck coming down the road towards the promenade. It stopped outside the terrace steps and she recognised it immediately. A minute later Lloyd got out.

'If it isn't the wood nymph of my dreams,' he said. 'Come to insult me some more?'

'I've come,' Gaby replied with as much courtesy as she could muster, 'hoping we can start again.'

He grabbed a laptop from the back seat. 'Start what again?'

'What do you mean?'

'What do *you* mean? You're the one asking me to start something again, so I want to know what it is.'

'Look, I just want to be civil. You're going to be a part of this village so it's silly for us to be at odds.'

'So *you* are the entire village? And everyone has to be your best friend? What do you do if they're not?'

'That's not what I mean!' Gaby checked her already rising temper. 'It's a small place and grudges take up a lot of room. So we make an effort to get along if we can, and I'd like to get along with you.'

'Well I can't say that's not a tempting offer, but is that it?'

'Yes. So we're good?'

'Maybe...' He regarded her with a faint, wry smile. 'Aren't you related to the guy who owns the fish shack?'

Gaby tried not to frown, despite the sinking feeling that was taking hold. 'He's going out with my sister. Why do you ask?'

'So this sudden desire to be my friend isn't you trying to find out what my plans are so you can tell him?'

'Would you tell me your plans if I asked?' Gaby asked coldly.

'No.'

'Then there's your answer. You might assume I'm that stupid, but I'm not.'

'I never assume anything of anyone. You can't blame me for asking.'

'I hardly imagine you'll be competing for the same customers anyway, so I shouldn't think it will matter.'

'That's true. Though with your shack, the fish and chip shop, and now me, there's only so much fish a village can eat. The way I see it, one of us will end up having to go. Perhaps it will be your chip shop, eh? I've heard he's got one foot in the grave.'

'Where are you going to buy your fish from?' Gaby asked, choosing to ignore what sounded like a veiled threat.

'I have a good supplier.'

'Only we have a supplier here you might want to try. Robin goes out every day; you'd struggle to get fresher, and Cormac's always been happy with what he buys.'

'If I see Robin I'll be sure to tell him you tried to sell his fish for him, but I'll stick with my man if it's all the same to you. I'm after a bit more than the odd pilchard.'

'Oh... well if you need—'

'Thank you,' he cut in. 'I appreciate your efforts, but I know what I'm doing.'

She'd have loved nothing more than to tell him exactly what she thought of him, but as it was hardly complimentary, Gaby held it in. Her opinion of him certainly hadn't improved since their last meeting, despite her best efforts to give him the benefit of the doubt.

'I'm sorry to have bothered you; I'll let you get on.'

'Thank you. Not that you haven't brightened my morning, of course. It's a long shot, but I take it you're still happy with that meathead I saw you with last weekend?'

This time, Gaby couldn't help her outraged expression. 'Are you talking about my husband? What kind of question is that?'

He gave a lazy shrug. 'You can't blame a man for trying, can you?'

'Well you're certainly trying.'

'I get the feeling that your meaning is not the same as mine there,' he said, a smile growing.

'I won't bother you again,' she said.

'Aww, don't say that!' He laughed as she walked away. 'And anyway, you will – they always say that and they always do!'

CHAPTER TEN

It had only been a matter of time, but Elijah and Fern had both caught the water sports bug and they'd been pestering for another day out on the kayaks. Ava was surprised Gaby hadn't seen it coming – after all, the Morrow sisters had loved nothing more than messing around on the sea as they'd grown up. Ava had seen a good Sunday in the forecast, so it seemed like the perfect opportunity to satisfy the kids' demands.

Gaby sat with Jill and Clara on the sand and watched them on the water. Killian was helping Cormac fix a tap at the shack and Harry was working on a new cider with his dad, leaving the Morrow women with an increasingly rare hour without their men. Gaby watched as Clara shifted to get comfortable. 'We ought to have brought a seat down for you – I never thought of it.'

'It's fine,' Clara said. 'Honestly, I think I might have broken it with the size I am now.'

'You're not that bad,' Jill said.

'Well I feel like an elephant.'

'I think you look gorgeous,' Gaby said. 'Far healthier than I did with either of mine.'

'That's not true but thank you; I appreciate your efforts to make me feel better.'

Across the bay, the sounds of metal on metal clanking and of drilling could be heard, accompanied by the whistles and shouts of workmen. Gaby cast an eye across to the source of the noise – Betty's. No longer Betty's of course, and causing quite a commotion in Port Promise in more ways than just the dust and noise of the renovations.

'So much for a peaceful day by the sea. How much longer is he going to be? It's been weeks and weeks and it looks nowhere near done to me.'

Clara rubbed her tummy. 'He did say big changes. I suppose if his plan is to make it somewhere a bit posh he has a lot of work to do. We all loved Betty's, but nobody could accuse it of being upmarket.'

'I have to say, I'm a bit surprised at how well you and Cormac are taking this,' Gaby said.

'What else can we do? We missed out on the cafe and that's that. All we can do now is work with the options we have left. And, to be honest, we've got more pressing things to think about. We both wonder now if taking on the cafe with a baby on the way might have been biting off more than we could chew.'

'That's true,' Jill said. 'And it won't be long now. Will Logan be coming for the birth?'

'I doubt he'd get here on time.'

'You say that but it's a first one so you might be ten, twelve hours, even longer. He ought to be able to.'

Clara paused. 'I know he ought to be; he's the father, but is it bad I'm sort of hoping he doesn't make it? If only because having him and Cormac there together will be bloody awkward.'

'That's something to concern those two, not you,' Jill said. 'You'll be otherwise engaged when the time comes and it won't be your job to referee them. They're grown men, aren't they?'

'I know,' Clara said. 'I know even if he doesn't make it for the birth he'll be down shortly afterwards. It's just going to be weird.'

All three looked round as a voice hailed from the promenade. Marina was waving at them.

Jill got up. 'I'll go and say hello.'

'We'll come too,' Clara said. 'I could do with moving a bit.'

All three made their way across the sand to Marina, who greeted them brightly. Today, her long white hair was braided in two plaits with little red hearts fastened at the ends. On anyone else her age it might have looked a bit bonkers, but somehow Marina made it work.

'Morning, darlin's! What are you three doing down here so early? Looks like a witches' plot to me!'

'Nothing so exciting.' Jill smiled.

The sound of an electric saw screamed through the air. Marina rolled her eyes in the direction of the cafe. 'I'll be glad when that racket stops.'

'We were just saying the same thing,' Jill said. 'We understand he has to do the work but...'

'Doesn't mean we have to like the disruption,' Gaby finished.

'It hardly looks like the same place at all now,' Marina said.

'No...' Gaby turned her gaze to the building standing above the beach on its terrace. 'I wonder what Betty would think if she saw it.'

'I know what old Betty would think,' Marina said.

'Betty's grandma, you mean?'

Marina nodded. 'It's a mercy she's in that wheelchair now and can't get down here so easy to look – she'd be so upset.'

'But this is progress, isn't it?' Jill put in. 'It comes whether we like it or not.'

'It does,' Marina said. 'But nobody said we had to take it lying down.' She was pensive for a moment, which was most unlike her, until she snapped out of it as she seemingly remembered something important. 'In any case, I came over to say I sorted some raffle prizes for Flag Day for you, Gaby.'

'That's brilliant. Thanks. I don't have much room at the house right now, but—'

'Don't worry – I can keep them in my stockroom until you need them,' Marina cut in. 'Figured as much with your place being so small. Just thought I'd tell you I got them and they're ready whenever you want them.'

'That's perfect; thanks so much, Marina. If only everyone was as on the ball as you. I have a feeling there's going to be a lot of chasing in the days before the event.'

'Have you got much pledged yet?'

'Not so much money. I have lots of people saying they'll help with goods and services, but cash donations are always more challenging. Honestly, I could do with something big and impressive. I feel... after the horrible tragedy with those young boys, the guys at the station could do with a win to lift their spirits. I'd love to wipe the floor with last year's fundraising and get a ton more. It'd be something to celebrate, and I feel as if we all need that.'

'That was an awful thing,' Jill agreed, 'but the last few months haven't been all bad.'

'Of course not,' Gaby said, 'I just think in lots of ways it's been very tough at the station, and nobody can deny that. If it's been the same for everyone else as it's been for Killian, then I can't imagine how they've even got themselves on the boats when there's been a shout. I've honestly never seen him like that.'

'But he's getting better?' Clara asked. 'He seems better. Cormac says they're all trying to move past it now.'

'It's tough,' Jill said. 'It didn't happen often, thank God, but I remember what it was like when your dad couldn't save someone. He'd beat himself up about it for months. I don't think he ever got over a single one, not really. He said all he could do was try to file it away in his brain so he could focus on the next shout.'

'He never really talked about it in front of us,' Clara said. 'But I do remember times when he seemed sad and it would last for weeks. It wasn't until I was older that I understood why.'

'The hard side of the service,' Gaby said. 'I still don't know how best to support Killian through these things. Even though he seems better, I can tell he's distracted. Little things, like he's said he'll pick up some wood or something, and then I go out to the car and he's at the wheel staring into space. At what point do I think this isn't just Kill being sad but needing something I can't give him? I just don't know.'

'None of us do,' Jill said. 'I could only do my best for your dad; I never knew if it was what he truly needed. But I think he understood that it was hard for us too.'

Marina nodded sagely. Then she gave a slow smile. 'I'll tell you who is worth a bob or two and ought to be making himself more popular with folks than he is.'

Gaby frowned slightly and Marina pointed to the cafe.

'No!' Gaby scoffed, half laughing and half appalled by the idea. 'I can't ask him!'

'Why not?'

'I just can't! Anyway, how do you know he's worth a bob or two?'

Marina tapped the side of her nose. 'Oh, I have my sources. You seen that great big white and glass house on the cliffs round the other side of Promise Point? What's it called now...? Ah! Trenvaren or something like.'

'I'm not sure what it's called, but I know the one.' Gaby's eyes widened. 'That's his house?'

Marina looked quite proud of herself for being the keeper of such obviously impressive information. 'And he has two more restaurants – one as busy as you like in Newquay. By all accounts he's doing nicely, thank you very much.'

'If he has a busy place in Newquay why would he want to open somewhere as quiet as this?' Clara asked.

Marina answered this like a keen pupil giving the answer to a question in class. 'Wants something very different and exclusive. Thinks he can bring people here and make the village famous just for his food.' Marina tutted. 'As if it ain't nice enough here anyway without his restaurant.'

'How did you find all this out?' Gaby asked.

'I told you – I have my sources.'

'Can your sources find out why he's such an insufferable arse all the time?'

Marina chuckled. 'I can certainly ask.'

'Some mysteries can't be solved,' Jill said. 'Some people are the way they are just because.'

Marina smiled in the direction of the sea. 'Is that your Elijah and Fern there?'

They all turned to see the kids waving madly from their kayaks. Ava raised a hand too, and everyone waved in return.

'They're growing up so fast,' Marina said.

'Don't I know it,' Gaby replied.

Marina turned her smile to Clara. 'And you next, my darlin'. The next generation of Morrows springing up right before our eyes. Jack'd been so proud to see 'em growing.'

Clara stroked a hand over her belly. 'I wish he could have met little William or little Matilda, but I suppose it's a regret we're going to have to live with.'

'Them's your names?' Marina asked.

'For now,' Clara said. 'I'll probably change my mind a dozen times before they're born.'

'I like what you have so far.'

'Me too,' Gaby agreed.

Marina glanced at her watch. 'Well I could stay here all day chatting but I have to go. I'm meeting the ramblers in an hour.' She mock-frowned at Jill. 'And they haven't forgotten that you haven't been out with us for weeks now.'

'Oh, I know, I'm sorry. I've had so much to do,' Jill said.

'Like sitting on this beach?' Marina arched an eyebrow.

Jill laughed lightly. 'I have to take it easy sometimes.'

'Mind that you make an effort for us soon – we'll all forget what you look like!' Marina kissed them all on the cheek. 'And think on what I said about tapping old Rockefeller up there for some money, Gaby. A donation to the lifeblood of the village is the least he can do as far as I can see, and he ought to be keen to do it if he wants to be on people's good side.'

'I don't think he cares about good sides either way,' Gaby said. 'But I'll think about it. I'm not sure I'm the person to ask, though; he's not exactly my number one fan.'

'I'm sure you could bring him round with those womanly wiles of yours,' Marina said blithely.

'What womanly wiles?' Gaby asked with a light laugh.

'There's two of them looking very impressive in that dress today.' Marina gave a pointed look at the cleavage at Gaby's V-necked bodice.

'Marina!' Jill spluttered.

'Only saying what I see. You know me well enough by now – I can only ever be straight.'

'Too straight sometimes,' Jill said, pretending to be annoyed but clearly not. She was still shaking her head as Marina said her goodbyes and left them, a smile on her face. 'One in a million, that one.'

'And probably for the best,' Clara said. 'I don't think the world could cope with two Marinas.' She turned to Gaby. 'It's not a bad idea, though.'

'What isn't?'

'Asking Lloyd for a donation. If he's as rich as Marina says, it shouldn't be a problem for him to bung you a couple of hundred pounds towards Flag Day.'

Gaby shook her head. 'You haven't met him properly yet, have you? Somehow I don't think he'd give two hoots about the lifeboats or making friends here. And if he's got that great big house, he was probably able to buy it by not giving his money away.'

'All people with big houses can't be like that. There are loads of rich people who like to help charities.'

'I'm sure there are; I just don't think he's one of them.'

'It's got to be worth a try.'

'I'm with Clara on this,' Jill said. 'You can only ask and the worst he can do is say no.'

'I'm more worried about what he might want in return if he says yes,' Gaby said darkly.

'Don't be daft!' Clara said. 'Don't listen to what Marina says about him eyeing you up. She sees affairs and lust everywhere; it just brightens up her day to think she's in some bodice-ripping novel!'

'She wishes she was in a bodice-ripping novel,' Jill added.

'Exactly. Lloyd knows you're married, and you haven't exactly given him cause to think you might be up for anything even if he asked. In fact, you've done the opposite.'

'I still don't like the idea of being indebted to him.'

'*You* wouldn't be; the lifeboats would be. And even then it's hardly being in his debt. A donation's a donation, right? People give them without expecting anything back – that's kind of the point, isn't it? Go on...' Clara broke into a mischievous smile. 'I dare you.'

Gaby started to laugh. 'You little minx! You had to go and play the challenge card, didn't you? You know I can't resist it!'

'That's why I did it. And when he swells up your fundraising, you'll thank me. He might not be a natural supporter of charity, but if one person can get cash out of him, it's you.'

'I appreciate your faith...' Gaby's gaze went to the cafe, where the sounds of a cement mixer had kicked in. 'But we'll see. I wouldn't be so sure this time.'

Gaby had wondered whether to tell Killian about her plan to try and get a sizeable donation for the lifeboat service from Lloyd, but in the end he was so distracted and she was so frustrated by his stunted attention span that she didn't bother. There had been another shout that evening, just as they'd sat down to eat, another capsized boat, and although this one had been straight-forward with everyone safely taken ashore, Killian had seemed withdrawn and irritable when he got back. She supposed it had something to do with the nature of the shout; how it must have reminded him of the terrible mission that had ended with the deaths of those two boys.

To Gaby, it felt as if every time he made a step's worth of progress getting over the sailboat tragedy he took two back again. Harry had tried to talk to him, as Gaby had asked him to, but hadn't had much luck. Ava tried and had even less, and Vas said he felt as if he'd got through, but Gaby doubted that too. She knew her husband – he could look OK when he really wasn't and he knew what to say to avoid scrutiny.

In the end, it didn't matter that Gaby hadn't told Killian about her plan to approach Lloyd. She'd accepted Clara's chal-lenge, but Lloyd's absence for the following week meant she couldn't do much about it. The contractors had no idea how to contact him when she'd asked – at least they'd said so, though Gaby suspected they were under instruction to tell villagers they couldn't contact him so he didn't get complaints about the work. Meanwhile, the renovations continued on the new restau-rant apace. New windows were installed – sleek with slate grey frames and wide panes – the outside walls were rendered and painted a paler grey and the roof replaced with wide, gleaming tiles. Its modernity didn't really fit with the quaintness of the other village buildings, but there was no mistaking it looked good. Lloyd meant business, and like Marina had said, he seemed to be aiming for exclusivity and style. Gaby had no idea what the changes were like within, but they had to be in the same vein and just as extensive.

Betty had sent a message mid-week to ask how everyone was, and Clara had told her about the changes to the building and sent her a photo. She'd told Gaby afterwards that Betty said it was no longer her concern and good luck to him, but she thought that, between the lines, Betty was secretly a little sad to see her cafe gone forever.

That weekend they were due to meet Harry and Ava at the Spratt. Ava had news – Gaby got the impression Killian knew what it was already. She'd asked him, and he'd said maybe, but he didn't want to steal Ava's thunder, and so it was with a mix of pride and trepidation that Gaby was forced to conclude Ava had finally qualified for the lifeboat's seagoing crew. She'd been on the home stretch with her training for some weeks now, and it had only been a matter of time.

When they arrived, Harry and Ava were already there, sitting with Harry's dad Sandy, Jill, Clara and Cormac, Marina and Bob, and Vas, Maxine and Shari from the station.

'Always the last to arrive,' Ava said as everyone cheered Gaby and Killian's entrance. It looked as though a few drinks had already been consumed, judging by the glasses on the table.

'Some of us have children to farm out before we can go anywhere,' Gaby said, kissing Ava, Marina, Jill and Clara in turn. 'And they've got a reputation by now.'

Jill laughed. 'Tell them, reputation or no, they're always welcome at Grandma's house.'

'I would,' Gaby shot back, 'but Grandma is here with a large brandy and lemonade, so...'

Everyone laughed as Jill gave herself a playful slap on the wrist.

'What are you having?' Killian asked Gaby.

'A gin please.'

'Right...' He looked around the table. 'Anyone else want anything while I'm at the bar?'

Everybody said they were fine, so Killian left them and went to the bar while Gaby pulled a spare chair from another table to join them, squeezing in between Ava and Jill.

'So what's this big news?' she asked her youngest sister. 'And don't tell me to wait until Killian comes back because I'm sure he already knows. Does everyone know?'

'Not yet.' Ava beamed. 'Some of you do, and I suppose the rest of you can guess.'

'You qualified for the boat crew?' Clara glanced at Vas, who gave a slight nod.

Ava's smile grew so wide it seemed like she could barely contain it. 'Yes! I'm done, fully trained, ready to go out and save lives!'

There was a chorus of congratulations that had everyone in the pub stopping to look and then a queue to hug her. Not a very orderly one, with people bumping into each other and tripping over each other's feet and laughing as they did, but what it lacked in order it more than made up for with enthusiasm.

Gaby squeezed her. 'That's fantastic news! Really great.'

'Do you mean that?' Ava asked as she let go. 'Because I know how—'

'Yes, I mean it. There's no point in pretending – especially not to you – I had my reservations, but I know how hard you've worked for this and how much you want it, so how can I be anything other than happy for you?'

'Thanks, sis,' Ava said. 'That means a lot to me.'

Gaby held on to her smile, though inside she was full of doubts and fears. She would never stop worrying about her sister, as she'd never stopped worrying about Killian, but she couldn't say so.

Killian returned with the drinks. 'I take it the news is out?' he asked, glancing at everyone's smiling faces.

'I didn't give it away,' Vas said to Ava.

'No, but it didn't take a genius to work out,' Killian replied as he put Gaby's drink in front of her. 'Either these two were getting engaged or having a baby, or Ava had qualified, and as Harry hasn't bitten his nails down to stubs, I could only assume it was the last one.'

'Oi!' Ava squeaked. 'Cheeky! He'd be lucky to get me to say yes!'

'It's true.' Harry laughed. 'I know when I'm punching above my weight.'

As the evening wore on, more and more people got to hear Ava's good news, and it felt as if people who hadn't been in the Spratt when it had been announced had even got to hear about it and had gone up especially to offer their congratulations. That included Robin, local fisherman, long-time family friend and owner of trawler *The Deidre*. This was a big deal, and Gaby recognised just what it had taken for him to come, because not only did he prefer his own company since his wife died, but he was also the reason the lifeboat had gone out the night her dad had been lost at sea.

'Your father would have been right proud,' he said, giving Ava a pained smile. 'Shame he ain't here to see.'

'Thanks, Robin!'

Ava threw her arms around him in a hug that clearly took him by surprise. When she let go he looked utterly shell-shocked.

'Well I'll be off then,' he mumbled. 'Wanted to say something, but I done it now.'

After nodded acknowledgements of everyone at the table, he left. It was then Gaby noticed Lloyd leaning against the bar with a pint, watching proceedings with his usual look of wry amusement.

Gaby got up. 'I'm going to have a word,' she said, nodding in his direction.

Clara gave a knowing look, and Ava got up too. 'I'll come with you.'

'What for?'

'We're going to invite him to sit with us, right?'

'No—' Gaby began.

But Jill stopped her. 'Ava's right. Better friend than enemy. Let's see if we can't soften him a bit too, then maybe you can ask him that favour you're after.'

'What favour?' Killian asked.

'I'm thinking I might get a donation from him for Flag Day.'

'Good luck with that,' he said.

'Maybe I should go over with Ava and ask him,' Clara said.

'I'll go,' Gaby said. 'It's me who wants something. And if you're worried about something kicking off, don't be. Nobody will put me in a bad mood this evening.'

'Not even the man you said has his photo next to the definition of facetious in the dictionary?' Clara asked with a wry smile.

'Even him.'

Gaby and Ava went over to the bar. That constant, sardonic grin Lloyd seemed to wear was very much in evidence at their approach.

'Life really is one long party here, isn't it?'

'Hi,' Ava said. 'I don't think we've met properly – I'm Gaby's sister, Ava.'

'I can see that,' he replied.

Ava shot an uncertain glance at Gaby, who tried not to sigh with impatience. Did this man ever give a normal, straight, courteous reply to anything?

'We're all over there having a drink and we thought you might like to join us, save standing here on your own,' she said.

He looked at the table and then back at her. 'What makes you think I don't like standing on my own?'

'Nothing,' Gaby replied stiffly, dying to add that he was so annoying, doubtless he was used to drinking alone because nobody could stand to be around him for more than two minutes. 'We're just trying to be friendly.'

'I thank you for your concern, but I'm happy where I am. I quite enjoy watching parties I haven't been invited to.'

Another dig at the incident at Betty's party? Gaby ignored it. 'It won't make you any less focused on your business just to make the odd friend in the village. Even if you think so. It might even make life easier for you.'

'You mean you won't try to hound me out of town if I play nice?'

'I mean it's a supportive community. We rally around for our friends.'

'I'm sure you do, but being in everyone else's pocket is really not my style I'm afraid. Sorry, but that's just the way I am and you can't change forty-five years of that.'

'What are you afraid of?' Gaby demanded.

For the first time since she'd met him, he seemed mildly taken aback by a question she'd asked.

'Nothing.'

'Then there's no harm in having one drink with us, is there?'

Ava touched her arm. 'It's all right,' she said to Lloyd. 'It was only a friendly invite but there's no pressure. Maybe another time?'

'Maybe,' he said.

As they left him, Gaby could feel her irritation levels at

maximum again. Despite her promise, he'd managed to ruin her good mood.

'He really winds you up, doesn't he?' Ava said as they went back to their table.

'Yes, and surely you can see why.'

Ava shot her a sideways glance she couldn't interpret. 'He's antisocial and, you're right, he's arrogant as hell, but you can just choose to ignore him if he bothers you that much. You don't have to have anything to do with him; you can stay out of his way. It's like you go looking for the conflict – and I don't know much about him yet, but from what I've seen so far, he strikes me as just as bad.'

Gaby wondered what Ava was trying to say, because there was a definite subtext and she wasn't sure she liked what it might be.

'I don't know what it is,' she snapped. 'Something about the man just makes my blood boil.'

'I can see that. Forget the lifeboat donation – probably best if you try to stay out of his way from now on. Nothing is worth that much stress, even your fundraising.'

'Staying out of his way won't be so easy when the restaurant opens.'

'He might not be here all that often if he has others to run as well.'

'We can only hope so.'

Clara looked up as they got back to the table. 'How did it go?'

'Don't ask,' Gaby said, sending her gaze back to the bar where Lloyd was lifting his glass to her in a mocking toast.

Killian noticed it and looked at Gaby sharply. 'What did he say to you?'

'Nothing much,' Gaby said. 'He made it clear he doesn't want to be friends, that's all.'

'With us?'

'With anyone.' Gaby reached for her drink. 'Forget him – I already have.'

But as the conversation turned to other things, Gaby couldn't forget him. Their interaction kept going round and round in her head, making her angrier and angrier. What was his problem? What made him think he was so much better than everyone else? More than anything, she wanted to go over to the bar and try again, and keep on trying until she got through. She was used to winning, to getting what she wanted, to getting to the bottom of any conundrum, any problem that stood in her way, and the fact that she couldn't this time irked her more than anything else.

'Even Ava said he was arrogant,' Gaby said to Killian as they walked home. 'And Ava is chill with everyone. I mean, you should have heard him.'

'Forget him,' Killian said. 'Don't keep dwelling on it; there's nothing you can do. If the guy wants us to leave him alone then we'll leave him alone.'

'I'm not dwelling on it.'

'Sounds like it.'

'I'm just telling you about it. We're married; it's what we do – tell each other things.'

'And you have told me about it, more than once. You're fixated on him.'

'I'm not!'

'You are; you're obsessed with what he does and says.'

'That's ridiculous!'

'Is it? Would you listen to yourself for five minutes? Do you fancy him or something?'

'Of course not!' Gaby yanked her hand from Killian's. 'Don't be stupid! What kind of thing is that to say?'

'Because if you do, it's all right; I won't get stressed about it.'

'I don't doubt that for a minute,' she snapped. 'Sometimes I think you've forgotten you have a wife at all.'

'Now who's being ridiculous? As if I could forget I have a wife – you wouldn't bloody let me.'

'Are you trying to start something here?'

'No, you are. Going on and on about that new guy. Leave it. We don't need to be his friend and we don't need whatever that favour is.'

'I wanted to get him to donate to the lifeboat station.'

'And while I appreciate that, you'd probably be wasting your time anyway. Men like that don't do charity. He'll never need the lifeboats, so why would he give his money to contribute to the safety of others? I've met tossers like that before and it's always the same.'

Gaby wanted to argue, but that was just because she was worked up. In her heart, she knew Killian had a point. And perhaps she had made far more of this than was necessary. 'You could be right.'

'I know I'm right.'

She shot him a sideways glance. 'Now you sound just like him.'

'Maybe that's why you fancy him,' Killian said airily.

Gaby frowned. 'Stop saying that!'

He reached to take her hand again and grinned. 'I would, but the way it makes you so angry is too entertaining.'

'Ugh!' Gaby said, pulling her hand free again. 'Then let me entertain you with a slap because you're really pushing it now!'

Killian's grin was visible in the light of the bulbs strung along the promenade. It broadened briefly but then faded again. That darkness that he'd been struggling to shake off over the past couple of months hadn't taken long to return.

'Harry and Ava seem OK now,' she said after a moment of silence.

'Shouldn't they be? They'll be made up now Ava has qualified.'

'I didn't mean that. They took losing those two kids really badly.'

'I know. But they understand that we can't let it get to us. If we do, we're no use for the next shout, are we?'

Gaby mused over his words for a moment. It didn't seem to her as if he was taking his own advice. Outwardly he was dealing with the tragedy, but she wondered if that was all show. His moods were up and down – one minute she would think he was moving on; the next she'd be convinced that he needed to see someone professionally – though he'd never admit that, even if she said so.

'And Harry took it badly when we lost Dad, but he seems to have dealt with this better, which is weird when you think about it.'

'That was the first time he'd ever lost anyone on the boats and it was one of our own. And he's older now – he's grown up fast in the past year and a half.'

'Then how come you've taken this one worse?'

'They were kids, Gab! I'm a dad – of course it's going to get to me.'

'I get that, but my dad—'

'We're not getting into this again. This is you, fixating. If it's not on the new owner of Betty's then it's this, and if not this it will be something else. Why do you always have to be obsessing over something? Why can't a thing just be without you trying to analyse it out of existence? It was different – different circumstances – and that's all.'

'I just want to understand. And there's no shame – it's normal to be affected.'

'I know that.'

'Do you?'

He turned to her. 'Yes. But if you're saying I'm not fine you're wrong. I am.'

'OK.' Gaby faced the path again, orange bulbs leading them down the coast, tailing off into the distance, a stiff breeze coming in from the sea.

'Believe me or don't,' Killian said. 'I can't do much to change your mind when you've made it up; I know that well enough.'

Gaby thought she might say something in reply, but nothing would come that seemed right, so she didn't.

CHAPTER ELEVEN

There had been a run of five days straight where the lifeboat had been called out for one reason or another. One had been a hoax call – which had disappointed Ava greatly because it had been her first as a seagoing crew member. They'd gone to check the area anyway, realised the facts didn't stack up and, satisfied there was no need of them, had headed back. Ava had considered it a very inauspicious start. The second one was to go out to a coasteering group who'd reported that one of their party had got a foot stuck between two rocks and was unable to get free. One was a surfer who'd been thrown against some rocks when caught by a rogue wave – thankfully only cuts and bruises, and everyone agreed it could have been far worse. One was for a dog that had swum out too far and was then taken by the currents, leaving their owner in a blind panic as they watched from the shore. And the final one had been to bring back an inflatable crewed by two teenagers that had been caught out in a similar way to the poor dog.

Killian had called it Ava's baptism of fire, but she'd been only too happy to muck in. It was what she'd joined for, after all. To Killian, it was just another sign that summer had arrived, bringing with it the tourists keen to enjoy the sea but not always aware of its unpredictable moods.

Gaby had only just dropped the kids off at school when she noticed the lifeboat launch for the sixth consecutive day and stopped to watch. The smaller inshore boat was being taken by tractor to the water's edge, ready to go. She was on her way to see Marina, who'd called early that morning to say she had some more fundraising ideas and did Gaby want to chat about them over a cup of tea. And even though Gaby had a million other things to do, she was glad of the excuse to get some fresh air and take a walk in the gentle morning sun.

Seeing the boat go, she assumed Ava, Harry and Killian would be aboard. Cormac was back on duty but not yet qualified as sea crew, and as the shack was still locked up, she assumed he'd answered the call and was helping from the control room. The sun glinted from the waves as the boat sped off, a haze on the horizon blurring the line between sky and sea. Gaby wondered what they'd been called out for this time – she couldn't see any signs of a vessel in distress. Perhaps it was something less dramatic – though her dad had always said that any emergency was dramatic to the person in need of their assistance.

Her thoughts were interrupted by the sound of her phone ringing. Taking it from her handbag, she frowned slightly at the unknown number.

'Hello?'

'Is that Gaby?'

'Yes, who is—?'

'Lloyd Turner.'

'Lloyd?' Gaby's frown deepened. 'How did you get my number? What do you—?'

For once, there was no patronising, mocking or facetious tone in Lloyd's voice. He sounded deadly serious and, if Gaby wasn't mistaken, a little worried.

'It's your sister.'

'Which—?'

'Clara. I'm at the hospital with her now, but you need to let her partner know she's here.'

'What's happened?' Gaby asked sharply.

'I don't know. One minute she's outside the restaurant bugging me about something and the next... I can only tell you something seems to be wrong and I think they're taking her into surgery any minute.'

'Something's wrong? With the baby?'

'I think so.'

'Right...' Gaby's thoughts were a jumble. She rarely got panicked, but she was dangerously close now. 'OK, thanks... I'll see if I can get hold of— Shit! The lifeboat has gone out.'

'What does that mean?'

'Cormac will be on duty.'

'Can't you come? I mean, I'm doing my best here, but I'm not exactly the right person to—'

'I'll be straight over. Don't feel you have to stay and wait for me; it was good of you to be there at all.'

'I'd rather stay until you arrive. I'll wait for you at the entrance of the maternity unit so you know where to go.'

'OK, I'll be there as quick as I can.'

As she ended the call she was torn. Should she go and get Cormac? What about her mum? What about calling Logan – he'd want to be there.

Quickly she decided the most important thing she could do was to get there herself, and as she'd left her car at home, she started to run back. She got a few curious stares as she did, but that wasn't something to concern her right now. She was focused on getting home, and the only thing she needed to worry about was Clara and the baby. She would let everyone else know as she was on her way to the hospital. It might not be the best decision, but it was the only one she could make.

The nearest maternity unit was twenty miles out of Port Promise, and Gaby had been held up by roadworks, so she arrived ninety minutes after Lloyd's call, frustrated and impatient. She'd used the time in traffic to contact everyone she could – everyone who wasn't currently at the lifeboat station working on a rescue, as Cormac was, at least. He couldn't be there right now, but the message would get through as soon as the crew were done and they would make sure Cormac got to Clara's side, where he would want to be. Meanwhile, Jill was following in her car, having rushed over from the allotment, and Logan – the baby's actual father – was heading for the motorway out of London, though it was likely to be very much later in the day when he arrived.

Gaby parked her car in the first space she found and raced for the entrance of the maternity unit. As he'd promised, Lloyd was outside. At her approach, he stubbed out his cigarette on a wall and dropped it into the nearest bin. Usually, Gaby would have made her feelings clear on the fire hazard, but her mind was elsewhere today.

'She's still in theatre,' he said. 'Not sure what's going on... Is it meant to take this long?'

'It depends what the complications are,' Gaby said tensely. 'It doesn't sound good.'

'I'll show you where the waiting area is,' he said, heading for the doors.

Gaby followed him. 'Are *you* all right?' she asked.

Lloyd looked faintly surprised at the question. 'I'm not the one in theatre.'

'No, but I guess it must have been a stressful morning.'

'I've had better, true.'

'Thank you for bringing her in.'

'I could hardly do anything else.'

'You could have just called an ambulance and then gone about your day. Or got one of us to bring her.'

'If you'd been there, you'd have seen that there was no way she could have waited for an ambulance or anyone else to get to her.'

'Right...'

Gaby was suddenly filled with dread. She'd been desperately worried, of course, but things must be bad if even Lloyd was as shaken as he seemed to be. She didn't know a lot about him but imagined he was a man who didn't get easily spooked.

'I'll leave you here if it's all the same,' he said, gesturing to the doors of the ward. 'This is where they'll be bringing her after surgery as far as I know, but you may want to check on that.'

'I'll ask at the desk,' Gaby said. 'Thanks again.'

'No problem. I hope everything is OK. Not that I know her well, of course, but she seems nice, your sister... I mean, when she's not hassling me at the restaurant about my business plans like she was today.'

'Nicer than me, you mean.'

He gave her a faint smile. 'I didn't say that; you did. But I'd like to hear how she gets on.'

'I suppose it's lucky for her that she was at your restaurant today hassling you about business plans – you probably saved her life and the baby's too. If she'd been alone...' Gaby gave a helpless shrug. There was no point in spelling it out and she suspected Lloyd wanted to hear chilling alternatives even less than she wanted to speak them. 'We'll call by sometime when you're at the restaurant. I know I keep saying it, but thank you – I dread to think what might have happened if you hadn't been there.'

'I expect someone would have done something. As you keep reminding me, Port Promise is that sort of a place.'

He turned and left. Almost as soon as he'd disappeared from sight, Jill dashed down the corridor.

'I've just seen Lloyd leaving; he said you were here. Any news?'

'I've only just got here myself, so I was just about to ask at reception.'

'OK. I'd better come in with you then.'

Lloyd must have broken the sound barrier, Gaby decided, when they discovered how perilous Clara's condition had been and how time had been against them to save not only her baby but possibly her as well. There had been a diagnosis of severe placental abruption, and an emergency caesarean section – though perilous – had delivered Clara's son safely some time later. After a few tense hours, mum and her newborn baby were over the worst of it. Clara was in a room recovering, while baby was in the neonatal unit – though the doctors didn't expect him to be there for long. Not out of the woods, but out of immediate danger at least. Whatever their previous feelings about Lloyd, the entire Morrow family had to be grateful for the part he'd played in the drama.

Only Cormac had been allowed to see Clara at first, having arrived shortly after Jill. But as Clara was still out after a general anaesthetic, there wouldn't have been much point in anyone else going in anyway, so Jill had said, even though Gaby could see she desperately wanted to.

Killian had phoned Gaby to say he was staying in Port Promise, conscious of the fact he might have to be there to pick the kids up from school and that while there were more than enough people in attendance for Clara, Port Promise was already one lifeboat crew member down – two if Ava decided she wanted to drive over to the hospital. For now, the youngest Morrow sister was in discussion with Harry about what to do for the best. Like Killian, she didn't want to leave the team short, but she was desperate to see Clara. She'd phoned and spoken to Jill, who'd told her there was little she could do even if she did come, and Clara hadn't yet come round from her anaesthetic anyway.

Logan had arrived a few hours later looking ashen and agitated. Cormac had had to be removed from Clara's room so Logan could go in, which had resulted in extra tension nobody had needed, though Cormac understood the situation and seemed to deal with it better than Logan.

Gaby had just watched him go to the canteen when her phone showed Killian calling. He was at home with the children, having collected them from school. But it wasn't him – it was Elijah and Fern both yelling excitedly down the line.

'Mum! Has the baby been born? Is it a boy or a girl?' Fern asked once Gaby had got them to calm down so she could understand their garbled questions.

'She's had a little boy named William.'

'She said she was going to call him William,' Elijah said. 'Yes!' Gaby could just picture him punching the air. 'A boy! I wanted her to have a boy!'

'I think you might have to wait a while before he can play football with you,' Gaby said with a smile.

'Can we come and see him?' Fern asked.

'If Clara is in for more than a couple of days, we can try and sort something. But it might be better to wait until she's back home. Hospitals are busy and you don't get a lot of visiting time.'

Clara would be exhausted for some time too, if Gaby knew anything about it, and perhaps a room full of children wasn't quite what she needed to recover. But she didn't mention this. Her two would just have to be patient, as everyone else in Port Promise would have to be.

'So we can't come?' Fern asked.

'We'll see,' Gaby said. 'Let's wait until tomorrow. If Clara is feeling up to it, maybe I'll bring you over.'

'Can we see pictures?'

'I suppose I could send a photo later,' Gaby said.

'Shall I make a card?' Fern asked, and then Gaby could hear Elijah telling her that babies can't read and that she was stupid, and she could imagine a lot of bickering once they got off the phone. For once, she was quite glad Killian was doing the child-care, though goodness knew what they were going to do if there was a lifeboat shout.

'Is your dad there?' she asked. 'Can you put him on the phone?'

'He's on his laptop,' Elijah said.

'Can you get him?'

'The door's closed.'

'Oh...' Gaby frowned. Perhaps he'd some last-minute stuff to do for work. 'I'll call him later – when the door opens tell him I need to speak to him, won't you? Has he said what will happen if there's a shout?'

'No,' Elijah said.

Fern cut in. 'But Marina came over and told dad she was in all night.'

'Hmm.' Gaby nodded slowly. 'She might be able to help then. I'll phone her and check. I'm going to ring off now because I need to sort it.'

'OK. Love you, Mum!' Fern said.

'Love you both more.' Gaby smiled before ending the call.

She was about to call Marina to put some contingency plan in place when her thoughts turned, unbidden, to Lloyd. Gaby was sure she'd had him figured out, but then he'd gone and done this, going above and beyond to save Clara and her baby. It wasn't like he had any connection to her, and he gave the impression he didn't give a stuff about anyone in the village, but when she'd spoken to him earlier that day he'd almost seemed like a real, caring, normal human being. And as much as the idea rattled her, the Morrows were in his debt, not to mention every other person who cared about Clara. It was a strange turn of events, one she would never have foreseen had she been asked to predict his actions, and she didn't quite know what to do with that. One thing was certain – she'd been forced to look again, to evaluate everything she'd believed about him and to see him in a new light. But in doing that, she realised she now didn't know anything about him at all.

There was something almost comical about the sight of Clara being fussed over by Cormac and Logan, both trying to be the most helpful. Logan had long ago accepted that he was no longer her partner, of course, but that didn't stop him trying to outdo Cormac, who clearly wanted to prove his worth as a surrogate dad and as Clara's new partner. As they led her into Seaspray Cottage after her discharge, where Clara was living after the sale of the flat she'd previously shared with Logan, Cormac was supporting Clara, and Logan, despite having William in his arms, was trying to muscle in by touching a hand to her other elbow, even though it wasn't doing much.

'Concentrate on William,' Clara said. 'Don't worry about me... Watch his head, Logan! Don't let it flop!'

Gaby had been sitting in the front garden with Jill waiting for them to arrive. It was a week since Lloyd had rushed Clara to the hospital, and although she looked tired as she got out of Cormac's car, Logan pulling up seconds afterwards and racing him to take the baby inside, she also looked happy.

'Finally!' Gaby got up from the bench to greet them. 'We were beginning to think you wouldn't get discharged today after all.'

Clara winced, putting a hand to the caesarean scar running across the lower part of her tummy. 'If they hadn't let me out today I'd have knotted some old sheets and climbed out of the window. Not that I don't appreciate what they did, but I've definitely seen enough hospitals these past few months to last me a lifetime.'

'I second that,' Cormac said.

Gaby caught a look of desperation from Logan. She had to feel sorry for him really. Cormac had done this hugely heroic thing in saving Elijah from a speeding car the previous winter, and the fact he'd nearly died in the process perhaps made him even more heroic, and if Logan hoped to compete, he was going to find it very difficult.

'Let me have him!'

Gaby held out her arms like an impatient toddler waiting for her birthday present. Clara gave a tired grin as Logan – with obvious reluctance – laid William gently into her arms.

'I might have known you'd be champing at the bit,' Jill said with a fond look.

Gaby gazed down at the baby. 'He's so perfect. Feels like ages since I was able to hold either of mine like this. I never thought I'd miss it, but...'

'Uh-oh!' Clara laughed. 'Should Killian be worried?'

Gaby rocked William, making gentle shushing noises as he grimaced and snuffled, perhaps deciding whether he felt like crying or whether he'd rather go back to sleep. Seeing him, so small – tinier than either of her children had been – so delicate, so utterly dependent on her, took her back to the first time she'd held Elijah like this. She and Killian hadn't really planned to have a child – nor had they not planned it. In a surprising twist for two people who both enjoyed control, they'd barely discussed it at all, and when she'd fallen pregnant, while they hadn't been expecting it, neither had they been worried. But then Elijah arrived and everything had changed. Their obsession with each other was suddenly secondary, and they'd been forced to concentrate on someone else, someone who relied entirely on them, someone far more important. They were forced to see that the world was bigger than them, and in the

end it had been a good and healthy progression for their relationship. Killian had fallen in love with Elijah the instant the
midwife had placed him into his arms while they made Gaby
comfortable. Gaby recalled his face now – softer than she'd ever
seen it, even for her. She'd been bowled over by that look in his
eyes, and then again when Fern had come along. They'd
decided two was enough, but looking at William now, perhaps it
wasn't, if only because Gaby would give almost anything right
now to see that look on Killian's face again. She looked up to see
Logan watching her cradle and coo, though he only had eyes for
his son. The look on his face wasn't a million miles away from
how Killian's had been as a new father.

'I've made a steak pie,' Jill said. She looked at Cormac and
Logan. 'You'll both stay for some, won't you?'

Clara looked faintly horrified at her mum's suggestion, but
both men nodded eagerly.

'Sounds good,' Cormac said.

'That would be great, Jill,' Logan added, and Gaby noted
how he used her name almost in a bid to show Cormac that he'd
been there first and longest, and how he was the one they all
knew best. Perhaps the fact that Cormac and Clara weren't yet
living together gave him cause for hope too, though it was ill-
founded and ultimately a waste of time. Clara adored Cormac
and he felt the same about her, and even though she'd once been
engaged to Logan, anyone could see there was a world of difference in her relationships with each of the men.

'Lovely,' Jill said. 'Let's get Clara comfortable and William
settled and then we can eat.'

'He was asleep as soon as we put him in the car seat,'
Cormac said. 'Must be tired out.'

'He does sleep a lot,' Clara said as Cormac and the rest of
them followed her inside. 'It worries me a bit, but the midwife
said he was OK.'

'I'm sure there's nothing to worry about,' Jill said. 'It's all new to you – you're bound to be anxious at first, especially after the birth you had.'

'I didn't really have one,' Clara said ruefully. 'One minute I was talking to Lloyd and the next I was waking up with a baby in an incubator. I almost feel as if I've cheated.'

'Believe me, you didn't cheat,' Gaby said, rocking William, almost without realising she was doing it. 'I had two long and difficult labours and I'm not sure which would be worse.'

'Shall we sit in the living room for now?' Jill asked. 'Might be more comfortable for you, Clara?' Jill fussed over cushions on the armchair to make sitting easier.

'I could get used to all this attention,' Clara said. 'You might have to stop or it will go to my head.'

'You deserve it,' Cormac said.

'Yes,' Logan said. 'You do deserve it.'

Gaby looked from one to the other, and it was all she could do not to laugh at the absurdity of their competition. She'd imagined many scenarios when she'd thought of them having to meet for the first time as a pair of dads to the same child, but this certainly hadn't been one of them.

'Can I have him?' Logan asked, looking up at Gaby expectantly. 'Only...'

Gaby nodded and took William over. She understood, as everyone did, that his opportunities to spend time with his son would be less than theirs. It was only fair not to deprive him while he was in Port Promise.

'I'll go and make some drinks,' Jill said. 'Everyone all right with tea, or would you like coffee?'

'I'll have coffee if that's OK, Jill,' Logan said, gazing down at William as he rocked him.

He was smitten, and Gaby knew Clara would be relieved about that. Much as it complicated things, having Logan disinterested in his son would have destroyed her. But they were no longer together and he had a new life in London, and she'd confided to Gaby that she was afraid that might happen. It wasn't for herself she feared, but for what it would mean to William as he grew up. Gaby told her Cormac would more than make up for that if it happened, and Clara knew he'd do his best, but seeing Logan now, they needn't have worried.

After drinks Logan was persuaded to put William in his carrycot and they went through to the kitchen to eat. Clara didn't manage much, but Cormac attacked his with enthusiasm.

'This pie is incredible,' he said to Jill as he munched. 'I can't remember the last time I had something this good.'

'Aww...' Jill waved away the compliment, though she was very obviously pleased.

'It's delicious,' Logan said. 'As always. I used to love your steak pie.'

He didn't, Gaby thought as she watched him and Cormac battle to be the most agreeable man in the room, because Clara had once told her he dreaded their family's 'stodgy dinners'. But Gaby wasn't about to ruin the goodwill filling the kitchen right now. Goodwill to everyone else, of course, because beneath the truce between Cormac and Logan there was very definitely tension. It was one of the reasons Killian had decided to stay away. He'd wanted to see Clara but was mindful of the past relationship he'd had with Logan, which could never have been called close, and he didn't want to make Logan feel cornered by two men who were good friends and who served on the lifeboats together and who, it would seem, would set out to undermine his position as the proud father. Gaby had been impressed by his logic and had agreed with it. Ava was due to call by later, having lessons booked that she couldn't get out of, and she was going to come without Harry for exactly the same reasons, even though Harry and Logan had always got on better than Logan and Killian. As for Elijah and Fern, Gaby had decided it might be better to delay their visit until Clara had been home for a couple of days and had settled. They'd be excitable and hard work.

Clara frowned slightly as she pushed her plate away. 'Is that someone's phone?'

Everyone stopped talking.

'Not mine,' Logan said, 'but I can hear it too.'

'Not mine either,' Cormac said.

'I'll go and check my bag.' Gaby got up.

'Don't wake William!' Clara called after her as she went into the living room where she'd left her handbag. There was no danger of that – she looked into his cot and little William was out like a light.

'Hello...'

'Hi, Gaby... it's Lloyd.'

'Oh, hi!' Gaby had realised straight away that the number she didn't recognise and had forgotten to store in her phone the first time was probably his. 'Is everything OK? Did you need—?'

'I just wanted to ask if Clara's OK. I saw the car passing – she's home now?'

'She is, thank you. And doing well – she and William both are.'

'William? I would have thought she'd have called him Lloyd.'

Gaby couldn't help but smile. 'I'll run it by her; perhaps she'll change her mind.'

'I think it's the least she could do.'

'Why don't you come over? We're eating dinner, but you'd be welcome to join us – Mum always makes too much.'

'No, I couldn't...'

'Or would you like to speak to Clara—?'

'No, not really. I was just checking.'

'It's good of you to think of her.'

'I wasn't just thinking of her.'

Gaby frowned, unsure what to make of his statement and what to say to it.

'I'll let you get back to your dinner,' he said.

'How's the restaurant renovation going? I haven't seen you there in a while.'

'Yeah, been busy out of town, but it's going OK. I should think we'll be open at the end of the summer. A bit later than I'd like, but that's the nature of the beast.'

'Are you worried about missing out on the tourist season?'

'Oh, I won't need to worry about tourists; I'm quite sure people will come anyway.'

'Confidence – I like it. I suppose that's why you're so successful.'

'I suppose it is. But if I don't have faith in my ventures, who else will?'

'Your...' Gaby wanted to say wife, partner, family, friends. But why did everything she'd seen of him lead her to believe he didn't have much in the way of any of those. That he wasn't like Cormac had been when he'd first arrived in Port Promise, simply alone because he hadn't yet found his people, but out of choice.

'Rely on yourself in this life, Gaby, because you can never rely fully on anyone else.'

She didn't know what to say to that either. Being stumped by him was becoming a regular occurrence. She was so used to being able to work out anyone and any situation that she wasn't entirely sure she liked it.

'Thanks for calling. I'll tell Clara you were asking after her,' she said.

'And I expect to hear she's changed the baby's name. Not that I have any issue with William, but it will have to be his middle name.'

'Right,' Gaby said, smiling again. 'I'll tell her that too. Bye, Lloyd.'

He ended the call without saying goodbye in return, but that didn't offend or even surprise her. It seemed to be his way, that he found normal social interactions a chore or, at the very least, a waste of breath. But she was beginning to understand that maybe he was a lot deeper than he wanted people to know.

CHAPTER TWELVE

Gaby noticed the date on the calendar as she rushed past it in the kitchen, trying to get packed lunches ready for the children while avoiding Killian, who'd chosen that exact moment to get his morning coffee. Without realising it, she let out a groan.

'What's wrong?' Killian looked round from his spot by the window where he'd been yawning and staring out at the early morning mists that lay over the sea.

'Mum and Dad's wedding anniversary – I totally forgot it was coming up. I'd better go over and see if she's OK. She struggled last year, and I don't want her to be alone if it can be helped.'

'She won't be – she's got Clara and William to occupy her.'

'But still… it's hardly fair to Clara to leave her to deal with it. She's still not 100 per cent herself and she's got her hands full – William's got colic, so he's a bit of a nightmare right now. I'll pop over later.'

'Need me to come?'

'No, I know you've got a lot of work to do. It might be better if it's just us anyway.'

'You mean you and your sisters?'

Gaby nodded as she stuffed an apple into each of the two lunch bags she was filling.

'Well don't forget you can call me if you need me.'

'Thanks, but it should be OK. I'm hoping she'll be better than she was last year.'

'You would think so. She seems to be moving forward these days.'

'I'll message her to see what she's planning today. She might be going to the allotment first thing. If not I'll go straight after the school run.'

'If I were her, I'd stay at the allotment all day, not give myself time to dwell on things.'

'Avoidance. Yes, that is your usual way, isn't it?'

Killian looked up from the kettle he'd just set to boil. 'What's that supposed to mean?'

'I don't think I need to explain it, do I? But that's not how Mum deals with things. She'll want to talk about it.'

'This isn't still...' Killian grimaced. 'Gaby... look, I'm fine.'

'Yep, sure you are.'

He let out a sigh of impatience and went to get a mug from the cupboard.

'I'd better go,' Gaby said, leaving the kitchen. 'The kids will be late for school.'

Clara called as Gaby waved off Elijah and Fern at the school gates.

'Hey, are you busy this morning?' Clara asked.

'Nothing I can't put off. What's up?'

'You know what today is, right?'

'Yes, and I was going to call to see if Mum wanted some company.'

'I'd say that's a yes.'

'Is everything all right?'

'Well...' Clara paused, and Gaby could hear the beginnings of William set to burst his lungs crying in the background. 'I'm not sure. I think I might need some backup. Ava will come over when her lessons are done for the day, but if you could be here a little earlier...'

'So Mum doesn't have plans to go to the allotment?'

'She hasn't said so, and she doesn't seem to be getting ready.'

'Then *what is* she doing?'

'Um...' At that moment, William let rip. 'I'd better go,' Clara said. 'So you'll be over shortly?'

'As soon as I can.'

When nobody answered the front door at Seaspray Cottage, rather than let herself in with her spare key, Gaby went to the gate that led to the back garden and pushed it open. Clara was walking the garden with William. The day promised to be warm and calm, but this early there was still a chill on the air, the last of a lingering mist in the hollows of distant hills and a haze over the sea.

'Hey.' Clara gave a tight smile. 'You got here quicker than I thought.'

'I came straight over. Where's Mum?'

'She's gone up to the chapel to put some flowers on Dad's memorial stone. I told her you'd be dropping by, but she didn't expect you to be this early either, I suppose.'

'How does she seem?'

Clara shushed William, who was grumbling. 'It's hard to tell.'

'Did she say how long she'd be at the chapel?'

'No, but I don't imagine it will be all that long.'

'Is William about to kick off?' Gaby asked.

Clara gave a faint smile. 'I'm sure it's due. I wouldn't blame you for running out on me when he does.'

'But are you all right?' Gaby asked, serious now. 'I know how hard it can be; stressful, and you're not exactly well yet after...'

'I'm fine, I think. I've had Mum to help and of course Cormac is here when he can be. Actually...' Clara repositioned William so he was lying across her chest, his cheek on her shoulder. 'Cormac has asked us to move in with him and I think I'm going to say yes. The only reason we haven't done it sooner was because I felt we hadn't been together long enough to make that sort of commitment. Cormac didn't see it that way, of course, and as he keeps pointing out, it's not like we didn't know each other before. I suppose I'm being too cautious and it's silly. I kept wondering if he wouldn't want a baby around all the time too, but honestly, I'm still gobsmacked every day at his patience, especially considering William isn't even his. So I don't see the point in putting it off... well, actually, I see one point, and that's leaving Mum alone again.'

'Mum has always understood that it wasn't going to be forever.'

'That's true, and I do worry that William can be quite disruptive, especially when he has one of his screaming fits. Stupid colic.'

'I remember those months only too well,' Gaby agreed. 'But if it's any consolation, though it feels as if your life has gone down the toilet right now, this stage will be over so quickly you'll hardly think about it in years to come.'

'That's what Mum says, and it's only clinging on to that hope that's keeping me sane.'

'Any time you need a break, don't feel as if you can't ask. We'd love to have him for a few hours, even overnight. The kids can't wait to start babysitting, so don't think it would be a burden.'

'Thanks, Gab. I might just take you up on that. I'm going to try to put William down shortly, so don't worry about staying here – go up to Mum. She might appreciate the support and probably needs it more than me today.'

'You're sure?'

Clara nodded. 'I'll see you both when you come back down.'

Gaby had always imagined that the little stone chapel standing high above Port Promise looked exactly the same now as it had done back in Iziah Morrow's day. If she squinted, she could see the fishermen and their wives and children filing in through the doors in their Sunday best, greeted by the parson, their voices ringing out across the clifftops as they sang the same hymns they sang every Sunday, and then the chapel emptying straight into the Spratt. Now it was usually silent. Though the vicar did his best on the upkeep and a couple of women from the ramblers tended the gardens and churchyard for him, unless there was some occasion like a christening, wedding or funeral, nobody much went. Sunday was still for sermons, but the congregation could often be counted on two hands. People didn't go to church anymore, and that was just modern life.

Pushing through the old wooden gates she noticed that the doors to the chapel were open, though it didn't seem as if anyone was in there. She supposed the vicar had left it so in case anyone fancied a bit of spiritual solitude, though, again, most in the village were too busy to come up here for that. It was a shame, Gaby mused as she made her way to the little graveyard at the back, where wildflowers bordered the path, and were dotted amongst the headstones and monuments, while birds sang in the trees that shaded the far corners, because this kind of peace and tranquillity was probably what a lot of them didn't even realise they needed.

As she emerged from the shaded walkway into the church-yard proper, she spotted Jill standing over a small square stone.

It was newer than most of the headstones and angels close by, though Gaby recognised many of these as the final resting place of a few of her ancestors. As she drew closer Gaby could see there were fresh roses laid on its flat surface.

'Hi, Mum.'

Jill looked up and dried her eyes. 'Oh, hello, my love. I didn't expect to see you here.'

'Clara told me you'd come up. I just wondered if you wanted company. I mean, I can go if—'

'No, of course – there's no need to go now you've climbed up here. I suppose you're checking up on me, making sure I'm coping. With today being our anniversary, I mean. Clara's been fussing, but there's really no need.'

'Clara fusses – it's what she does.'

'And you don't?'

'I've been known to, but she's the worrier of the family, isn't she? I'm a hard cow, or so Killian tells me.'

Jill smiled sadly. 'A bit of tough love isn't always a bad thing. There's a time when worrying works and a time when hard truth works instead.'

'Which do you need today?' Gaby put an arm around her mum's shoulders and looked down at the stone.

'I'm not sure. It's funny, I can feel myself moving on, a little bit more every day, but I feel as if it's wrong. I feel so guilty about it.'

'That's only natural, and it's also OK.'

Jill nodded slowly. 'Then why do I feel so guilty about it?'

'I suppose that's natural too.'

'Knowing that doesn't make it any easier. Everyone talks – quite rightly – about how hard it can be on the lifeboat crew, but nobody ever spares a thought for the people they leave on shore to worry about them, do they?'

'We don't do the hard bit, I suppose?'

'Don't we? I'd say in many ways we do. I always felt powerless when your dad went out. He had some control over the way he did things at sea; he could make decisions that affected the outcome of the mission...'

'He couldn't control everything – that's why we lost him.'

'True. But all we can do is wait.' She turned to Gaby. 'How is Killian these days? I know that shout where they lost the young boys hit him hard.'

'Oh, that... you know Killian – bottles it up. God forbid he'd confide in his wife.'

'Your dad was the same. Didn't want to worry me.'

'I don't think it's that...'

Jill turned to her. 'Then what?'

Gaby gave a lame shrug. 'I wish I knew.'

CHAPTER THIRTEEN

The anniversary had passed without too much drama in the end, and Jill had seemed to cope. All the Morrow girls had been relieved about that. A couple of days later, life was as it had always been, apart from the welcome distraction of a new baby in the family. It was almost enough to make Gaby broody, and when she'd told Killian this she'd had to laugh at the faint look of horror on his face.

'Don't worry,' she'd said. 'Two's definitely enough.'

Gaby had spent the afternoon fussing over William and had left her mother's cottage feeling content. She'd noticed the girl with the rucksack climbing the hill of their street as she'd been driving home, but the sounds of her two bickering in the back seat as they went back to Thistledown Cottage had shattered her peaceful mood and had her on edge again. So apart from noting vaguely that the girl was a long way out of town and seemed young to be out on the hills alone, that was as much attention as Gaby paid her.

At the house, the kids tumbled out of the car, still arguing about who was more scared of spiders. Gaby was getting a headache and she still had a ton of maths marking to do for her students who were due to sit exams that summer.

'Go on in and get your homework done,' she said, opening the door for them before going back to the car to retrieve some plants Jill had given her. As she opened the boot she heard a voice from behind.

'Excuse me... is this Thistledown Cottage?'

Gaby looked round the open boot to see the girl with the rucksack standing there. She was dark-haired, eyes of blue so deep they could almost be mistaken for brown, and though her tone was hesitant Gaby got the instant impression of someone who could hold their own if they had to, despite looking as if she couldn't have been more than fourteen years old.

'Yes.'

'Does Killian live here?'

'Killian?' Gaby's frown deepened. 'What do you want him for?'

'Are you Gaby?'

'Yes.'

'I'm Meredith.'

Gaby stared at her. 'Sorry, I don't... Have we met?'

The girl's hopeful smile instantly faded. 'Oh, he hasn't... I'm sorry.' After a moment of hesitation, the girl began to walk away.

'Where are you going?' Gaby called. 'Didn't you want to see Killian? Is it something to do with the lifeboats?'

She turned back looking puzzled. 'Lifeboats?'

'Well... did he rescue you or something? He's not home, but I'm sure he won't be long if you want to wait. I mean, you did come all the way up that steep hill.'

She paused, seemingly torn.

'You're more than welcome to come inside and wait,' Gaby said. 'Did someone at the station tell you where we lived?'

The girl shook her head. Gaby was relieved no one had been that lax, but the mystery only deepened.

'Have you come far?' Gaby asked.

She nodded. 'Bristol. I had to get a train; it took ages, but you have no station in Port Promise, so I walked the rest of the way.'

Gaby's mouth fell open. Not because she knew the girl's walk from the neighbouring village with their closest train station must have taken her hours, though that in itself was impressive, but because she'd said she was from Bristol. Slowly but surely, gears were cranking in her brain, the facts slotting into place. The more she thought, the more obvious it was, but she didn't want to believe it could be true.

'How old are you?'

'Nearly fifteen.'

She studied the girl more closely. Dark hair, blue eyes... surely not?

'How do you know Killian?' she asked. 'It's nothing to do with the lifeboats, is it?'

The girl looked utterly mortified, as if she realised she'd blundered into a situation that was about to get a whole lot worse because she was here.

'He's my dad.'

Gaby grabbed for the roof of the car to steady herself.

'Sorry,' the girl said. 'I guess you didn't know.'

'Is...' Gaby stammered, 'is your mum and Killian... Are they...?'

'Oh, they're not together!' the girl said, and this time smiled as if she'd offered Gaby a wonderful gift. 'No way! They were together for, like, two weeks or something before I was born.'

'But he's your dad?'

'Yep.' She dug her hands into her pockets and gave Gaby another of those hopeful smiles. 'I've heard all about you. Dad says you're amazing. And Elijah and Fern too... are they here? Will I be able to meet them?'

'Killian's never mentioned you,' Gaby said, the world seeming to spin around her. 'Sorry. I've forgotten your name...'

'Meredith,' she repeated, seemingly unfazed by Gaby's reaction to her arrival. 'I don't know why he didn't say anything about me. I guess he was getting around to it or something...'

'So...' Gaby's thoughts were like swarming wasps. Much as she tried, she couldn't get a hold on a single one to make any sense of it. Meredith was quiet as she waited for Gaby to finish her sentence. But then Fern appeared at the front door.

'Mum!' she whined. 'Elijah says he's going to catch a spider in the garden and—' She stopped short at the sight of Meredith and, rather than finish her complaint, gave a shy smile.

'Hi,' Meredith said. 'You must be Fern?'

'Go inside!' Gaby ordered. Fern looked confused and as if she might protest until Gaby gave a scowl of warning so severe that she turned tail and raced back in. Then she rounded on Meredith. 'What are you doing?'

'I'm sorry, I didn't know I wasn't supposed to talk to her.'

'You have to leave!'

'Now? But you said I could wait for my dad—'

'He's not your dad!'

'My mum says he is.'

'How does your mum know? You said they were only together for a couple of weeks!'

'What does that mean? If she says it's him then it's him. Calling my mum a slag?'

'No, but...'

Gaby was drowning. She didn't even know where to start with a situation which had caught her like a sudden storm at sea. She wanted this girl to disappear, for her life to go back to where it had been only ten minutes before, but at the same time she had so many questions. How could Killian do this to her? To the family? She didn't understand much, but already she understood that they could never go back to how they'd been before. Meredith had arrived, and in one sentence, three small words, everything had changed. She'd said she didn't believe Killian was Meredith's father, and yet one look at the girl made it plain that he was. There was so much of him in her, more than either Elijah or Fern, and it was heartbreaking to see.

It was Elijah's turn to interrupt. It was likely Fern had told him about the girl on the doorstep who seemed to have their mum in the strangest of moods and he'd wanted to see for himself.

'Mum, I—'

'Go in!' Gaby snapped.

Without another word he scuttled away.

Gaby turned to Meredith. 'What do you want Killian for? Why have you come all this way? What's so important that you needed to see him here? Presumably he's always come to see you in Bristol.'

'Once,' Meredith said. 'He's been to Bristol once.'

'Only once? A few months ago; like about February time?' Gaby asked, rapidly putting the pieces together. It would explain the mysterious journey that had landed Killian the speeding fine.

Meredith nodded.

'So where do you usually see him?'

'Nowhere. That was the first time I met him.'

'I don't understand.'

'I've never seen him before that. Didn't even know who my dad was. Mum didn't want to say.'

'Why not?'

Meredith shrugged vaguely. 'She's like that sometimes.'

'And after fifteen years of not telling you she suddenly just changed her mind?'

'She's got a brain tumour. She didn't want to die and leave me with nobody so she decided to find him.'

'She's dying?'

As angry as she was with Killian, Gaby's heart went out to Meredith as the enormity of the girl's circumstances sank in. Meredith hadn't asked for any of this. Gaby couldn't know why Meredith's mother had chosen to keep Killian's identity a secret from her for all these years, but she understood why a mother would fear dying and leaving her child alone in the world. She'd tracked Killian down so that Meredith would at least have one parent. Gaby would have done exactly the same.

'Maybe. There's an operation she can have, but they say it's fifty-fifty.'

'She's going to have it though?'

'She doesn't know. I think she's a bit scared. She might be all right for years without it, but nobody can say.'

Gaby nodded slowly.

'I guess I should have called ahead,' Meredith said. 'I thought my dad would have told you about me. I just wanted to surprise him.'

If Meredith had called ahead, the chances were Killian would have arranged to meet her somewhere away from the house and Gaby might never have found out about her. For some reason he'd chosen to keep her a secret. That hurt, but what hurt more was the lying. He'd been a bit too good at that. Gaby had to wonder what else he'd kept from her over the years. If he'd managed to hide something this big – although, admittedly he hadn't known about Meredith all that long – there was no telling what else he might be keeping from her.

Gaby gestured at Meredith's rucksack. 'That's all you have with you?'

'Yes.'

'Where were you planning to stay? Bristol is way too far to go back to now.'

'I know...'

'Oh...' Gaby said with the faintest smile now. 'You thought you might stay with us?'

'Is that not OK?'

Gaby studied her. How could she turn her away? How could she refuse her a bed knowing who she was and how far she'd come? But letting her into the house was like knocking over another support from the certainty of the ordered family life that Gaby knew and loved. Letting her in, letting her bond with Elijah and Fern, letting her get close to them all felt like trouble.

'Of course it's OK,' Gaby said finally. 'But please don't tell Elijah and Fern about your dad.'

'What do you mean?'

'Don't tell them Killian is your dad – not yet.'

'Why not? They're my brother and sister.'

Gaby baulked as Meredith's argument sank in for a moment. As if things didn't seem difficult enough, it hadn't properly occurred to her until that moment that Meredith was their half-sister. Acknowledging it suddenly made everything feel far more immediate.

'It's just that they don't know and they're young, and I think it would be better if Killian talks to them about it first. I realise it's a big ask, but could you keep it to yourself for just a short while, until he gets a minute?'

'I suppose...' Meredith said.

Gaby gave a tight smile. 'I appreciate that.'

And then she led Meredith into Thistledown Cottage. What else could she do?

Gaby got Meredith to store her rucksack in the airing cupboard. They had no guest bedroom – the cottage was barely big enough for the four of them – and so she would have to sleep on the sofa. Then she took her to the kitchen and made her a sandwich and ordered a curious Elijah and Fern upstairs to do their homework, then went out into the garden to phone Killian while she had the chance.

'Where are you?' she asked.

'I'm just giving Harry a hand with some roof repairs at his place... I did say I'd be coming over—'

'I need you home.'

'I can't come home yet. I'm doing—'

'I don't care what you're doing! Apologise to Harry and come home!'

'Gab, what the hell is this about?'

'You'll find out when you get here.'

'I'm not just going to drop Harry in the shit if this is something—'

'Fine,' Gaby snapped. 'I didn't want to have this conversation over the phone but you're not making it easy to do anything else. There's a girl sitting in our kitchen who's travelled all the way from Bristol and says she's your daughter. Is that a good-enough reason to come home?'

There was silence on the line. It lasted so long Gaby half wondered if the connection was lost. But then Killian spoke.

'I'm on my way.'

Gaby waited for Killian at the front gate. She wanted to speak to him before anyone else did – especially Meredith. He looked tense as he hopped out of Harry's van. Gaby aimed a distracted wave at Harry as he pulled straight out again. Ordinarily he'd have stopped to say hello. The fact that he didn't made her wonder how much – if anything – Killian had told him. She imagined he'd have given some kind of reason for having to cut his assistance short, and while part of her cared what he'd said, there wasn't time to dwell on it now. She waited until Harry's van had got to the end of the lane before rounding on her husband.

'Care to tell me what the hell is going on?' she asked coldly, glancing back at the house briefly as she did. 'Is it true? She's your daughter?'

'Yes.'

Even though she'd known what his answer would be, it still shocked her to hear him put it so bluntly. There was no sign of shame, no remorse, seemingly no insight into how this news might affect her or their family.

'How?' she demanded. 'How is this possible?'

He raised his eyebrows slightly and it made her want to slap him. 'You really want me to explain the mechanics?'

'You bastard!' Gaby hissed. 'This is all a big joke to you, is it? Are you even sorry at all?'

'For what? I can't help that she exists.'

'But you could have *told* me she exists! I don't know... It might have been quite nice not to arrive home to a stranger on my doorstep telling me you're her dad! She's almost fifteen! You've had our entire married life to tell me about her!'

At this, he seemed to soften. 'I didn't know about her, Gab, I swear. I only just found out a few months ago.'

'And you went to Bristol to see them? Her and her mum?'

He nodded, reaching for a hand that Gaby snatched away.

'I get why you're angry,' he said.

'When were you going to tell me?' she demanded. 'If she hadn't come here today, would you ever have told me?'

'No,' he said.

Gaby stared at him.

'Only because,' he continued, 'I was scared it would affect our life here and I didn't want that.'

'So what was the plan? Keep on sneaking over to Bristol for Christmas and birthdays? Keep your idiot wife in the dark?'

'You're not an idiot—'

'Then why do I feel like one?'

'I'm sorry; it wasn't my intention to make you feel that way. I only did what I thought was right for the family.'

'Clearly your oldest daughter had other ideas. Is it true her mum's dying?'

'Nothing is certain, but she is ill. It's why she decided to reach out.'

'And you really didn't know she'd had a baby?'

'I swear to you on the kids'—'

'No!' Gaby said. 'Not that. Just swear to me you didn't know.'

'I swear the first I knew was a few months ago.'

'How the hell did this woman find you? You didn't even live in Port Promise back then.'

'Apparently, if you search hard enough on Google, you can find just about anything. I'm mentioned on the lifeboat reports that are online; all the crew get a mention from time to time.' He shrugged. 'Says she figured it out from that. She knew the village, but honestly, she didn't have our address, so I don't know how Meredith managed to find the house.'

'She only had to ask in the village – anyone would have told her, I suppose.'

'Not anyone,' Killian said. 'My money's on Marina or Tanika.'

Gaby couldn't hold back a faint smile. Her money would be on one of those two as well.

'I should go in and see her,' Killian said. 'She's come a long way, after all. Has she told you why she's come?'

'She only said she was hoping to stay.'

'How long for?'

'How should I know? I was too busy getting my head around the idea you have another kid to worry about setting another place for breakfast.'

'I suppose we'll find out more as we go along.'

He began to walk the path, but Gaby called him back.

'I don't want you to tell Elijah and Fern,' she said.

He turned with a frown. 'We have to.'

'Why?'

'Because now she's here and you know about her, they ought to know too. They're naturally going to ask questions. She's their sister and they have a right to know now it's all out in the open. She has a right to get to know them as a sister too.'

'Who says?'

'Anyone would say.'

'I don't want it. They're too young and it's too big a shock—'

'You're being ridiculous!'

'I don't care! Let me be ridiculous! They're my children and I don't want them to know!' Gaby could feel her head spinning.

'They won't thank you for keeping them in the dark when the truth comes out.'

'Why does it have to come out? Keep them in the dark forever as far as I'm concerned.'

'Isn't that just what I wanted to do? I seem to recall you weren't very happy about the prospect.'

'This is different.'

'How?'

'It just is! They're children and this is too much for them right now.'

'You're being ridiculous. They can handle this – they lived through losing your dad so they can handle anything.'

'Exactly! Haven't they been through enough over the past couple of years? My dad, Cormac almost dying saving Eli... and then we nearly lost Clara and the baby...' She shook her head vehemently. 'It's too much; I won't land something else on them.'

'I'm not keeping it from them – it's stupid. They'll find out sooner or later. They all have a right to form a relationship.'

Gaby threw her hands in the air. Her voice was getting

louder but at this point she didn't care. 'Then at least don't do anything until we've discussed it!'

'What's to discuss?'

'Plenty! This will destroy everything they thought they knew! Who knows what it will do to them – what problems it will create for them in the future?'

'They still have to know, Gab.'

He turned to go in, and she followed.

'Please just not now,' she said.

'It's as good a time as any – it'll only be worse the longer we keep it from them.'

'It's a pity you didn't have that attitude when you kept it from me!' she yelled.

He swung to face her, the familiar steel that she'd always admired in him there to mock her now. 'I didn't tell you because I knew you'd react like this!'

'How else did you want me to react?'

'Like a grown-up.'

'I hate you! That grown-up enough for you?'

'I'm getting that impression, yeah. But can you keep hold of it until I've spoken to Meredith. It's not her fault you're pissed off with me and it's not fair to put her in the middle of our domestic.'

'This is not a domestic, Killian! This isn't just you forgetting to put the bin out!'

'I know, but you losing it isn't helping anyone to deal with the situation. She's here now and I can't do anything about that. All I'm saying is leave her out of the blame game, because nothing is her fault. She didn't ask to be in the middle of this.'

'She came to our house to find you!'

'And you're saying she was wrong to do that?'

'No!' Gaby tried to swallow a rage that was building and building. She felt as if she was about to blow, and even as the red mist descended she could see that wasn't a good thing. As she looked at Killian now, she wondered if she might actually hate him for real. She couldn't remember a time when she'd felt such anger towards him – and theirs had been a tempestuous marriage with plenty of arguments in the past. 'Of course I'm not saying that, but she must have expected some friction when she did.'

'She came because she's in a weird and vulnerable place right now. I'd have thought you, of all people, would understand that, Gaby. I always thought you were practical and compassionate and they were qualities I loved in you, but now...' He shook his head sadly. 'Now, I don't even know where that woman is. My wife wouldn't treat a young girl in need like this.'

'But she's not just any young girl,' Gaby said, fighting angry tears. 'She's your *secret*. There was a time when I thought you were open and honest and that you could trust me with any bombshell, but it looks as if I got it wrong too. It's not even that she's here, Kill, it's that you never told me about her... that's what hurts. You could have told me about her months ago, but you chose to lie. How could you do that to me?'

'Now's not the time,' Killian said. 'We can talk later. I'm going in; she'll be wondering what's going on out here and I don't want her to come out and hear this.'

Killian strode inside, and Gaby could tell by his tone that although she was desperate to battle this out, he wasn't going to indulge her. She couldn't decide whether that made her feel even angrier, though she also couldn't see how she could possibly be angrier than she was. What she'd told him was true, and she understood it now – she didn't care that he had a daughter with another woman – after all, it was before they'd met and he hadn't even known about her – but she cared that he hadn't shared this news with her as soon as he'd discovered it. The cut was deep. Not only did this affect their family, but he must have been shocked when he'd found out. He must have tussled with his new status as father to another daughter, with new responsibilities, and Gaby would have wanted to support him through that, but he'd chosen to exclude her from what was a huge change in his life. He'd even admitted that if Meredith hadn't come to Port Promise to find him, he'd never have told Gaby of her existence. She barely recognised the man entering their home as her husband right now. The man she loved and respected, the man she thought she knew inside and out was a stranger to her. There was another in his place, one who lied and didn't care for the consequences. One who wasn't a bit sorry for what he'd done.

Meredith looked up from her phone as Gaby followed Killian into the kitchen. Her worried frown cleared like storm clouds chased from the sun and she beamed at him. She didn't get down from the high stool at the breakfast bar to hug him, but gazed at him with a sort of awed shyness as he took the stool next to her.

'Hi, Dad.' She gave an awkward wave. 'Surprise!'

'Does your mum know you're here?'

'Yeah.'

Killian fixed her with a look of obvious disbelief.

'No,' Meredith said, her smile fading. 'Are you going to send me back?'

'Not right now; it's too late. But we do need to tell her where you are. She'll be worried and she has enough to worry about.'

'Yeah.' Meredith's shoulders visibly slumped. 'Remind me how everything is about that.'

'I'm sorry, but it is. She's seriously ill and, whether we like it or not, until that situation is resolved one way or another, everything will be about that.'

Gaby folded her arms tight and leaned against the kitchen doorway. She had to be impressed by the way Killian had just dealt with Meredith. He didn't condescend – he spoke to her with respect as an equal. In a way that only made things worse – she couldn't help but feel that he was treating Meredith with more respect than he had Gaby only moments before.

'I just needed to get away,' Meredith said. 'I needed some head space. I didn't know where to go, but you said it was so nice here and...' She shrugged.

'This was the first place you thought to come?' He reached to pat her on the shoulder. 'Take some time out here – you're always welcome – but then you need to go home. I know it's hard, but your mum is going to need you. You may not think so now, and you may feel as if you just want to run away – nobody would blame you for it – but if you shirk that duty, you'll regret it for the rest of your life.'

Meredith nodded slowly. 'OK,' she said. 'But I can stay tonight?'

'We're hardly going to send you back to Bristol tonight.' Killian offered a tense smile. 'Square it with your mum and we can maybe do a few days; give you that head space you need. Then you can go back and support her. And you know you don't have to do that alone – I'm always on the end of the phone. When it gets too much, call me. You don't have to run away from home.'

'I didn't run away from home,' she said with a sullen edge to her voice.

Killian raised his eyebrows with that look of disbelief again.

'I didn't,' she insisted. 'I only wanted to get out for a while.'

'Don't you have any family in Bristol?' Gaby asked.

Killian fired her a warning look but she ignored it. 'It's a reasonable question,' she said to him.

'I had my dad... my other dad,' Meredith said in answer to Gaby's look of confusion. 'The dad I called Dad from when I was little. He died when I was twelve. I used to see his family but when he died they stopped coming round and I don't see them now.'

'So your mum got married?' Gaby asked.

Killian fired one of those looks at her again. Perhaps she was fishing for information, and perhaps it was more about her position as Killian's wife than anything else, but she had a right to know these things, didn't she?

Meredith shook her head. 'They just lived together. He was nice, though. He didn't mind that he wasn't my real dad.'

'You always knew?'

'Yes.'

'Didn't you ever want to know where your real dad was?'

'Mum told me she didn't know who he was.'

'It must have been a shock when she told you she'd lied about that.'

'I don't know.' Meredith shrugged. 'A bit.'

'Did she tell you why she'd kept it from you?'

'She didn't want me to go looking for him because she said he wasn't the right sort of man for our life. She wanted to bring me up herself. They'd only been together for a couple of weeks so it wasn't like she loved him or anything. She said she didn't need some stranger interfering with the way she did things...'

She offered Killian a vague look of apology, but if Meredith had known him better, she'd have realised there was no need. Killian looked unmoved by the notion that he hadn't been loved by this woman. Then again, Gaby mused, he'd be far too practical for that sort of thing, even if he had been offended.

There was a light tap on Gaby's arm, and she turned to see Fern standing behind her. 'How long have you been there?' she asked, perhaps too sharply as she noted Fern back away.

'I've finished my homework and Eli says he's hungry.'

'Has he finished his homework?'

Fern nodded.

'Go and fetch him down,' Killian said. 'We'll eat shortly.'

Fern shot a furtive look at Meredith before scampering away. Goodness only knew what she was making of all this, but even at her young age there was no way she could fail to realise something huge was happening and that this newcomer was at the centre of it.

'I don't know what we're going to eat,' Gaby said obstructively. 'I haven't been able to even think about a meal with all this going on.'

'We'll go to Cormac's if it's a problem.'

'All of us?' Gaby's tone held a note of alarm. There was no way they could take Meredith down to the shack. How would they explain who she was?

'We've all got to eat, haven't we? And if you don't have time to—'

'I'll cook,' Gaby said firmly. She went to the freezer, and as she inspected the contents she heard Fern come back with Elijah in tow. Shutting the door, she was horrified to see Killian put his arm around Meredith and smile at his two other children.

'This is Meredith. She's come to stay with us for a few days.'

'Hello...'

Both Elijah and Fern studied her with some shyness and a lot of curiosity. They weren't naturally shy children, and Gaby could only put it down to that sense of something big happening. It was hard to see how they wouldn't notice that there was something very different about Meredith than their other visitors.

'So...' Meredith pointed to them in turn. 'Elijah and Fern, right?'

They both nodded and then she looked at Killian expectantly.

'Why not?' Killian said. He turned back to the children and before Gaby could utter a word of protest, he simply told them. 'Meredith is your half-sister.'

CHAPTER FOURTEEN

Gaby didn't want to hate Meredith. It was petty, unfair and unbecoming, and she ought to be above such negative reactions, but try as she might, she couldn't shut out her feelings of resentment. It was almost made worse by how agreeable Meredith was. She was every bit her father's daughter – confident, reasonable, intelligent and pragmatic – but made extra impressive by the traits that must have been passed to her from her mother, Vicky.

Vicky sounded like a free spirit, a strong character who knew her own mind and didn't subscribe to anyone else's view on how she ought to live her life – it was no wonder Killian had been attracted to her. Whatever they'd had, no matter how brief, Gaby would bet it had been intense, even if it hadn't been love, and the notion made her jealous in a way she couldn't explain. After all, there was no need. She was married to Killian and it was her he loved. He'd made a life with her in Port Promise, not with Vicky in Bristol, so why should she be jealous?

But she couldn't shut out the *what if* thoughts. What if Vicky had told him about her pregnancy at the very start? What if they'd had longer together? What if Killian had discovered

Meredith years ago, before he'd met Gaby or before they'd married or had their own children? Would Gaby have him now, or would he have chosen a different life?

It didn't help that Elijah and Fern were captivated. They'd taken the news of their new sister far better than Gaby could have imagined. They were in awe, full of questions and eager to share the details of their lives in Port Promise with her. They were endlessly fascinated – Fern in particular couldn't take her eyes off Meredith all through their hastily prepared dinner.

As they cleared away, Meredith offered to help. Gaby was about to refuse when Killian smiled.

'That'd be great, thanks.'

So Meredith busied herself handing the plates to him to load the dishwasher while Gaby quietly seethed as she put the pots in the bowl to soak.

'Can I help too?' Fern asked.

Killian laughed. 'You never offer to help. Meredith must be a good influence – she'll have to come over more often.'

Gaby glared at him. How could he be so relaxed? Couldn't he see what he'd done?

An electronic bleep stopped him in his tracks. He pulled his pager from his jeans pocket and looked at it.

'What's that?' Meredith asked.

'Lifeboat pager,' Elijah said with obvious pride. Pride that he knew something Meredith didn't or pride that his father owned such a thing? It was hard to tell. 'It means Dad has to go out and rescue someone.'

But Killian didn't run for the door as he would usually do. He paused and glanced at every face in the room. He seemed torn. For a moment, Gaby thought he wasn't going to go. He clearly didn't want to. Was this because of Meredith? He'd never ignore a page, not for anything. He'd gone out Christmas morning one year as the kids had been opening their presents.

'I'd better go,' he said finally. 'Will you be OK here?'

'I'm usually OK,' Gaby said shortly. 'Don't know why today would be any different.'

He didn't have time for an argument, but Gaby supposed he wouldn't have been drawn into one even if he had. He raced out, leaving her with Elijah, Fern and Meredith.

'What does he have to do?' Meredith asked. 'Does he have to go on his boat?'

'Yes,' Elijah said. 'They're going to see if they can save someone. One day I'm going to do it.'

'Sounds cool,' Meredith said. 'Can anyone do it?'

'Ava does it,' Fern said. 'So do Harry and Cormac, and our grandad used to do it too.'

'But he died,' Elijah said solemnly. 'He fell over the side of the boat.'

Meredith's eyes widened. 'Your grandad? So my...'

'My dad,' Gaby put in briskly. 'Not Killian's.'

'Oh. But still cool.'

Gaby wanted to say that it wasn't cool. She wanted to tell Meredith that it was tragic and heartbreaking and it had torn her family apart, but in a totally different way than her arriving in Port Promise was doing right now. But she didn't, because, tough as it was, she had to keep reminding herself that none of this was Meredith's fault. She'd only wanted to find her dad, and it sounded as if life in Bristol was hard for her right now, and so nobody could blame her for wanting a breather from it. Gaby had to be gracious, as she knew she was capable of being. She only wished she could find that grace right now, because she couldn't recall a single occasion where she'd struggled quite so much.

'Are people allowed to watch?' Meredith asked. 'I've seen it on telly but never seen a lifeboat in real life.'

'Can we go down, Mum?' Elijah asked.

'You know we don't go down unless—'

'Yes, but Meredith is here and she's never seen it,' Fern cut in.

'And it looks so cool when it splashes into the sea!' Elijah added.

'They might be going out in the inshore,' Gaby said. 'That doesn't splash in – it's driven in on a tractor.'

'But it's still cool,' Elijah said.

'I don't want to be a bother if we're not supposed to be there,' Meredith said.

Despite her words, Gaby could see her obvious disappointment. Not only had she recently found her dad, but she'd also discovered he was something of a hero. Rational Gaby, the one who hadn't just had her life tipped upside down by the arrival of a teenager, would have seen that all too plainly and probably would have been a lot more indulgent. Of course Meredith wanted to see Killian in action.

'Anyone can watch from the beach,' Elijah said. 'It's allowed as long as you don't get too close.'

Gaby let out a sigh of resignation. She could be bigger than this, and maybe she simply needed to force it.

'OK. Get your jackets. We'll have missed the launch, but we'll see if we can catch them coming back in.'

Darkness had fallen by the time the lifeboat got back in. Killian would need to hose down his waterproofs and see to his kit before he could return home, so they left the beach without him to wait at the cottage.

'False alarm,' he announced as he walked in to where they were all watching television. Elijah and Fern were meant to be in bed, but with Meredith there and Killian still not home, Gaby hadn't had much success in getting them there. In the end, she'd decided it wasn't worth the hassle and she was in no mood to care either way. 'Someone saw a body in the water, only it wasn't a body; it was a lost lilo, so...'

'No one was out there?' Elijah asked, looking bitterly disappointed.

'I'm happy enough about that,' Killian said, going to the kitchen. 'I'd take a lost lilo every time over a body in the water.'

'We came to watch,' Meredith said. 'It was cool. I've never seen a lifeboat before. I mean, on telly, but not for real.'

'You did?' He put his head back around the kitchen door and gave her a tired smile. Then his gaze went to Gaby. She detected the faintest hint of surprise in it. 'You took them down to the station?'

'Well,' Gaby said briskly, 'like she said, Meredith had never seen one before.'

Killian turned to his youngest children. 'What are you still doing up?'

'They wanted to wait for you,' Gaby said. 'And we have other distractions...'

'Sorry.' Meredith looked sheepish. 'I guess that's my fault.'

'Well,' Killian said, 'it's not every day you meet a new sister, is it? I suppose it's to be expected.'

His words scratched at the edges of Gaby's already raw patience. Every time he referred to Meredith as his daughter, so naturally and casually, she found it jarring. Would she ever come to terms with the fact that she wasn't the only – or even first – mother of a child from him? She felt it diminished her, made her less important, and it made her feel like she was less *to* him. And the way he dropped it into conversation already like it was nothing... couldn't he see that? Couldn't he understand how it might make Gaby feel?

Her head was swimming, but as well as all this, she still had marking to do for her students. It was getting late and she was tired and tetchy and hardly in the mood to concentrate, but that wasn't going to mean a thing to some anxious student waiting on her feedback.

'Elijah, Fern...' She looked at them. 'Time for bed.'

'But...'

'You wanted to wait for your dad to come in; he's here now so you have no more excuses.'

'Can't we stay up a tiny bit longer?' Fern asked, glancing shyly at Meredith. It was clear she was already in awe of her. Perhaps, being the youngest, the new status quo was a lot easier for her to get her head around.

'I've got work to do and I can't do it with a house full of people making noise,' Gaby said. She looked to Killian for support but he'd already gone into the kitchen. She heard him fill the kettle and switch it on.

'Please—' Fern began.

'Bed!' Gaby repeated.

Both children slid from the sofa looking sullen.

'I'll see you in the morning,' Meredith said.

'Will you still be here?' Fern asked.

'Of course!'

Great, Gaby thought. *Just what I need.*

CHAPTER FIFTEEN

It felt far too early when the alarm went off. Killian was up first. He was fully dressed by the time Gaby rolled over and opened her eyes.

'Want me to take the kids to school today so you can finish off your stuff?'

'I did it last night.'

'All of it?'

'Yep.'

She'd stayed up until midnight trying to mark, though her mind was hardly on it. She'd been using the home office and had been able to hear Killian talking to Meredith in the living room, though she couldn't make out what they were saying. Eventually she'd heard him go to bed, gone downstairs to see that Meredith had everything she needed for her night on the sofa, then went to bed herself. Killian had already been asleep – or he'd been doing a good job pretending to be. Gaby had climbed in beside him, but sleep wouldn't come to her. An hour later, she'd given up and gone to finish the rest of her papers.

Gaby yawned and got out of bed, reaching for the dressing gown hanging on the back of the bedroom door. 'I'll take them.'

'I'll do it,' Killian said. 'Meredith can come.'

Gaby looked sharply at him. 'What?'

'Why not? I don't have to tell anyone who she is.'

'But this is Port Promise! They're going to bloody well wonder and most of them are good at finding out!'

'It'll come out soon enough anyway. You think Eli and Fern are going to keep their mouths shut at school about her? We might as well face it head on and get it out into the open. Otherwise it looks like we have something to hide.'

'Explain to them that we need to keep it between us and nobody needs to know.'

'They're not going to do that – they're kids!'

'I don't want everyone knowing about this!'

Killian's expression darkened. 'You're ashamed or something?'

'Yes!' Gaby yanked at the tie on her dressing gown. 'Yes, I'm ashamed! Have you ever stopped to consider how humiliating this all is for me? What will people say?'

'They'll think I have a past where I did stuff before I met you. It's not that big a deal.'

'It is a big deal! I don't want their pitying looks and them pretending not to be talking about me when I know they are! I don't want them thinking I was your second choice, that you loved someone before me!'

'Do you know how ridiculous you sound?'

'Yes! I don't care! If it's ridiculous, then I'm sorry but it's how I feel! How can you not understand that? How would you feel if it was the other way around? How would you feel if I suddenly produced a child I'd had with another man?'

'Cormac raises Logan's—'

'It's not the same and you know it! How dare you patronise me, Kill! How dare you make me the unreasonable one, like my reaction is a failing in me!'

'I can't do anything about the fact she was born.'

'But you could have warned me! As soon as you knew about her you could have told me. I would have had time to get my head around it and to talk to my mum and sisters.'

'What's it got to do with them?'

'Everything! She's not related to them but she's yours and you're a part of my family, so that makes it everything to do with them! If you can't see that then you really are clueless.'

Killian studied her for a moment, but his expression gave nothing away. 'I did what I thought was the right thing at the time and I'm sorry if you think I got it wrong.'

'If *I think* you got it wrong? What does that mean? *You* don't think you got it wrong and so, once again, it's irrational Gaby overreacting?'

'You're never irrational and you never overreact and, to be honest, that's why I don't get what this is. I understand it was a shock, but I don't see why you're still struggling so badly with it.'

'Well you wouldn't, would you? Because this doesn't affect you like it affects me. It's just one more kid to hero-worship you while I get to pick up the real-life pieces.'

'There are no pieces.'

'Maybe it looks like that now, but how do you know where this is going? What about when her mum dies? What then? I know you; you'll be pushing to move her here and when I finally agree you'll go about your life like nothing has changed and I'll have to pick up the slack. I'll be the wicked stepmother; I'll be the one living with a stranger I never asked for!'

'I never imagined you could sound so selfish.'

'It's not selfish to be angry about something forced on you that you never wanted; it's human. If anyone's being selfish here, it's you.'

'For helping when my daughter comes to ask for it?'

'For making her think you can have a normal relationship like other dads and daughters have. For making her think she can just slot into our lives here, because it doesn't work like that. She can't just turn up and be an instant part of our family.'

'Why not?'

'She just can't! We don't even know her!'

'I know her—'

'You met her like a few months ago, Killian. Once, for an hour in Bristol or whatever it was. Get real – you don't know the first thing about her or her mum. How can you even be sure she's yours? How do you know this Vicky woman didn't just look up all her old boyfriends and peg you as the sucker to dump her kid on?'

'I'm not listening to any more of this bullshit.'

He shoved Gaby out of the way and stormed out. A moment later she heard him shout for Elijah and Fern to get up. It meant there was no more discussion to be had for now – although discussion was hardly the word. All-out war was more like it.

She went to sit on the bed, hating herself for every single thing she'd just said to him. Maybe she felt much of it, but maybe she shouldn't have said it. Too late now – the spiteful words were out and couldn't be taken back. And no matter how she tried to convince herself and Killian that there might be some elaborate con going on here, one look at Meredith had left her in no doubt that she was Killian's. She wasn't sure whether that made things worse or better.

Gaby suspected that Meredith had overheard them arguing, and even if she couldn't hear what they were fighting about, she'd probably worked out that she herself had featured heavily. While Killian took Elijah and Fern to school, Meredith packed her rucksack. Seeing it made Gaby feel even worse. She didn't necessarily want Meredith there, but she didn't want to hurt her either. In any other circumstance, she'd have liked her, and it was plain that Elijah and Fern liked her too.

'You don't have to go today,' she said as she handed Meredith a plate of toast.

'Dad said that, but I already told my mum I'd come back today.'

'So you're not leaving because of anything we...'

'It's all right,' Meredith said. 'I get that you must have been shocked. I never would have come if I'd known Dad hadn't told you about me. I'm sorry if I messed things up for you.'

'You didn't,' Gaby said, filled with a sudden shame. Meredith was acting like the mature woman here when it should have been her. 'I *was* shocked, but that's not your doing. Your dad likes having you here and so do Elijah and Fern. Now that everything is out in the open you can visit whenever you want. Although, a bit of a heads-up might be nice.'

'Got it.' Meredith gave a slight smile as she bit into her toast. 'Mum had a right go at me about it yesterday when I phoned her.'

'I'm sure I'd have done the same. Wasn't she worried about the fact you'd jumped on a train and come here by yourself without telling anyone?'

'Not worried – I do loads of stuff on my own. But I think maybe she was hurt. I tried to explain, but...' Meredith shrugged.

Gaby tried to imagine how she'd feel in Vicky's shoes, but she couldn't. She couldn't imagine for a moment knowing you might die any day and leave your teenage daughter fending for herself, to see that daughter struggle with her reality and feel such huge guilt for your part in it. Meredith deserved better than she'd been given. And when Gaby really looked into her heart, she could see that it had never been Meredith arriving unannounced that had made her angry – it was all about Killian.

'It must be hard,' she said.

'She gets really ill some days.'

'I meant for you.'

'Oh...' Meredith chewed silently for a moment. 'I suppose.'

Killian appeared at the kitchen doorway. He barely looked at Gaby and even his smile for Meredith was tense.

'Ready to head off soon?' he asked her.

'You're driving?' Gaby asked.

'Yes,' Killian said. 'That OK with you?'

Gaby tried not to take offence at the obvious barb in his comment.

'Of course,' she said. 'I just wondered, because of the distance. You don't like being away from the station if you can help it.'

'Well this time I can't help it. Vas knows I'll be missing for a few hours and Ava's on the crew now, so...'

Meredith crammed the last of her toast into her mouth and stood up. 'I'm ready.'

Killian was right about one thing – no matter how hard they might try to keep Meredith a secret, their kids would have other ideas. It wouldn't be long before they let slip to a friend, and then a friend would tell a parent and, as was the way of things, the whole of Port Promise would know. Better for Gaby to come clean, at least with her family, so that they'd hear it from her before someone else.

Jill had sounded vaguely surprised when Gaby phoned and asked if she could visit her at the allotment. Gaby could imagine why – she'd normally wait until Jill got home; it was her place of work after all. But she didn't want to put off telling her mum about Meredith. It was one of those things that she wouldn't be able to put out of her mind until it was done. She'd arrange to meet up with Clara and Ava when she could, unless Jill beat her to it, of course. Which Gaby wouldn't mind at all. There would have to be a conversation, but it seemed easier, somehow, not to have to keep introducing the subject. It felt weird enough to be saying the words: *Killian has another daughter* the once, without saying them over and over.

'Why do I get the feeling this isn't purely a social call?' Jill asked as Gaby found her in the greenhouse taking cuttings to start new plants.

'Was it that obvious?'

'A bit. What's wrong?'

'Nothing...' Gaby picked up a newly potted palm and looked at it. 'Actually, everything. I think my marriage might be in trouble for a start.'

Jill halted and looked up at her.

'I know,' Gaby said. 'Sounds a bit dramatic, doesn't it?'

'Has something happened?'

'Something, yes, but things have been weird for a while now and I can't really explain it. This has just made everything that bit harder.'

'Do you need me to take a break...?' Jill started to take off her gloves but Gaby held up a hand to stop her.

'No, I don't want to disturb you and this bit won't actually take long. I just wanted you to hear it from me before anyone else. I discovered yesterday that Killian has a daughter from a previous relationship. In fact, I met her for the first time at the same time as I discovered it.'

Jill's forehead creased into a deep frown. 'You're joking?'

'I wish I was. She turned up at the house asking for him. Out of the blue. I had no idea she even existed until that point.'

Jill stared at her. 'Killian must have known?'

'Meredith says he didn't know about her until a few months ago. She didn't know about him much before that either. Apparently her mum had always told her she didn't know the identity of her dad. I have no reason to believe that isn't true.'

'So Killian only met her yesterday too? He must—'

'Oh, no, Killian's met her before. He went to Bristol when the mother first contacted him. A few months ago. He neglected to tell me about that bit.'

Gaby wanted to tell her mum about the lies, how he'd hidden his reasons for travelling to Bristol, how she wouldn't have known he'd been there at all if he hadn't been caught speeding or had Meredith chosen not to visit, about how all that made her feel, but for the sake of her family she didn't. Telling Jill about the full extent of Killian's cover-up would only cause resentment and she didn't want bad feeling between her mum and her husband. It was easier to keep the peace and trust that at some point it was the right call to make. Things were going to be awkward enough for a while without making it worse.

'Well...'

Jill's expression was so full of pity that Gaby didn't know how to feel. Was it a cause for pity? It was the one reaction she hadn't wanted from people when they heard the news, because it implied that she'd been treated badly, that there was a reason to pity her; it implied that she was weak. It reminded her that Killian wasn't the man she'd thought he was, and of her fears that perhaps his love for her hadn't ever been as complete as hers was for him.

'I'm not sure what to do with this information,' Jill continued. 'Where is she now?'

'It gets more complicated – she ran away from home. Her mum has a tumour of some sort and it's touch and go whether she's going to make the end of this year. So she came to find Killian, hoping she could stay, have a break from it all. I feel a bit sorry for her really. She's a nice girl and she's having a rough time. I know what Dad would have said about it. Anyway, we let her stay last night but Killian persuaded her that she needed to be at home for Vicky and he's driving her back as we speak.'

'Vicky is her mother?'

Gaby nodded.

'And how old is Meredith?'

'Almost fifteen. There wasn't anything serious between her mum and Killian, so they say. A short fling. When Vicky found out she was pregnant she'd already lost touch with him and chose not to find him; wanted to raise Meredith on her own.'

'What on earth would she want to do that for?'

'No idea. I'm sure she had her reasons and it's none of my business.'

'Is that how you really feel?' Jill's study of Gaby was shrewd.

Gaby sighed. 'It's crazy, but I'm jealous of this woman and I have no idea why. She was with him for two weeks and she didn't want him even after she discovered she was pregnant. Now she's literally dying, and yet I feel as if I'm somehow in competition with her – it's stupid! Tell me it's stupid, Mum, please; tell me to get a grip.'

Jill pulled her into a hug. 'You're only human, even if you try to pretend you're not. She was with Killian before you and they have a person bonding them together – that's a connection that can never be broken. But he chose you and he loves you.'

'Lately I have to wonder if he does. Sometimes I don't feel that from him at all. He's always at the station or doing something in the house, making excuses when I try to spend time with him. I know it's been a tough year in so many ways for him, but I'm so lonely, Mum. I know I have the kids, and you, Clara and Ava, but it scares me that he's moving further and further from me. I worry I'll lose him and I'll be all alone. A different kind of alone, you know?'

'I know,' Jill said, letting go of her.

Instantly Gaby felt shame. She'd poured out her heart, whining and entitled, completely forgetting that her mother was forced to live with the loneliness that Gaby was so afraid of every day.

'I'm sorry, I shouldn't be going on about it to you—'

'You absolutely should!' Jill said firmly. 'If you can't confide in me, then what good am I to you? You're my daughter, I love you, and while I have breath in my body I will be there for you.'

Gaby fought back tears. She had no right to them and she had no right to burden her mum, no matter what Jill said.

'You don't know what it means to me, just to be able to say it. I can't talk to Clara and Ava about this stuff.'

'Why not?'

She shook her head. 'I don't know. I just feel...'

'Like you have to be the sensible one?' Jill gave a wry smile. 'I'm fairly sure they realise you're only human. You're there for them to confide in all the time and I'm sure they'd want to do the same for you. You don't have to go through this alone.'

'That's just it; I'm not really going through anything compared to some, am I? In the scheme of things it's not that big. I'm not dying or anything.'

'Don't be so hard on yourself. I can't imagine how I would have felt if I'd discovered something like this. It changes everything you believed before.'

Gaby shook her head. 'I know it's stupid, but I keep thinking, what if he'd known Vicky longer than he did? Would he have loved her? Would he have loved her more than he loves me? Would she have been better? Was it her who was meant to be with him instead of me? Am I second best? Would he want her now if—'

'Stop it!' Jill said. 'Forget all that! You will never know the answer to those questions and the fact remains that he married you and he loves you. That's all you need to know.'

'Yes, but is that why he didn't tell me about her? He's never mentioned her, not even when we've talked about old partners. Why? Is that because she was someone to worry about? Because she meant more to him than he says?'

'If he was only with her for such a short time then perhaps

he really didn't think she meant anything, not even enough to merit a mention. They parted after only a couple of weeks and she didn't contact him to tell him about her baby, so that says all you need to know about how much they meant to each other.'

Gaby's gaze went to the windows. Beyond the humid air of the greenhouse was a lush quadrangle of greenery, the hills of Port Promise like scenery on a stage behind it. 'I know you're right,' she said. 'My brain knows you're right – I just wish my stupid emotions could see it too.'

'Give it time,' Jill said. 'You'll get through this, as you always get through everything, and when you do your marriage will be stronger for it.'

Gaby looked at her and forced a smile. 'I'll do my best. I don't have much of a choice, do I?'

Gaby went to see Ava and Clara after she left her mum. Ava had been between lessons so there hadn't been time for anything but the barest details. Although she'd been shocked to hear the news, she didn't seem to think it was something to worry about. If anything, she was intrigued, and wanted to know more about Meredith and her mother's situation. Gaby assumed – given how close Ava and Killian had become since Ava had joined the lifeboat crew – that she'd talk to him at some point to get his side of things, and perhaps that would be a good thing. Hearing his side in a far more neutral way and then relaying that back might give Gaby much-needed perspective. God only knew she needed some of that right now.

Clara was at Cormac's shack, William in a sling fastened to her front as she did her best to assist her partner.

'I've told her to go home,' Cormac said in answer to Gaby's faint look of disapproval. 'I've told her she ought to be resting but she says she's bored. I can't do any more than that – see if you can.'

'There's no need,' Clara said stubbornly. 'I'm fine, and if I'm moving around William shuts up.'

Gaby raised her eyebrows.

'He never stops crying,' Clara said.

'You know I'll take him from you any time so you can have a break,' Gaby said. 'I could take him tonight if you want.'

Clara stroked William's head gently. He was sleeping and looked so peaceful Gaby couldn't imagine him making a fuss at all, but she knew Clara wasn't the sort of woman to exaggerate. If she said she was struggling, then it was probably a lot worse than that.

'I know you would,' she said. 'But I have to do this. I can't keep asking everyone else to do it all for me.'

'There's no shame in asking for help,' Cormac put in from where he was chopping some fennel. Gaby could smell aniseed even over the sea salt on the air.

'Says you.' Clara shot him a withering glance. 'The man who has to do everything himself.'

'That's different,' Cormac said.

'I don't see why.'

'Honestly,' Gaby said, 'I'm with Clara on this one... sorry, Cormac. But you are very stubborn about anyone doing anything for you.'

'Well,' Cormac said with a low chuckle, 'that's me told.'

'But if you can spare her for ten minutes,' Gaby continued, 'I really wanted to have a word.'

'What's up?' Clara asked as she gestured for Gaby to move away from the shack and followed her out.

'Got time for a quick walk?' Gaby asked, glancing back to where Cormac was still in earshot. It wouldn't be long before he found out about Meredith and so there was no reason to hide this conversation from him, but that didn't make Gaby feel any less awkward about it.

'If I'm moving, William's more likely to stay asleep, so that's fine by me.'

They began to walk the road that hugged the curve of the bay, out towards Promise Rocks where the beach was quieter.

'So what's up?' Clara asked.

'We had an unexpected visitor yesterday. She's—'

'Is this the girl who was asking where Killian lived?'

Gaby sent a sideways glance her sister's way. 'I shouldn't need to ask, but how did you know about that already?'

'Tanika.'

'She told her where we lived?'

'I called at the holiday park this morning and she told me about it. I'm so sorry – that was a really stupid thing for her to do, giving a complete stranger your address. She could have been anyone. I said so and, if it's any consolation, I think she realised afterwards. But she said it was only a young girl and she didn't see what harm it would do. So who was she?'

Gaby took a breath. Here she was, saying those words one more time, and it never got any less weird. 'Killian's daughter.'

Clara was silent for a beat, and then she nodded slowly. 'I had wondered if it might be something like that.'

'Really?'

'It just seemed one of the most likely things. It was either something to do with the lifeboats – someone who'd been rescued – but then I thought they'd just go to the station, or it had to be someone looking for him for something very specific. And as Tanika said she was really young...'

'I suppose it's obvious when you look at it like that.'

'Well, no. I didn't seriously think it would be that; I'm saying I'm not surprised, given the facts. So I guess our family just got a bit bigger. Is she staying with you?'

'Killian's taking her home to Bristol. She ran away and came straight here.'

'Wow, things must be bad at home if she ran away and this

was the first place she thought to come. I mean, she must have been uncertain what sort of reception she'd get as she'd never even spoken to you before. So, you want to tell me about it? Has Killian explained why he's never told you about this girl?'

'He didn't know about her.'

'And you believe that?'

'It's what Meredith – his... his daughter – and Killian are saying so I have no reason to doubt it.'

'So the first thing he knew about her was yesterday when she arrived? That must have been a hell of a shock for him too!'

'No, he's known for a few months. He went to Bristol to meet her.'

'So how long have you known?'

'Since yesterday.'

Clara sucked in a breath. 'I bet you loved that.'

'You could say I didn't take it as calmly as I might have done.'

'And it's just the one?'

'One what?'

'Child. He's only got the one extra?'

'Jesus, Clara! I didn't even think of that and now you've planted another seed of doubt!'

'It's a reasonable question,' Clara said. 'I don't know... was he with her mother for a while? Did they have more than one child together? Were there other women who had babies with him? I mean, he was well into his twenties when you two got together and that's plenty of time.'

'Great – thanks for that. I'm *so* glad I came to talk to you! Now I have to have the conversation about how many other children I might expect to come looking for him!'

'Probably none,' Clara said, hastily backpedalling. 'I didn't mean that; I just meant is that the only thing you don't know about his past?'

'That's making it worse not better! Don't you think I've

already considered that he might be keeping a whole load more secrets? Don't you think I'm already paranoid enough? Since I found out about Meredith I can't trust anything that has ever come out of his mouth – or not come out of his mouth. I don't know what else might be in his past and it terrifies me.'

'So what are you going to do?'

'What can I do? I have to suck it up.'

'Not really.'

'I do if I want to stay married. Meredith is a part of our lives now whether I like it or not and he's made it clear that if I want to be with him I have to accept her. I can't tell you, Clara... it's like he's already so proud when he looks at her. I feel things I shouldn't feel about it. I know it's not her fault, but I feel as if she's somehow pushed our children out of his heart, as if he has just that little bit less love to give them because now he's giving it to her. I feel sad and angry, and I don't even know what, but I just feel for Eli and Fern.'

'He adores those two – nothing would change that.'

'I know. I know it's silly to think there's this standard pot of love that will only go so far but...' She shrugged, unable to finish the sentence. Saying it all out loud did make it sound ridiculous but that didn't change her feelings.

'I'm assuming Elijah and Fern met her?'

'Yes.'

'And you told them who she is?'

'I didn't want to but Killian did it anyway.'

'You didn't want to? But isn't that just as bad as him not telling you about it?'

'I wanted to give them time.'

'For what?'

'I don't know...'

'Sounds like it was you who needed time, not them. Imagine how much weirder it would have been if they'd got to know her as this random girl who'd come to visit and then suddenly, oh, by the way, she's your sister but we didn't tell you because we thought you needed time. That would have been way worse. I hate to say it, but I think Killian was right to be up front with them.'

'He could have been a bit more upfront with me. Why does everyone else deserve it but me?'

'Maybe he was afraid to tell you.'

'This is Killian we're talking about – the king of plain speaking. I doubt that.'

'There must have been a reason then. You're right – he's always so straight about everything. Perhaps that's what you ought to be trying to figure out. He doesn't shy away from anything that needs saying, so why this?'

'He says he knew I'd react badly.'

'That's never stopped either of you before.'

Gaby was silent as she pondered Clara's words. Out in the bay, the clouds had moved in to obscure the sun, the atmosphere was heavy and humid and it felt like a storm was in the air. Clara was right: Killian never shied away from uncomfortable truths – it was one of the reasons they argued so often. It was also one of the things she grudgingly admired about him. She appreciated people being straight and frank with her, and perhaps that was what really needled her about this deception. It wasn't like him at all. Unless she'd never really known him like she'd thought she had. Perhaps this *was* the real Killian, a man who seemed straight but who kept secrets. After all, just twenty-four hours previously she'd thought she'd known everything there was to know, she'd felt like she'd understood him, body, mind and soul. But the appearance of Meredith showed the lie of her confidence, and she didn't quite know what to do with that notion.

CHAPTER SIXTEEN

Killian was already home by the time Gaby got back. She found him cutting logs to season for the winter and use on their log burner, which was what he did every summer. Ordinarily, Gaby would have taken a moment to admire his muscles as he worked, and perhaps to tease him about being a caveman. But today she took no pleasure in the sight of him working.

'The roads must have been good,' she said. 'Didn't expect you to be back so soon. How was Vicky?'

'Didn't stay,' he grunted, bringing the axe down on a chunk of wood. 'I dropped Meredith off at the door; thought they needed to talk some stuff through.'

'I've been to see Mum. Ava and Clara too.'

'Oh?'

'I told them about Meredith.'

'And what did they say? I suppose I'm the villain now?'

'It wasn't like that. I had to tell them – what else was I meant to do? You said yourself people will find out soon enough – better they heard it from me than from Marina or Tanika.'

'So they're not telling you to divorce me?'

'Of course not!'

'Still, I'm surprised my ears haven't been burning.'

'Killian, we need to talk.'

'I'm listening.'

'Properly.'

Killian paused and looked up at her. 'OK. What do you need to say that you haven't already said?'

'I wish you'd told me about Meredith sooner.'

'Huh…' He started to chop again. 'I did what I thought was best.'

'You really thought hiding her was for the best?'

'Yes, and I was straight with you about why I did that.'

'But can't you see why that's bad?'

'Not really. I'm right you'd have been happier not knowing, aren't I?'

'That's not the point.'

'That's exactly the point.' Killian scooped another log from the stack and set it on the block. 'Where has you knowing about her got us? All it's done is caused all this strife.'

'Do you really think you could have kept her a secret forever?'

He looked up, his face a mask that Gaby couldn't read. 'Yes,' he said simply. 'If she'd never come then I would have kept her from you.'

'Why?' Gaby asked, tears of anger and frustration squeezing her throat. 'I'm your wife; I had a right to know!'

'Life would have gone on as it always has. You'd have been blissfully unaware and I wouldn't be feeling like a total bastard for something I had no control over—'

'You had control over it!' Gaby snapped, rage getting the better of her. 'You slept with her mum! You made the baby! You left that woman high and dry!'

'I didn't know she was pregnant!' Killian yelled. 'How is that my fault?'

'Well it's certainly not mine!'

He paused and fixed her with a look so cold, so full of contempt she could barely believe this was her husband. 'What do you want from me, Gaby? Do you want me to pretend she doesn't exist?'

'I want you to be sorry!'

'I haven't done anything wrong.'

'Unbelievable!' Gaby stamped her foot like a petulant toddler. 'You haven't done anything wrong? Are you really that clueless? You don't think driving to Bristol to meet the daughter you never mentioned to me and then lying about where you'd been was wrong?'

'I did what I thought was the right thing,' he repeated. 'You'd have been happier not knowing and so I didn't tell you. I kept it a secret for your sake.'

'So that backfired in a most spectacular way then.'

'Looks like it.'

Gaby stared him down, but he went back to his task. As she waited for something more, he offered nothing; he only continued to chop with such ferocity there was a danger he'd go through the block beneath the logs. With every swing of the axe there was a grunt, but there was nothing physical about it – it was the sound of pure frustrated anger.

Gaby pursed her lips, just as angry and frustrated herself, but she knew an impasse when she saw one. Killian was never going to apologise for this and she'd never make him see the damage his part in it had done. If it threatened to tear the family apart, he'd still never back down. There were a million answers she could give, a million more arguments, but what was the point? He was in no mood to listen and no mood to admit he was wrong. But she wasn't going to back down either. She'd let things go in the past, but not this time.

She wondered if it wasn't just stubbornness, if he really couldn't see what he'd done. She'd always known being married to Killian would be a challenge and it was one she'd relished.

She could give as good as she got, and, at times, in a strange and perverse way, she'd even enjoyed their conflicts. She loved him for the incredible strength of his convictions, for his strong sense of self-belief, for going with his gut even when it wasn't the popular choice, but this time it was a step too far, even for her. Unless one of them backed down, she really didn't see how this could end well, and it sure as hell wasn't going to be her.

CHAPTER SEVENTEEN

Other than the necessary communication to run the house, Gaby and Killian had barely exchanged a full sentence for three days. That was hardly anything new – they'd been known to have apocalyptic rows before – but the substance of this one felt more dangerous, somehow more insidious and damaging. Worst of all was the fact that Killian had offered no apology and didn't seem to recognise the hurt the affair had caused. In fact, he seemed to have no remorse whatsoever. Killian had never made life easy for Gaby – and at times she'd secretly quite enjoyed that loving him could be a challenge – but, even for her, this time he'd gone too far.

The lifeboat station's annual fundraising Flag Day was a matter of weeks away, and Gaby was so busy preparing for it, she almost didn't have time to worry about whether Killian was speaking to her or not. She'd taken on the task in her dad's memory, and at first that had been her primary motivation, but it had since grown into something else. Yes, she was also doing it for Ava, Harry, Cormac, Killian and the other crew who relied on the money she was raising for vital equipment and maintenance to keep them safe and the service running, but now, she also felt she had a point to prove. She'd didn't need to be Killian's wife to be someone. She didn't need his approval or support. She was going to smash her targets almost as an act of revenge. He thought he was someone, strutting around Port Promise, Mr Black and White, Mr Holier Than Thou, Mr Everyone's Moral Compass – well she'd show him she could better him every time. She was someone around here, and he ought to be grateful she'd married him at all.

And so, with the summer days now sticky and fierce, Port Promise filled with tourists with sunburned shoulders wafting wasps from their ice creams and the beach packed every day, Gaby set out from Thistledown Cottage by way of the harbour to see what Marina had in her stock room for the Flag Day raffle, and to chase up one or two other people who had pledged to help.

Just like every summer, there were boats moored in the harbour that Gaby didn't recognise. Many were small, meant for messing around close to the shore; some were bigger, meant to go further afield. A group of children and their parents were pointing at one, a sleek yacht, with awed gasps.

Gaby stopped to get a better look. It was beautiful – there was no denying it – with pristine rigging, a gleaming walnut deck complete with loungers and a glossy white hull. It had to be forty, maybe forty-five feet, though she couldn't say for sure. It was the sort of yacht people would stop and admire as it sailed elegantly past them, perhaps heading for warmer climes, on the sort of escape that was very appealing to Gaby right now.

'Do you like her?'

She spun round to see Lloyd standing behind her. 'Jesus! You scared the life out of me!'

'Sorry. I noticed you admiring my new woman and thought I'd say hello. She's beautiful, isn't she?'

'It's yours?'

'I took delivery yesterday. Thought I'd give her a run out so decided to sail over here today rather than drive. I have to say, it's a far nicer way to get to work – you should try it.'

'Well, as I don't have a boat and I work from home, I'll take your word for it.'

'You work from home? Interesting... so you call the shots. You can take time off whenever suits you?'

'Hardly. I'm not sure I remember what free time is.'

'So what are you up to right now? Not at home working – I can see that.'

'On a mission. I'm organising a fundraising day for the lifeboat station, so I've got my hands full enough.'

'How commendable of you.'

'Not really. It's kind of what my family does. We've always been connected to the lifeboats, and those of us not on the crew do what we can in other ways.'

'Of course... I had heard you lot practically run it. You're like the Port Promise mafia, aren't you?'

'I wouldn't go that far, but, yes, quite a few of my family and friends are on the crew.'

'So you're a seagoing family? Then I suppose my lovely new boat won't impress you at all. It's a shame – I was hoping it would.'

'Oh?' Gaby glanced at the yacht and then back at him with a wry smile. 'And where would that have got us?'

'Let's just say a man can dare to dream.'

Gaby shook her head, that faint smile still fixed on her face. 'You don't give up, do you?'

'I didn't get where I am today by giving up. I see something I want and I resolve to get it, no matter how impossible it might seem.'

'I suppose I can relate to that.' Her small smile spread as an idea seized her. 'That's why I'm going to ask you to donate to the lifeboats.'

He got out his wallet with a grin of his own. 'I like your style. Let's see, twenty... fifty pounds? Would that be enough?'

'I was thinking more zeros than that. And before you argue with me, I know you can afford it.'

He arched an eyebrow at her. 'May I remind you that I've just bought a boat?'

'And may I remind you who will be coming to rescue you when you run aground because you're not as good a sailor as you think you are?'

His grin spread, and there was something like lust in his eyes. 'God, you're good!'

'I know.'

This was dangerous territory, and Gaby could see where it might go, but perhaps that was the reason she was suddenly enjoying his advances so much.

'So you think I can't sail?' he asked as he put his wallet away.

'Have you sailed much before? You said you've only just got the boat.'

'But I never said it was my first.' He looked at her for a moment. Sizing her up, perhaps, issuing a silent challenge – or so it felt to Gaby. Who would dare go the furthest to get what they wanted? 'What are you doing today?'

'Today? I told you, I'm running around collecting donations. Why?'

'Is there anywhere you have to be this morning?'

'Loads of places.'

'But you don't have a schedule?'

'I have my own schedule.'

'But you can change it however you like.'

Gaby pursed her lips. 'How bold of you to assume I don't have anything important to do? I might not run a chain of fancy restaurants but I still have plenty of work.'

'I didn't say that. But you must be able to juggle your terribly important commitments. I mean, you do owe me.'

Gaby folded her arms. 'Do I?'

'Yes.'

She tried not to show he'd won, but he was right – she did owe him. He'd saved Clara, after all, and whatever else happened that would always stand with her.

'I suppose I might owe you a little.'

'Then let me take you out and you can judge if I can sail.'

'No thanks.'

'Scared you might enjoy it?'

'Scared I might drown.'

'It does float, you know.'

'It does if you're sailing it right.'

'I just told you I can handle her.'

'Still...'

'Your husband won't have to know, if that's what you're worried about.'

'Should I be worried about that? Even if I said yes there'd be nothing else in it other than an hour round the bay.'

'Then what are you worried about?'

'I don't have time to go off around the bay.'

'Come out with me. You said you wanted to be my friend – here's your chance to get to know me. If you say yes, we'll talk about your lifeboat donation while we're out there. Think about it; I'll be a captive audience and you can screw as much money out of me as the station needs.'

'How do I know you won't change your mind about that once we're at sea?'

'Is there anything I can say that would reassure you I won't?'

'Not really.'

'Then it's up to you. How much of a gambler are you?'

She bit back another smile. Though she hated to admit it,

she was enjoying their verbal sparring. And if there was a little flirting in there, she had to admit to enjoying that too. Didn't they say it was good for the ego? And God knew she could do with something to soothe hers these days. 'I don't take risks.'

'Perhaps it's time you started. Life can be more fun when you do.'

'I'm hardly dressed for a trip round the bay.'

He looked her up and down. 'Jeans and trainers – looks fine to me.'

Gaby opened her mouth to argue. But then she closed it again and let out an impatient sigh. This was a bad idea, and yet, she did want to go. She wanted the money he'd promised, but she also wanted the adventure. It was no lie when she'd said she didn't take risks. Once, she would have done, but those days were over. Now she was a wife and mother, a dutiful daughter and an upstanding member of the community. All that was fine, but nobody could be all that all the time, not even Gaby. It felt like such a long time since she'd done something this spontaneous, and she did love to be out at sea, to feel the waves lifting the deck of a boat, the wind in her hair, the spray on her face... and the weather was certainly perfect for it. She could get on that beautiful yacht now and everyone in the harbour would be watching and wishing it was them.

'One hour,' she said. 'I can't be out longer than that.'

'Deal! Ready to go now then?'

'I suppose there's no time like the present. And perhaps I ought to get on board before I change my mind.'

Gaby was filled with misgiving, but by the time it had occurred to her that she ought to be worried, the sand and rocks and clifftops of Port Promise were miles away and getting smaller with every mile the yacht travelled out to sea.

'Relax!' Lloyd said as he steered the boat. 'You look as if you want to jump overboard.'

'I'm just thinking about all the things I ought to be doing instead of this.'

'Don't worry; I'll have you back in time to do all that stuff. You promised me an hour round the bay – you can't back out of your end of the deal now.'

'I know.'

Gaby stood next to him, the wind whipping her hair round her face, salt on her lips, the sun burning down – though the edge was taken off the heat by the speed with which the prow of the boat cleaved through the waves. The sea was choppy but nothing to worry about, petrol-blue peaks topped with silver. Being out here reminded her of trips out with her dad as a younger girl. He hadn't had a fancy yacht like this, but he had owned a little cuddy cabin that he loved to take out when he had a spare afternoon, where he'd drop anchor out in the bay and throw a fishing line over the side, or take sandwiches and simply enjoy bobbing about doing nothing. Often, he'd fall asleep, and his daughters would laugh as they played and chatted on deck. Once, Ava even drew a fake moustache on him as he slept and he didn't notice it until later that evening, having sailed back to the village and greeted many friends on the way to their cottage. Gaby recalled it now with fondness. They'd expected him to be furious, but he'd laughed so hard at how long the joke had lasted that they'd been almost fearful he'd stop breathing.

'It's fast,' she said, glancing at Lloyd.

He grinned. 'Where do you want to go? How about I show you where I live?'

'As long as you show me from the boat, that's fine.'

'Your wish is my command.'

Sending spray across the deck, he turned the boat sharply in the direction of Promise Rocks. That was the name given to the headland beyond Port Promise's beach. Ava had once come unstuck there trying to help a father and his son trapped on them, and many a boat and surfer had done the same. But Lloyd seemed to be keeping a safe distance as he passed them and rounded the headland into open water.

'So you do know what you're doing a bit,' she said.

'Did you doubt me?'

'Yes.'

His face split into a grin again. And then he pointed towards a spot on the sea ahead. 'Dolphins!'

Gaby strained to look, and at first couldn't see anything. But then she spotted two dorsal fins, skimming the water, appearing and disappearing.

'I see them!'

But then the fins disappeared again. Gaby went to the prow of the boat to look closer, trying to see where they'd gone. And then she let out a squeal of delight that Fern would have been proud of as she saw them again, this time keeping pace with the boat as they swam alongside. They seemed to be racing the yacht. One of them leaped out of the water, while the other was doing barrel rolls, showing its belly to the sun every so often as it went through the water like an arrow. 'There they are again! I wish the kids could have seen this!'

'You'll have to tell them all about it.'

Gaby glanced up at him. That wasn't going to happen and he must have known that. She couldn't tell any of her family about going out with Lloyd, especially Killian. People in the village loved to gossip and they loved to come to the worst possible conclusions, so she'd rather avoid any scrutiny of her motives for being out here, however noble. In fact, she'd taken great care to make certain nobody she knew had seen her go aboard, even though she hadn't told Lloyd that was what she was doing.

Part of her didn't know why she felt the need to hide it – she was doing nothing wrong. And yet, she did feel that need. In fact, there was a strange residue of guilt on everything she was doing today. Why was that? Perhaps it was because she was enjoying herself – and Lloyd's company – just a little too much? Perhaps because, if he pressed hard enough, she might find herself succumbing to his flattery? But she was stronger than that, surely?

After a few minutes the dolphins began to peel away, out towards the open sea. Gaby left her post on the foredeck and went back to Lloyd.

'They've gone?' he asked.

She nodded. 'I'm sorry, I could have taken the wheel if you'd wanted to have a closer look.'

'You sail then?'

'I have done – mostly when I was younger. My dad used to take me out every now and again, and other people in the village too. I wasn't very good, but I could steer a boat well enough. Although, this is a big one to handle solo. You might want to think about a crew if you're going any distance in it.'

Gaby went to the foredeck again, letting the wind blow through her hair as the boat raced over the waves. They sailed on, following the shape of the coast but staying out of the way of the rocks and sandbars that made the shallower waters perilous. Every so often she'd glance back at Lloyd. His gaze was always straight ahead, but he looked relaxed and content. Perhaps he was enjoying this taste of freedom, this all too brief respite from the weight of everybody's expectations, as much as she was. Whatever he was thinking, it softened his features in a way she'd never seen before.

After a while they slowed and Lloyd let down the anchor, so that they drifted gently, swaying this way and that, the boat lifted and dropped by the waves in a sleepy rhythm. Out here now, she could see why her dad often felt the need to nap.

'There,' he said, joining her at the bow, pointing towards the distant cliffs.

Almost as if it were clinging on to a sheer drop stood a stark white, angular house. It had something of an art deco feel to it, though the vast glass panels cut across the upper level were as sleek and modern as anything Gaby had seen along this coast.

'That's your house?'

He folded his arms and gave a short nod, looking with pride at the structure.

'It's gorgeous,' she said.

'Yes. I like it.'

'Looks big.'

'It's a decent size.'

'Too big for just you?' She turned to him. 'You've never actually said – is there a Mrs Turner?'

'What do you think?'

'I don't know; that's why I'm asking.'

'Do you think I'd be out here with you if there was?'

'I don't know that either. And what does that say about me if I'm out here with you when I have a husband at home?'

'But you have an ulterior motive.'

'And you don't?'

'I suppose I do,' he said, turning to her with a faint smile. 'But I'm beginning to see it might be more of a challenge than I'd expected. That's all right, though. I like a challenge.'

Gaby silently appraised him for a moment. 'You work hard on this act, don't you?'

'There's no act.'

'I think there is. You know, a lot of people around here would respond better to a bit of honest vulnerability than they do to all your bluffing and posturing.'

'That's not my experience. People don't like vulnerability – they see it as a weakness – and they certainly don't want honesty. You walk down the street and ask someone how they are – do you want them to answer honestly? Or do you want them to tell you they're OK and then leave you to go about your day? Nobody wants honesty – they don't have time for it.'

'No, but why are you alone? You have money, success, you're passable in the looks department—'

'Only passable?'

'I can just about stand to look at you.'

He smiled.

'But you're alone,' she continued. 'How is that? I don't get it – how is a man like you alone?'

'I choose to be.'

'And yet I'm on this yacht at your request, so I don't think you like being on your own as much as you say.'

He walked starboard side and gazed back at the curve of the headland. Gaby followed him.

'I never asked,' he said. 'How's your sister doing?'

'Clara? Brilliant, thanks to you.'

'And the baby?'

'Healthy. His lungs definitely are – he's crying a lot, but that's what they do. In fact, Clara's in a really good place for once. She's had a rough couple of years – we all have.'

'Oh? What happened?'

'Lots of things really. It started with my dad being lost at sea after he fell from the lifeboat while on a mission.'

'I didn't know... I'm sorry to hear that. So I guess that's why this fundraising means so much to you?'

She nodded. 'It's one amongst many reasons, but yes. My dad dedicated his life to saving others, and in the end he lost it doing just that. The lifeboats mean everything to the community here and they're a huge part of my life.'

'OK,' he said slowly. 'Fair's fair. You came out here, so you'll get your donation from me. I'll call my PA when I get back to sort something. Just tell me where it needs to go – I presume there's an account I can transfer to?'

'Yes. And thank you. You really have no idea how much it means to me – to everyone around here. The lifeboats are like part of our DNA.'

'Ten thousand sound OK?'

Gaby stared at him. 'Ten thousand? *Pounds?*'

'Yes.'

'Oh my God! More than OK! Are you sure?'

'Like you said before, I've got to keep the villagers onside.'

Gaby couldn't stop staring. Who was this man? Why was she finding him more and more fascinating with every minute she spent in his company?

'So that's settled,' he said.

'Thank you so much!'

'You've already thanked me.'

Gaby broke into a broad smile. 'While we're talking about keeping the village onside—'

'Surely not something else?' He leaned on the guardrail and gave a sideways look. 'You're never satisfied, are you?'

'It's just that everyone is so fond of Cormac – maybe don't go out of your way to bankrupt him when the restaurant opens? There must be enough room for you both.'

'I never said I was going to do that.'

'But you sort of implied it. I suppose this is you winding me up for a bit of fun again?'

'Maybe. But don't worry; I'll leave your sister's lump out of my plans for global domination.'

'You know,' Gaby said slowly as another idea occurred to her, 'Clara is trained as a chef and she's a grafter. You might do worse than to have her come and work for you.'

'Doesn't she work at the shack?'

'She was before William was born, but that was only because she lost her other job – long story and not really her fault. But I don't think Cormac really makes enough to pay her what she's worth, even though he probably needs the help. It might make more sense for her to take a better-paid position elsewhere and he could hire someone to train up.'

'What makes you think I'd pay a better wage?'

'I'm making some bold assumptions. I mean, you're supposed to be a top-notch outfit, aren't you?'

'Touché. I'll think about it.' He glanced back to the white house on the cliffs. 'Want to go ashore? I could let you have a proper look around up there.'

Gaby shook her head. 'We agreed on an hour – remember? Even now we're going to overrun – I really ought to get back.'

'Shame.'

'But I've enjoyed the trip.'

'Enough to come again?'

'I don't know if that's such a good idea... Killian—'

'Doesn't have to know.'

Gaby raised her eyebrows. 'Clearly you haven't spent enough time in Port Promise yet to work out that there are no secrets. Sooner or later, you're found out.'

Her mind went back to Killian's secrets and part of her wondered why she ought to care about having secrets herself. So what if she snuck out with Lloyd on his boat? Would Killian have any right to complain if he found her out? It wasn't like she was planning on having an affair, and if she was forced to take Killian's word on his relationship with Vicky then he ought to do the same for her. Perhaps it was flawed logic, but Gaby couldn't acknowledge that right now. She was sick of being taken for granted, for being played a fool by her husband. It was nice to be on the receiving end of some flattery, no matter how wrong or right it was.

'But there's nothing to find out here, is there? It's just two friends on a yacht together – all perfectly innocent.'

'Hmm...' Gaby paused as she appraised him again. She seemed to be doing a lot of that, but he was taking so much working out she couldn't help it. 'I don't know whether I ought to be flattered or furious.'

'Will either of them make you give in? Which should I keep working on?'

Gaby gave a deep frown. 'Sorry, but I need to head back.'

'Are you quite sure this hour is up?'

'Yes.'

'Well that must be the most expensive hour I've ever had then.'

'We struck a deal – don't be backing out now.'

'I wouldn't dream of it. I can't help thinking you might have got the better end, though.'

'Not me, the lifeboats. And as that's such a worthy cause, surely you wouldn't begrudge them that?'

He was silent for a moment, his smile fading. 'You asked me before why I was alone.'

Gaby nodded, suddenly eager to hear more but not sure why it mattered so much.

'I was married until last year.'

'What happened?'

'Oh, the usual. Husband and wife stop understanding each other and it all goes to hell in a handcart.'

'I'm sorry. So you're divorced?'

'Yes. And she's in New York dining out on half the money I worked for twenty-five years to make.'

'So you're bitter about it?'

'A bit, but in a strange way I'm also impressed by her. Proud even. She was single-minded, got what she wanted and she's set for life. How can someone like me fail to be impressed by that?'

Gaby blew out a breath. 'I wasn't expecting that.'

'You remind me of her.'

She looked sharply at him. 'And I certainly wasn't expecting that. I feel as if that's not a good thing.'

'No, it is. It's why I'm so attracted to you. There now, I've said it. Cards on the table. You wanted honesty and there it is. I'm attracted to you – as if you hadn't noticed already. And I think you're attracted to me.'

'No, I...' Gaby paused. 'No, I'm not.'

Was she? She shielded her eyes from the sun to look at him properly. He was handsome – there was no arguing with that. Infuriating, arrogant, ridiculously self-assured, a bit of an arsehole. And yet he had hidden depths that intrigued her. He could be kind and vulnerable in the right circumstances. In many ways he wasn't so different from Killian. Killian's intentions were nobler, his morals clearer, and yet there was that same conviction, that same supreme confidence that his actions and opinions were always right. And weren't those same qualities the ones she'd found irresistible when they'd first met?

'You can be married and still attracted to someone else, you know,' he said, cutting into her thoughts. 'It's only human.'

'I'm not,' Gaby said. 'You're wrong.'

He shook his head slowly with a wry smile. 'Whatever you say. Shall we get going?'

As they headed back to the harbour of Port Promise, Gaby's mood was more subdued than it had been on the way out. She couldn't stop thinking about what Lloyd had just said. She wasn't attracted to him, was she? So why had she felt so guilty about this trip out? Why had she been convinced that she shouldn't tell Killian about it? Was it because she was feeling things she knew she shouldn't? Was it because, despite her protestations to him and to herself, Lloyd might actually be right?

But she loved Killian, didn't she? No matter what came between them, she had to remember that she loved Killian and she'd made a commitment to him and their family. Did that matter? Maybe Lloyd had a point about that too – perhaps being married didn't stop you from wondering what it might be like to be with someone else, to kiss them, to feel their hands on your body...

She was shaken from her thoughts by a sudden crunch that threw her onto the foredeck. She scrambled to her feet again, staring at Lloyd.

'Are you OK?' he asked tersely.

'Yes. Why have we stopped?'

'I don't know; I'll get us going again – don't panic.'

Gaby let out a groan. 'I knew we were sailing too close to the shore. We've run aground, haven't we?'

Lloyd went to look over the side of the boat.

'And don't try to tell me everything is under control,' Gaby added. 'Because I know enough about these things to see that it's not.'

'I'm sure you know all there is to know,' Lloyd fired back, crossing the deck to look over the other side. 'I'm sure I'm about to get a lecture.'

'A lecture? Jesus, you know what this means?'

'That you'll have to suffer my company for a bit longer?'

'That the lifeboat will be called out!'

'And?'

'And? Killian will be on it.' Gaby waved a hand down herself. 'He's going to want to know why I'm here!'

'Why can't you tell him? We've nothing to hide.'

'You don't know Killian.'

'I think you're overreacting.'

'Don't. Now you sound like him. He's always—'

'OK, I'm sorry. Could you calm down for a minute? All we have to do is wait. I don't think we've hit rocks – we'd have heard more of a noise. It'll be a sandbar. Another hour or so and the tide will lift us off.'

'I wouldn't be so sure about the tide. I think it will be a longer wait than an hour. Do you have a chart on board?'

'I don't know.'

'What do you mean, you don't know? Surely you haven't sailed without some indication of the tides?'

'I didn't think I was going to need them. I'll go and look.'

While he went below deck, Gaby perched on one of the loungers. A minute later he came back up.

'Can't find anything. I'm sure it ought to have come with this stuff but don't know where it is.'

'Why would it have come with it?' Gaby asked with a resigned tone. 'How do the manufacturers know where you're going to be sailing it? Maybe there'll be something online if you look – that's if we can get any signal out here.'

Lloyd took out his phone and unlocked it. 'Were you always this much fun or have you put a lot of work in?'

'Suddenly you don't seem quite so funny as you did earlier.'

'Oh, so you were finding me funny?'

'I didn't say you were funny; only less funny now. And the thought of having Killian pick us up isn't funny at all.'

'I don't know what to say...' Lloyd held his phone in the air and frowned. 'You could swim for it. Or maybe hide below deck while they tow us back. That might be interesting.'

'If I didn't know better, I'd say you'd done this on purpose.' Gaby got out her phone. 'Yep, signal's crap here. So much for checking tides online.' She stood and held up a finger. 'We might have been able to raise the sails and have the wind haul us off, but it's blowing in the wrong direction. If I had a better signal I could have phoned my sister.'

'Clara?'

'Ava. If I could somehow get a message to her she might be able to get help that didn't involve launching the lifeboat. Only trouble is, she's a crew member now so she might not be happy to do that. Last time she tried to rescue someone under her own steam it didn't go that well – not for her anyway.' Though she knew it would be useless, she switched her phone off and on again to see if it would pick up any kind of signal but it was no good. 'If I could have got hold of anyone it might have helped. Even my mum or Clara.'

'What would they do other than tell the lifeboat crew?'

'I don't know,' Gaby said irritably. 'They could have got Robin to come out to us or something.'

'Robin? As in Robin with his fishing boat?'

'Yes. Maybe he could have pulled us free.'

'And wrecked my new yacht? I don't think so. Have you any idea how much this thing cost? We're waiting for the tide, not having some scruffy old trawler dragging us out.'

'Well it's all academic because we have no working phones. I suppose there's a radio, though?'

'Of course, though we've just established there's nobody we can call out who wouldn't be involved with the lifeboat in some way.'

Gaby chewed her lip as she looked back towards the shore. She could see a thin strip of golden sand, but it might as well have been a million miles away for all the chances of getting there right now. She was a decent swimmer, but that was definitely too far, even if she'd wanted to jump in and take her chances – which she didn't.

'I don't suppose you have a kedge anchor?' she said after a pause. 'If the water on the sandbar is shallow enough we could stand on it and tug the boat off with that.'

'No. At least I don't think so. I could take a look below – what does one look like?'

'I thought you said you'd sailed before.'

'Yes, I have, but I've never run aground before.'

'But you ought to have been equipped for the possibility that you might one day. Anyway, the yacht will have been equipped with one, I'm sure, when you bought it.'

'It might be. If you tell me what I'm looking for I'll be able to tell you whether I'm equipped, won't I?'

Gaby went to look over the side. 'It doesn't look shallow enough anyway.'

She went to sit down again and they were silent for a time. She wondered whether Lloyd was sulking. She imagined he wasn't a man who was told he was wrong very often, so he probably wasn't enjoying Gaby's criticisms all that much. Still, they were in this mess because of him and she stood to come out of it a lot worse – she was entitled to criticise a bit. She got her phone out again and fiddled with the settings while Lloyd walked the deck, crossing from side to side and from front to back to see if there was any change – or so Gaby presumed.

And then, the boat shifted beneath them. She looked up.

'We're lifting free,' he said. 'I told you.'

'No...' Gaby paused, as if listening. 'We're listing. The tide is leaving us more exposed and the yacht's going to tip if we're not careful.'

'Don't be—'

The boat shifted again, and this time the deck had a definite tilt that even Lloyd couldn't deny.

'Right,' he said, going below. 'Time to see first-hand what I'm giving ten grand to.'

'You can't call the coastguard!'

'What else can I do? You've just said it – we're listing!'

'But if the tide's receding it means the water will be shallow enough for us to go down there to try and free the boat from the sandbar. Go and see if you've got that kedge anchor.'

'I'm not going to risk wrecking my new yacht.'

'It won't wreck your yacht! I can't risk Killian finding me here!'

'You should have thought of that before you agreed to come.'

'*What?* You wanted me to come!'

'I did, but you wanted to come too. And no matter what you say, we both know why.'

'To talk to you about your donation!'

'Of course,' Lloyd said as he disappeared below deck. 'That's exactly why.'

'Dickhead!' Gaby slammed her hand onto the guardrail in a fit of temper, wincing as the impact shot through her wrist. This was bad, and yet, she couldn't see a way out except for him to radio the coastguard. Even if they sent out a Mayday and a passing vessel towed them out, there was still a good chance the story would reach Port Promise, and perhaps reaching Killian that way would be even worse. Perhaps honesty was the best policy. Once she explained why she was there, he could hardly be angry.

Lloyd came back onto the deck. 'I can't find that anchor – I did try. I'm sorry, but I've had to radio for help.'

Gaby gave a short nod. 'Yep, I thought as much. Maybe Killian won't answer the shout and he won't be on the crew who comes to us,' she added in a resigned tone. Of course he was going to answer – she was fooling nobody but herself trying to believe otherwise.

'Surely whoever comes is going to know you and would tell him anyway.'

'True. I'm screwed either way.'

'He's really going to be that angry?'

'Wouldn't you be?'

'Furious,' he said. 'But I know I have jealousy issues. I also know many men don't.'

'Killian isn't one of those. And... well, we haven't exactly been getting along. In normal circumstances he might have been more open to any explanation, but the way things are now...'

He sat next to her. 'I wish you'd told me your marriage was in trouble before.'

'Why? Wouldn't you have invited me out?'

'Of course I would. I'd have also tried harder to get you below deck with me.'

'Stop it, Lloyd. You're not fooling me with that playboy act for a minute. At first, maybe, but not now.'

'Doesn't mean I'm not serious about what I said though. I am ridiculously attracted to you. I know I shouldn't be but I can't help it. And I still think you feel the same way, and if there's a chance—'

'There isn't. I love Killian, no matter what else is going on.'

'What's that got to do with anything? I bet ninety per cent of people who cheat on their partners say they love them. It doesn't mean a thing.'

'It does to me. I made promises to him and I intend to keep them.'

He reached to take a lock of her hair and she shivered. She ought to have pushed him away but she didn't. The back of his hand traced her cheek.

'Tell me to stop,' he whispered as it travelled to her neck.

'Stop.'

'Tell me like you mean it.'

'Lloyd... please...'

'Please what?'

'Please... don't...'

He moved closer, his face right in front of hers, so close she could see how his hazel eyes were flecked with darker spots, almost black. And despite the arrogance and the bluff and posturing, they were filled with passion. She hated him, was frustrated at him, and perhaps that was why she wanted him. This close, she could no longer deny that she did. She ached for his lips, for his hands to travel her body. She could lie back on the deck and let him take her, right there, beneath the blue sky with the sea all around them and the breeze kissing their bare skin.

'Tell me you don't want this...' he murmured, moving in to touch her lips with his.

Gaby pushed him off and leaped up. 'This is not what I came here for!'

'It's not what you thought you'd come here for, but maybe it was what you wanted all along. Tell me I wasn't getting through just then. Tell me you didn't want me – I know it will be a lie. I could see it in your face; I could feel it radiating off you. You wanted me as much as I want you. Tell me it's not true, Gaby.'

'It's not true,' she said. She checked her watch. Six minutes had passed since Lloyd had radioed for help. The lifeboat aimed to launch in around that time, but they'd have had to get the message from the coastguard and then they'd have to get here. Maybe she had three, four minutes left until they arrived. Despite her fears about Killian finding her here, they couldn't come soon enough. The alternative, that she might do something here she'd regret for the rest of her life, was too terrifying to think about.

She moved away, down to the stern, as far away as she could get from him, and looked out to sea.

Come on... where are you?

Bang on schedule, a sliver of orange appeared, skimming the waves, and soon the lifeboat came into view. Silly as the suggestion had been, she almost ducked below deck, as Lloyd had joked she ought to. But instead she stood and watched as the lifeboat approached, running every conceivable conversation through her head, wondering what Killian would make of her being here and which one would actually play out. As it drew closer, she could make out Killian by his build – his features obscured by his helmet and safety visor. And then she recognised Vas, Ava and Harry in the same way and held back a groan. Three of the worst people who could have answered this particular shout had turned up. The universe really did have it in for her today.

Lloyd strode to the side of the boat and shouted down to them. 'Sorry about this.'

'Don't worry about it,' Harry called up as Vas killed the engine alongside the yacht. 'You're stuck then?'

'Regrettably,' Lloyd shouted back. 'Don't suppose there's any chance of a tow?'

Harry gave a thumbs up but then spoke to Vas quietly, so Gaby couldn't hear what they were saying over the sound of the stiffening breeze and the waves slapping against both boats. As she tried to figure out what was being said, she was aware of Ava and Killian watching her. She wished she could see their expressions behind their safety gear and had expected one of them to express some kind of surprise to find her there, but neither said a word.

'Might be easier for you to come back with us,' Harry said after a brief consultation with Vas and Killian. 'You look pretty stuck, but once the water rises you'll probably float free without our interference.'

Lloyd frowned deeply. 'But it's listing!'

'Not that badly.'

'Well... it will drift away!'

'Not if you use your kedge anchor,' Harry replied. 'Once she's off the sandbar you can get a lift back out to her. Honestly, it's probably the most straightforward and safest way for you and the boat.'

Lloyd shook his head. 'I can't find the kedge anchor and I'm not leaving her here.'

'We can sort your anchor if that's your concern.' Harry glanced at Gaby, and once again she wished she could see his face properly. 'I'd really advise you to come back with us now. You might be some time out here and the weather might turn. It doesn't make sense to be in any more danger than you need to be.'

Gaby went over to Lloyd. 'He's right. Best to take Harry's advice; he knows what he's talking about.'

'Might be the first time you've ever said that about me!' Harry replied cheerfully enough. If he was perplexed by any of this, he was doing a great job of hiding it.

Lloyd nodded uncertainly. 'I can't say I'm happy...'

'I'm sure you're not,' Harry said. 'Lovely boat like this – I wouldn't be either. But it'll be quite safe until you can get back to it.'

With obvious reluctance, Lloyd helped Harry secure the yacht, and then he and Gaby were helped aboard the lifeboat. She sat next to Ava, and Killian was across from her with Lloyd at his side. While Lloyd's gaze barely moved from the shrinking spectre of his yacht, Killian stared at Gaby.

'I don't know what's going on' – Ava leaned in to Gaby, finally addressing the situation – 'but I'm sure you've got a very good reason for being out with Alan Sugar on his poncey yacht.'

'I have,' Gaby said, 'and it's not what you think.'

'How do you know what I'm thinking?'

'Because it's the same as everyone will be thinking.' She glanced at Killian, who was still staring silently at her. If only she could open that head of his and see what was going on in there. If he'd been angry she'd have been able to deal with it, but this? This was far scarier.

Within minutes the station at Port Promise was in sight. Feeling more awkward and guilty by the second, and bristling under Killian's scrutiny, she didn't think she'd ever been so glad to see it. As they disembarked and Vas had a brief word with them, Killian remained silent, though he stared at her right up until the moment he went to remove his safety kit. Ava and Harry followed him and Gaby turned to Lloyd.

'Might be best to make yourself scarce.'

'Why?'

'Because...' She let out a sigh. 'Let's go outside; I can explain.'

But she couldn't explain. She had no clue what Killian might do next, but she knew she wanted Lloyd off his radar as quickly as possible. Things might blow over – they might even never start – but Lloyd being there would almost certainly make everything more difficult.

Like a sullen child determined to make a point, Lloyd followed her out into the sunshine. The beach was packed with families, the sounds of children playing, tinny radios and laughter everywhere, and the heat on shore felt heavy and oppressive after being at sea. Above them stood Lloyd's restaurant, where a team of workers were repainting the terrace walls.

'Look,' she began, 'I think... please, just lie low for a while.'

'Why should I do that?'

'Because... you know why!'

'I'm supposed to lie low because we needed to be rescued? Isn't that what you wanted my money for? So people like us can be picked up if we needed to? I haven't done anything wrong – why should I lie low?'

Gaby folded her arms tight. 'Are you being deliberately dense?'

'You think I ought to be intimidated by your Neanderthal husband?'

'Yes, you should...'

They both spun around to see Killian, back in his own clothes, striding from the station. He made for Lloyd and slammed him against the wall.

'You think I don't know what you're trying to do? What was that you called me? A Neanderthal? Well I'm not as stupid as you wish I was. I've had your game sussed from the start. The only thing I didn't see' – he turned to Gaby – 'was that my wife would be stupid enough to fall for it.'

'Killian!' Gaby hissed. 'You're making a scene!'

'Oh, am I?' Killian shoved Lloyd again before letting go of him. 'Terribly sorry, Gaby. I know how you value your reputation. Wouldn't want to blacken your good name, would we?'

'Maybe you should be thinking of yours,' she shot back. 'You're a crew member – act like one!'

'Right now, I'm not,' he growled. 'Right now I'm a husband who can see when some snake is trying to take advantage of his wife. So is one of you going to tell me what happened on that yacht? What should I know? How long has this been going on?'

Lloyd grinned and Gaby's stomach lurched. 'Maybe you should ask your wife what we did... Go on – I dare you.'

Killian pulled back his fist, and before Gaby could stop him, he fired it straight into Lloyd's stomach. Lloyd doubled over, but when he caught his breath again, he looked up at Killian and, to Gaby's horror and frustration, started to laugh. Killian almost roared with fury and pulled his fist back once more, but this time Harry raced from the station and caught his arm before the punch landed.

'What the hell, Kill!' he cried. 'What are you doing?'

'What does it look like?' Killian spat. 'I'm giving this prick what he's been asking for since day one!'

'This is not the way!' Harry urged, obviously struggling to hold Killian back. 'Think! Stop! Is he worth losing your place on the crew? Because if you do this you will!'

'It's already done,' Lloyd said, looking smugger than any man dangerously close to getting his head kicked in ought to. 'I only have to say the word and you're finished. Let's see how you like being a nobody again. Oh, wait... you already are! That's why your wife was so keen... She needs a real man—'

'You—' Killian shook Harry off and went for Lloyd again.

Gaby could have intervened, but it was as if she'd forgotten how to move. She could only stare at Lloyd. What was wrong with him? It was like he wanted Killian to pulverise him.

But Lloyd got in a punch of his own this time, and as Killian tried to counter, Vas and Cormac ran out of the station with Ava, and it took the entire crew to hold Killian off. Cormac spoke in his ear – low, urgent words that Gaby couldn't make out – and by degrees Killian seemed to calm. He was still furious, but at least the red mist had lifted.

Even as Cormac kept an arm firmly around Killian's neck, holding him close and talking him down, Lloyd squared up and opened his mouth to start again, and this time Ava cut him off.

'Don't!' she commanded. 'Just don't! Trust me; you really don't want to go there – not ever, but especially not today.'

'I'll get him fired – just you watch,' Lloyd sneered.

'Get him fired,' Ava said coldly, 'and you'll have the deaths of innocent people on your hands. Killian is the best this service has got and if you take him away from that, just because you can, we'll be that much less able to do our job. But fine, go ahead. Let's see if you can live with that on your conscience.'

'I don't think he has one,' Harry said in a tone so grim Gaby turned to him in shock. She'd never heard him speak like that before.

'Whatever,' Lloyd said. 'I've just donated ten grand to your service, so that will train someone else.'

'Ten grand doesn't buy all Killian's years of experience,' Ava said. 'It doesn't buy compassion or dedication or bravery. So if that's your attitude, we don't want your money.'

'Ava...' Gaby began, and this time Ava looked at her with such pity and disappointment, and something even close to disgust, that Gaby didn't know how to feel.

'You know what came in an hour ago?' Ava asked her.

Gaby gave her head a tiny shake.

'A letter from the parents of those boys we lost this spring.

They wanted to thank us. Imagine that! We didn't save their children, but they don't blame us for what happened, only themselves. Imagine us all reading that letter, and then having to go out and rescue that ungrateful shit!' She flung an arm at Lloyd. 'But we don't complain. We don't judge; we just do it because that's what we vowed to do. No matter who's in trouble we go out for them. But this time... we're only human and this is a step too far. I don't know what's going on here, Gab, but get a grip!'

Gaby had no reply. She could only watch as Ava walked off with Harry, and Cormac led Killian, every muscle still tensed so that everything about him screamed rage, back to the station.

'You'd better go,' Gaby said to Lloyd in a dull voice. 'You really shouldn't be here when he comes out again.'

CHAPTER EIGHTEEN

Gaby knocked on the door of her sister's caravan. She detected movement inside, and a few moments later Ava opened up.

'I wondered when you'd be over,' she said wearily. 'I must admit, this is quicker than I thought; I've barely got my water-proofs off.'

'Is Harry here?'

'No, he's gone back to work. You know, because we all have jobs as well as racing out to sea to save pricks with yachts... sorry, I should clarify that usually there are no pricks with yachts, only people who've suffered some misfortune, but today seems like a day for firsts.'

'Ava... I want to explain—'

'You already explained.'

'No, not properly.' Gaby paused. To be shrugged off by her little sister like this... it had never happened before. It was strange and unsettling and made her feel oddly helpless in a way that didn't happen very often. 'Can I come in?'

'Do I have a choice?'

'Of course you do! But I can't bear the thought of you

having the wrong impression about what went on today – I want to set you straight.'

Ava stepped back to allow Gaby entrance. 'Drink?' she asked, going to the kitchen area.

'No thanks, but you go ahead. I can't stay; I need to—'

'Save your marriage?'

'I was going to say I need to see Killian. But he was still inside the station when I left there. I think he must be trying to sort things out with Vas, and I think it's probably better if I let him cool off.' Gaby was suddenly troubled by an idea. 'You don't think Vas will give him his marching orders?'

'I hope not. You know as well as I do that, after Dad and Vas, Killian is about the best and most experienced we've got. I don't know what we'd do if we lost him.' Ava filled a glass of water from the tap and sat down. 'What the hell were you thinking?'

Gaby took a seat across from her. 'It was a boat trip – it wasn't supposed to be a big deal. I'm not allowed to have some fun every now and again like everyone else? I have to be sensible Gaby all the time?'

'Of course not. But with *him*? He's trouble – you were the first person to say so. In fact, I seem to recall you hated him when he first arrived. What the hell did he say to get you on that boat? It must have been good. And what did he mean by all those things he said to Killian? Gaby, please tell me you didn't—'

'Of course I didn't! He was winding Killian up; it's what he does.'

Ava sipped at her water, regarding Gaby steadily over the rim of her glass. 'I just don't get it.'

'Honestly, neither do I. I don't know what... well, I do. He promised a donation to the lifeboat fundraiser if I went out with him.'

'Oh, yes, the ten grand he was boasting about. But you

didn't think it was a weird demand, him asking you to go on his boat? You didn't see any ulterior motive?'

'I'm not stupid; I know what he was after.'

'But you thought you could play it smarter than him?'

'That's not how it was. I just wanted the money. And, yes, maybe I wanted to have some fun and maybe I was enjoying having someone want me, and maybe I wanted to piss Killian off for all the stuff he's done lately. I'm only human.'

'So is Killian. You must be able to see this from his point of view – at least a bit. He must have felt like a gullible idiot, and in front of his crewmates too, who mean everything to him.'

'It's not what I intended. But quite honestly,' Gaby continued, letting irrational emotions cloud her judgement yet again, 'he made me feel like a gullible idiot when he kept Meredith from me.'

'So that's what this is about? There are better ways to let him know you're pissed off than going out on a yacht with some slimeball who's clearly after breaking up your marriage. Killian can't change his past or the fact that Meredith came out of it. But you... If I didn't know better, I'd say you did this deliberately. And if you wanted to get back at Killian I understand, but this affects more than just you and him. We've all been dragged into this now.'

Ava shook her head. 'I don't know what's going on with you but I've always looked up to you, Gaby. To me, you were always what I ought to be – you always had a plan, always knew what to do, always saw the most sensible course of action in any situation. And it wasn't boring; it was something to aspire to. I never would have expected you of all people to do something like this, but I suppose it just goes to show that you never really know anyone, do you?'

Gaby let out a sigh. 'What do you want me to say, Ava? You want me to say I'm sorry? I don't feel I've done anything wrong.'

'Shouldn't you be telling Killian this?'

'I will, if he ever lets me, which he probably won't. It matters to me that you know the truth too.'

'And now I do.'

'I did it for a good reason.'

'To piss off Killian.'

'To get a donation from Lloyd.'

'Oh yeah...' Ava raised her eyebrows as if she didn't believe a word of Gaby's excuse.

Gaby was quite sure she didn't, and, if she was being honest, had the tables been turned, she'd have been sceptical too.

'Ten thousand pounds,' she insisted. 'That's a lot.'

'Was it worth what you had to do for it?'

'That's out of order!'

Ava held up her hands. 'All right, I'm sorry – that was uncalled for. Has he actually handed the cash over then?'

'Not yet, but he—'

'So he actually just said that to get what he wanted?'

'He didn't want anything! And if he had he wouldn't have got it!'

'It looks very much like he wanted something from where I'm standing.'

Gaby shook her head. The same idea had occurred to her more than once, but she refused to believe that she'd been played here. She'd have seen that coming, surely? She'd always prided herself on her judgement, on her ability to sniff out bullshit, to see through a scam. And if it had been a ploy to get her into bed, the idea that she'd come so close to falling for it horrified her now.

'No,' she said. 'That's not how it was. He's going to give us the money.'

'Well forgive me for not being more excited, Gab, but after today I'll believe it when I see it.'

'Don't be like this—'

'Like what? I'm not being like anything. Maybe that's your guilty conscience bothering you again.'

'You're taking Killian's side and you don't know the half of it.'

'There is no side, but if there was, he's looking like the safer bet right now – and God knows I never imagined I'd be saying that. He can be quick to judge and quicker to lose his cool, but this time I totally get why. And just wait until the gossip gets around – and it will. How do you think he's going to feel then?'

'Gossip has never bothered Killian.'

'It's never been that personal before. He's never had to defend you and your marriage before.'

'Nobody saw...' Gaby began, trying to convince herself more than Ava.

'Gab, everyone saw! Did you get sunstroke on that boat or something?'

'Maybe they did, but it'll last as long as gossip does around here – there'll be something else to talk about in a few days.'

'Probably, but let's hope the damage isn't already done by then. You may not think so, but I want you guys to work this out because I know that despite what you might feel now, you'd be miserable without Killian. He'd be miserable without you too, and I love you both too much to see that happen.'

Gaby was silent for a moment as Ava picked up her water.

'I'll go and see if I can find him,' she said finally.

Ava nodded. 'I think you should.'

'I'm sorry you had to see all that,' Gaby added as she stood up.

'Forget it – we all have our wobbles. It's probably good for me to see that even the people I think are perfect aren't – means there's hope for me.'

'You're more perfect than you imagine.' Gaby tried to force a smile but none would come. She bent to hug Ava briefly and then set out on the path back to the village.

. . .

Ava's words stung. Gaby could think of little else as she walked back to Thistledown Cottage, wondering what she might find when she got there. Nor could she get Ava's look of intense disappointment out of her head. It was as if her sister's eyes had suddenly been opened to some unbearable truth about the world that she'd never wanted to see, like everything good she'd believed in had been destroyed in an instant. It was desperately sad, and even though Gaby still maintained she'd done nothing wrong, she hated that she'd been the person to make Ava feel that way.

But was she as blameless as she would have Ava believe? She hadn't cheated with Lloyd, but the temptation had been there just the same. In the end, was thinking it as bad as doing it?

Killian was home by the time she got there. He was sitting in the garden, staring out at the cliffs beyond, a glass of something – perhaps brandy – at his side. He barely looked at her as she spoke to get his attention, almost as if he couldn't bear to.

'We need to talk.'

Killian picked up his drink. 'Do we?'

'I need to explain—'

'You don't. You told me there was nothing going on, right?'

'Yes, but—'

'Then I believe you.'

Gaby took a step towards the seat and hovered. But instead of sitting next to him, as she ordinarily would have done, she backed off again. 'That's not how it seemed at the station.'

'I was angry at him, not you.'

'I'm not sure I believe you.'

'He was lying, right? He does it to wind people up – you said it. You said you were on his yacht to talk to him about money. If you said so, then... I know you. You're not naive, and you're not a liar, so...'

'Killian, I'm so sorry.'

'For what? For being out there with someone you know to be poison? For betraying Cormac and Clara? Because you must know he's out to ruin them. For letting him say the things he did about you and him? Or because those things might actually be true? What are you sorry for, Gab?'

'I'm sorry that you had to come out to that situation. I tried to find a way to get us off that sandbar, but—'

'So I'd never have to find out you'd gone sailing with him?'

'No,' Gaby snapped, wanting to point out the irony of his accusation, to say that he was the one who kept secrets. But doing that would only make things much worse, might even take them to a point of no return, so she swallowed it back. 'So there wouldn't be a pointless shout.'

'No shout is pointless – you know that. I wouldn't have cared about that. We get called, we go, we don't judge.'

'But Ava said... about the letter from that family. She said—'

'We do our job,' Killian repeated. 'It doesn't matter what else happens.'

'He's going to donate ten thousand to the fundraising,' she said, knowing how hollow it sounded even as she spoke the words. She didn't even know if he would keep his word about the money, and did it really make anything better? Or was it just making her feel better to say it?

'So I heard.' Killian sipped at his drink, his gaze on the distant cliffs again. 'Congratulations on a job well done. You must have been very persuasive.'

'Aren't you a bit pleased? I did it for the service – for you!'

'I'm sure you did.'

'It'll make a huge difference.'

Killian's gaze went to the depths of his glass. 'It will. But what will he expect in return?'

'Nothing.'

'Men like him never do things expecting nothing back. Come on, Gaby, you're not a child – you must know that.'

'Whatever you think it might be, he won't get it.'

Killian drained his glass and got up. 'Then there's nothing more to be said.'

'Kill, please… we're not done—'

'I'm tired and I don't want to talk about it. I've got a report to finish for work and dinner to cook – I'm too busy to worry about that man's bullshit now.'

'Right,' Gaby said helplessly, wondering where this left them. 'I could cook dinner if it helps…'

'Whatever.' Killian wafted his hand vaguely as he went inside.

One thing was certain, she thought as the door closed behind him, she'd get no further with this today. She'd been married to Killian long enough to recognise that much. 'I'd better go and pick up the kids then,' she said, even though he was long out of earshot.

Gaby had been checking her emails and the fundraising account all week, but there was no sign of Lloyd's donation. She'd also been to the restaurant to see if she could talk to him, but to no avail. His workers didn't know where he was or when he'd next be on site. There was nothing to do but wait and try to keep her dwindling hope alive.

What had happened at the station the day the crew had been out to pick them up from Lloyd's yacht was bad enough, but if it had all been in vain, she didn't know how she'd bear it.

When she'd confided all this to Clara, who'd been far more receptive to her explanations and apologies than Ava, Clara had expressed the opinion that perhaps Lloyd had seen fit to lie low for a while. It would explain his absence and, Gaby was forced to admit, was probably the wisest thing he'd done since he'd arrived in Port Promise. But it didn't explain the missing donation.

Gaby was beginning to feel she'd been well and truly played, and being unable to speak to him was making her more frustrated and angrier by the day. She'd done some detective work and had found a number for his office – which was out of town – but the PA there knew nothing about any donation and had been instructed not to put any calls through to him. None of this quelled her unease, and when she thought about how close she'd come to making a huge mistake with him she could barely stand to look at herself in the mirror. Thank God she hadn't, but she feared the damage was already done.

The one bright spot in the midst of her misery was Cormac's qualification, finally, to the lifeboat crew. If anyone had fought for it, he had, and because he'd saved Elijah's life and because he'd given Clara so much happiness, and for so many other reasons, her entire family owed him so much that they all had a special place in their hearts for him. Just like Ava, he didn't want a fuss, but he did want to invite his friends to a barbeque at the shack.

For Gaby, something to celebrate was a welcome distraction, though she realised there might also be some awkward conversations. She wasn't yet sure how much of what had gone on when Lloyd's yacht had run aground was common knowledge, but knowing Port Promise, some of the details were bound to be out there. And it would probably be all the worst bits with people filling in the gaps however they liked.

Not only that, but it was now common knowledge that Killian had a daughter from a relationship long before Gaby. What people made of that was anyone's guess, but more than once Gaby had walked into a shop, or into the Spratt, or passed someone casually chatting on the front to find them stop mid-conversation with guilty looks her way, accompanied by overly enthusiastic greetings. It would pass, but Gaby didn't enjoy being the focus of so much gossip – though she had to admit some of that had been self-inflicted.

It was the end of August, with Flag Day just over a week away, and the weather had been hot, with stilted air over the beach and sticky heat shimmering from the promenade, but as the sun slipped down the sky, the day cooled.

Cormac closed the shack and set up a little way down from it on the sand. Everyone had brought camping chairs or blankets to sit on. Clara had just got William to sleep in the shade of the shack's eaves and was opening a bottle of champagne as Cormac put the first sausages on the coals to cook. They exchanged a look that was so full of happiness that Gaby was caught by a sudden pang of envy. She pushed it out of her mind – she had no right to begrudge anyone happiness, especially not her sister and Cormac, who'd both been through so much to get to this day.

As Clara handed out the glasses of fizz, Harry stood up.

'Speech!'

Cormac laughed. 'Go on with yer!'

'No, come on! We want a speech!'

Cormac wafted his request away. 'What for? Did you prepare one?'

'No.' Harry grinned. 'But if you don't make one today I'm going to do it for you, and you might not like what I have to say.'

'Be my guest!' Cormac looked to his griddle, shaking his head with a grin as everyone egged Harry on.

Harry cleared his throat as if about to burst into song, and everyone laughed.

'When Cormac arrived in Port Promise, my first thought was: there go my chances with any of the local women.'

Everyone laughed again and Cormac looked up.

'Ah, come on now...'

Harry's grin spread. 'Sorry, mate, but I thought you were a

handsome bonehead. And I was right...'

This was greeted by more laughter and Cormac pretending to be annoyed.

'But,' Harry continued, his expression more earnest now, 'you're the bravest, funniest, most loyal, handsome bonehead I've ever met and I'm glad to have you on the lifeboat beside me.'

As he raised his glass, Gaby caught a glimpse of Clara looking on with tears in her eyes, while Cormac steadfastly stared at the griddle. Perhaps he was overwhelmed with the sudden emotion of the occasion too – Gaby wouldn't blame him for that.

'To Cormac!' Harry said, and everyone raised their glasses with him. 'Here's to saving a few lives!'

'To saving lives!' everyone repeated, and then broke out into applause.

As it died down, it was Ava's turn to pretend to be cross. 'I didn't get all that fuss!'

'Yes...' Harry pulled her into a kiss. 'But you did get a more private kind of appreciation.'

'Oh my God!' Clara squeaked. 'Too much information!'

Killian glanced across at Gaby, but she couldn't read his expression at all. Once there would have been some recognition of their own love – but now? Was there any left in him? Had this all been her fault? She didn't want to admit it, and yet her judgement had been so off lately she hardly trusted she could see the truth, even if someone had presented it to her neatly wrapped with a bow and a label that said: this is the truth.

The worst thing was, the way she felt now she wasn't even sure she cared. She was just so tired, sick of conflict and second-guessing. If it all ended tomorrow, at least that would be an end. She'd be sad, she'd mourn what she'd lost, but she'd move on. As things were, it was a daily purgatory, moving neither forward nor back, stuck on the same old flash points: the secrets Killian had kept, the lies she'd told, her near infidelity, his lack of effort – and they both had tempers that were too quick and too sharp. And the children were stuck with them, unaware of the particulars but clearly aware of a change in the atmosphere of their home. How could they fail to be when it was so charged it felt ready to combust at any moment?

The smell of cooking meat soon hung on the air. Holidaymakers strolled over to take a look, saw that it was a private party and then left again. Cormac joked that he'd been selling the wrong food all this time and ought to do a nightly barbeque in the summer months, and everyone told him that was actually a brilliant idea, which made him suddenly thoughtful.

'You've started something now,' Clara said to everyone. 'I know that face – he's making plans.'

'But it's obvious, now I think of it!' Cormac said. 'And it would take away any competition with the new restaurant – for some of the time anyway.'

Another loaded glance from Killian came Gaby's way.

She leaned in. 'Just say whatever it is you're thinking,' she muttered.

'I would,' he replied, his voice low, 'but I don't think you'd like it.'

'I'm sure I wouldn't, but when has that ever stopped you?'

'Right now this is about Cormac – I'm not about to ruin his moment. Unlike some, I actually care about other people.'

Gaby pursed her lips and sat back in her chair. Though it riled her to think so, she had to admit he was right – again. Every word they exchanged lately escalated into an argument and now wasn't the time. She couldn't say whether he was right about his second point, however. She cared about others – at least she'd always tried to.

As Gaby got up to refill her glass, she caught a conversation between Tanika – Clara's ex-colleague from the caravan park – and her adult daughter, Zinnia. Cormac had extended the invitation to them on Clara's behalf after Clara had mentioned feeling guilty that they hadn't asked them along.

'Bold as you like! I'd like to know what was going on out there, but I bet it wasn't sailing!'

'But... she always seems so—'

'Strait-laced? They're always the ones you have to watch. And I bet there was a bit of revenge in there... you know, that business with the other kid...'

'I bet he was furious...' Zinnia nodded towards Killian.

'I don't know about that, but I do know she wants her head looking at. Why go out for hamburger when you have steak at home? And he's definitely one prime bit of steak!'

'Yes, but we all like a bit of dirty fast food sometimes, don't we?'

They both started to laugh, and not wanting to hear anything else not meant for her ears, Gaby cleared her throat loudly.

'Don't mind me – just getting another drink.'

Pouring a fresh glass as hastily as she could, Gaby then went back to her seat. She'd never been someone who let gossip get to her, but this time, she was consumed by shame and mortification. Her dalliance with Lloyd – well, it was the gift that just kept on giving, and it hadn't been much of a gift worth having in the first place.

She opened her mouth to speak to Killian, but before she could get a word out, he got up and went to talk to Harry and Ava. They all shot her a look she didn't much like – or was that only in her imagination? Gaby had to wonder whether that was the worst thing about this whole business – how people looked at her now. Not with admiration and respect as she'd become used to, but with pity. Killian would have told her that was all in her head – at least, he would have done in the old days. But these days, the way he looked at her seemed most changed of all.

CHAPTER NINETEEN

Gaby arrived at the lifeboat station early to direct operations for her fundraising Flag Day, thankful that at least the weather was still treating her kindly. It ought to have been fine – it was still August after all, but you never knew. Many of the attractions she'd booked were already setting up, including the carousel, bouncy castle, trampolines, donkeys for beach rides and a flight simulator based on a fighter jet. There would also be displays of Cornish and Morris dancing, a clown and a stilt walker, and a visit from a local bird of prey sanctuary who were due to bring some of their owls and falcons for people to look at. There was food and drink, of course, and a tombola and raffles, stalls full of bric-a-brac, guessing how many sweets were in a jar and other varied cheap and cheerful punts, and a chance for people to take a look around the lifeboat station and the boats.

Gaby had also set up a stall just outside the station selling lifeboat-themed merchandise: models of their boats, shopping bags, notepads, framed photos of the first station at Port Prom-ise, and many other things. Marina and Jill would help man it as Gaby would be called away often to do other things. She was grateful for them, and for the small army of helpers with buckets ready to suck up any loose change that might be troubling the pockets of visitors.

Gaby had chosen the last bank holiday of the summer precisely because it was the busiest weekend of the year for visitors to Port Promise, and she was determined to get as much from the event as she could. In the end, she'd decided against the auction for the services of lifeboat crew that Marina had been so keen on and which had turned a bit seedy the year before. The mood Killian had been in of late, one good-enough bid might see him move out with the bidder permanently.

The sea was playing well too, calm and clear, sunlight glinting from its crests like tiny diamonds. Out on the horizon, jet skiers were already zooming back and forth, while groups of children leaped over the waves as they rolled into shore, laughing and squealing as they landed each time with a splash.

It was already too hot for Gaby, despite being early, but perhaps that had as much to do with her frame of mind as the temperature. She had a lot to do and had to work quickly, and though she'd put on a pair of jeans this morning for practicality, she was beginning to wish she'd opted for something cooler.

As an olive branch, Gaby had suggested they invite Meredith to stay and allow her to get involved with the Flag Day. Killian had seemed pleased with this and Gaby could hear from his end of a conversation on the phone that Meredith was chuffed too. He'd been to collect her from Bristol and had spent a few hours with Vicky at Meredith's request, and had returned with reports that Vicky was doing well, all things considered.

As she'd left the house, Killian had said he'd bring the three kids down later, and that was fine by her. Since Cormac's barbeque, life with Killian had been another long round of misunderstanding, miscommunication and downright stubbornness on both sides. Gaby was under no illusions – she was far from blameless and accepted her part, but she didn't seem able to stop herself, even when she knew she was doing it. It was as if they'd both been programmed to self-destruct. Killian would never admit that, though, so perhaps she was doing better than he was.

Ironically, they'd got on better since Meredith's arrival the night before than they had for weeks, but with a visitor in the house, Gaby supposed they'd been forced to. But she couldn't allow herself to think about any of that now.

Vas raised a hand as he arrived to unlock the lifeboat station – the first of the crew to appear. 'Morning!' he called.

Gaby went over. 'All set?' she asked.

'We will be once I've been in and checked around. A lot of people about today – hopefully we can convince them to come and take an interest.'

'Personally, I don't care how interested they are as long as they part with their cash,' Gaby said briskly.

Vas laughed. 'Spoken like a businesswoman. I know you've got a lot on your plate, but I wouldn't say no if you ever wanted to come and sort my—'

'What am I missing?'

They both turned to see Maxine arrive, her hair tied up in its usual fluffy ponytail, her uniform sleeves rolled up.

'I was just telling Gaby what a legend she is,' Vas said.

'I've got a good feeling about today,' Maxine said. 'I think we're going to raise a lot of money. I mean, it won't be for want of trying if you don't beat last year's total, will it?'

Gaby nodded. 'I'm going to do my best.' She glanced back at her stand. 'And with that in mind, I'd better get on.'

'Yep, don't mind us,' Vas said. 'We'll be ready when you are.'

As the sun climbed higher, the beach and promenade started to get busier. Alongside the holidaymakers were friends and villagers who'd come to help Gaby and offer their support to the fundraising in whatever way they could. Gaby was grateful to see every one of them, but none caused her face to erupt into actual delight the way Betty's surprise arrival did.

'Oh my God!' Gaby squealed as she looked up from a to-do list on her phone she'd steadily been working down all morning. 'You never said you were coming!'

Betty raced over and threw her arms around Gaby. 'I wanted to surprise you all.'

'Well you certainly did that!' Gaby held her at arm's-length. 'You look amazing! New Zealand must suit you!'

'So does love,' Betty said, sending a shy smile to the man who'd now arrived to stand by her side. 'This is Liam. Liam – this is my good friend, Gaby.'

'You kept that quiet!' Gaby said with a laugh. 'Pleased to meet you, Liam.'

'You too.' He smiled. 'I've heard so much about you; I feel as if I'm meeting a legend.'

'Bloody hell!' Gaby raised her eyebrows at her old friend. 'What's Betty been telling you?'

'Only the truth,' Betty said with a fond smile. 'So where are the rest of the Morrows?'

'Not here yet – lazy lot! They shouldn't be long, though; Clara texted me to say they were on their way. Oh, you haven't met William yet, have you? You're going to love him!'

'I've seen him on FaceTime – he looks so cute. I can't wait to meet him in real life.'

Gaby shook her head. 'I can't believe you're here! Did you just decide to fly all this way or...?'

'Actually, we're going to Iceland,' Betty said. 'And we thought why not take a detour?'

'Iceland! Wow! That's one hell of a detour!'

'I know.'

'Will you see the Northern Lights?'

'I don't think so,' Liam said. 'I think it's a bit early. But there's still plenty of cool things to see and do in the summer and we decided to take advantage of some bargain flights. We're planning to try to see the Northern Lights somewhere else later in the year.'

Gaby's smile was so wide she couldn't have wiped it from her face if she'd tried. 'So you're doing all that travelling you wanted to finally?'

'I'm giving it a good go,' Betty said.

'I'm glad it's working out for you.' Gaby got her phone out. 'Let me tell Clara you're—'

'No way!' Betty said. 'You'll ruin the surprise! I want to see the look on her face when I tap her on the shoulder and say hello.'

'Well she'd better get here soon because I want to see that too!'

'So...' Betty linked arms with Liam as she looked around at the busy promenade. 'What have I missed?'

'Since you went?' Gaby could have told her all about Lloyd and his stirring, but she didn't want to ruin her good mood. As for Meredith, she assumed Betty had already heard that sorry saga and was being too tactful to mention it. 'Not a lot. Things here are as they usually are. Except for Ava and Cormac qualifying for the seagoing crew, of course, but I expect you already know about all that.'

'I do. It's really good news.' Betty glanced at the donation point Gaby was manning. It was really just an old decorating table draped in a cloth and adorned with bunting bearing the flag of the station, as were all the donation points she'd set up that day. 'How's it going so far?'

'It's early, but I think good. I keep having this recurring nightmare that I've forgotten something really important, of course.'

'If I know you that's never going to happen. You're the most organised person I've ever met.'

'I think that might make me sound very boring.' She looked at Liam. 'Sorry to have burst your bubble.'

'I would never say that,' Betty said. 'I've always envied how you seem to have everything under control, no matter what.'

Gaby silently pondered the notion that Betty might not have been quite so impressed had she seen her very chaotic behaviour over the last few weeks. But today wasn't about any of that. Today was about making this event a success, and all that other nonsense would wait.

'Betty!'

They both turned to see Maxine in her uniform rush from the station. She threw her arms around Betty.

'We didn't know you were coming home!'

'Nobody did,' Betty said. 'It was a bit of a spur of the moment decision.'

'Well,' Maxine said, 'you'd know all about them these days, wouldn't you?' They hugged again and then Maxine turned to Gaby. 'Sorry to talk shop when we have this lovely surprise, but I could do with your opinion on something.'

'I'll let you get on,' Betty began, but Gaby stopped her.

'No, it's fine.'

'Honestly, I'm going to show Liam around anyway and see who else we can surprise. But I'll be back later.'

'Right. We'll likely be in the Spratt after this if you fancy one.'

'You don't need to ask me twice!' Betty said. 'I'll see you up there if not before.'

As they walked away, Gaby noticed Killian arrive with Jill, Elijah and Fern. Gaby noted Meredith's absence. He bid them goodbye before heading into the station. He hadn't looked Gaby's way once, though he must have been able to see her. It was like a knife to her heart, but she tried not to think about it; she had to stay brave for Elijah and Fern, who were now on their way over with Jill.

'Where's Meredith?' Gaby asked her two as Maxine was momentarily distracted by a visitor querying what time the lifeboat would be on display.

'She went to take a look around by herself,' Jill replied for them.

'You met her?'

'Yes,' Jill said, 'we all walked down together but I think she felt a bit awkward so I told her we wouldn't be offended if she wanted to do her own thing for a while. I expect she'll find us when she's ready.'

'Well it won't be hard. I bet there are lawns in Bristol bigger than the whole of Port Promise.'

'I'm sure,' Jill said. 'She seems like a sweet girl,' she added carefully.

'She is,' Gaby said. 'I know it could have been a lot worse and I'm trying, Mum, I really am.'

'I know, love.'

'Mum!' Fern bounced on the balls of her feet. 'Where are our buckets? Do we get special T-shirts?'

'You do,' Gaby said, getting a box out from beneath the table. She rifled inside for the right size and then handed a navy T-shirt to each child. Elijah slipped his straight on, his face a picture of pride. He looked so much like Killian in that moment, dressed in the same navy as Killian's uniform, Gaby's breath caught in her throat.

'And buckets...' she added, shaking away the melancholy that had crept over her. She gave them both a lidded bucket with a slot in the top. 'Go forth and make lots of money.'

'I'll go with them,' Jill said. 'Do I get a T-shirt?'

'Sure, and you can have a bucket too,' Gaby said. 'Can't have you slacking, can I?'

Jill's eye roll was full of humour. 'Thanks.'

'There's Harry!' Fern squealed and ran over to where Ava and Harry were going into the station. They were both in uniform, just like Maxine and Killian. The crew had agreed to be on charm duty today, showing people bits of what they did in order to convince them to donate.

'She's not over that yet then,' Maxine said with a wry smile as she rejoined Gaby.

'Let's just say it's lucky she's not a bit older,' Jill said as they watched Fern talk to Harry. 'Ava might have some competition.'

'Oh, I don't think so,' Maxine said. 'I think the stars lined up Harry and Ava long before anyone else was thought of. I can't imagine how it took them so long to get together when they're so perfect for each other.'

'That's what we've always said,' Jill agreed.

Elijah followed his sister to where Harry and Ava were talking to Fern. Ava glanced across and gave them a wave. Gaby was glad for it; seeing Ava today had been one of the things she'd worried about without really understanding why. Her little sister had been different with her since the yacht incident, even though she'd reassured Gaby that she was over it, and though she couldn't put her finger on what it was exactly, the disconnect made her sad. But today, Ava seemed a lot more like her old self.

'Have you seen Betty yet?' Maxine asked Jill.

'Betty?' Jill frowned slightly before a huge smile spread across her face. 'She's here?'

'Maxine!' Gaby smiled. 'What happened to Betty's surprise?'

'Oh, stuff that!' Maxine grinned. 'Jill might have walked up and down this promenade twenty times today and not seen her; there are so many folks here. Now she knows to look out for her.'

'Hmmm,' Gaby said. 'Well I ought to go and make sure all the food people are here.'

'I saw Trevithick's setting up a minute ago,' Jill said.

'Brilliant.' Gaby nodded. 'I'll go and say hello to Sandy. It was really sweet of him to donate his profits from today, so I ought to make a fuss of him.'

'I expect Harry had something to do with that too,' Maxine said. 'Though Sandy is a darling and I'm sure he would have offered in any case.'

'Cormac's not opening the shack today?' Gaby asked Jill.

'Later,' Jill said. 'He thought it was more important to be here, and it's too much for Clara by herself.'

'She needs to be with William anyway.'

'Exactly.' Jill nodded. 'He's not worried, doesn't think there will be a lot of trade until later on in the afternoon.'

'I'm not sure about that, but I appreciate it,' Gaby said.

'Right then.' Jill surveyed the growing crowds. 'I'd better grab those grandchildren of mine and get collecting!'

Gaby turned to Maxine. 'You wanted me for something when Betty was here…'

Maxine glanced back at the station, where a small crowd was gathering, and then back at Gaby.

'I was going to ask whether we ought to do some sort of loudspeaker announcement to let people know when the station would be open for tours, but I don't think we need to now – everyone seems to be happy to hang around and wait.'

'Looks that way. Well if you don't need me, I'd better get out there and mingle.'

'Thank you,' Maxine said.

Gaby's forehead creased slightly. 'For what?'

'For all this you're doing today.'

'God, it's the least the rest of us can do! You're the ones who put your lives on the line – this is easy in comparison.'

'You say that, but I don't think anyone else would do half the job you're doing.'

'Don't let my mum hear you say that.'

Maxine grinned as she started to walk to the station. 'I won't tell her if you don't!'

. . .

Gaby made an effort to visit every stall and every attraction to thank them for attending and to see if there was anything she could do to make the day better for them. It was important to keep people onside – there would be many more years of fundraising and many more events where she might need them again. She walked past Lloyd's restaurant more than once and noted that although it looked almost ready – the scaffolding outside gone, the terrace newly landscaped and the tables inside dressed with lamps – there was no sign of the owner, or anyone else for that matter. She couldn't tell how she felt about that, but perhaps it was for the best. The missing ten thousand from her donation pot irked her, but him being here would definitely complicate things.

Outside the lifeboat station, the inshore lifeboat was on the sand, and a group of children were poring over it, with Killian and Cormac explaining all the bits and what they used it for. Meredith strolled over, obvious pride in her expression as she watched her dad in action.

Gaby was reminded that she'd been used to that kind of pride over the years, and perhaps she'd taken it for granted sometimes. Her dad had been a hero, as were Killian and Ava, and perhaps she didn't recognise it often enough. But watching Meredith now, seeing the wonder and the awe, she tried to imagine what it might be like to witness it for the first time. She couldn't exactly recall the moment she'd first seen her dad in his uniform and recognised what it meant, or the first time she'd seen him run to the station or stand on the deck of the boat as it sped out to sea – she'd seen it so often, many of her memories of the shouts she'd witnessed were tangled up with one another. And, like her, Elijah and Fern had grown up knowing only that their father went out to sea to save lives and it was as much a part of their family routine as homework or baths. What would she give to be Meredith now, to see it all for the first time, to be in the midst of a crowd hanging on the crew's every word and know that her dad was one of them?

Killian looked up for a moment and spotted Meredith, and she beamed as he called her out of the onlookers and used her to demonstrate putting on a lifejacket.

As Gaby watched with a faint smile, she heard her name spoken and turned to see Lloyd behind her.

'What's all this then?' he asked, his usual mocking tone very much in evidence.

'This is our fundraising day,' Gaby replied coldly. 'You know, the one you were meant to donate to.'

'Ah—' he began, but she cut him off.

'Not to be rude... actually, yes, I do mean to be rude – but are you here for anything in particular or have you just come to pour scorn on another of our village events?'

'No, I... Can we talk?'

Gaby folded her arms and glared at him. 'Go ahead. What is it this time? Come to promise more money you're never going to give to me? Or will you bypass the bullshit this time and just go straight for wrecking my marriage?'

'I realise I'm probably not your favourite person right now—'

'However did you get that impression? Was it something I said?'

'I just want to talk. Can we go somewhere more private?'

'Like your yacht?'

'Like the restaurant. It's empty right now so we won't be disturbed.'

'Oh, goody. Do I need to bring pepper spray?'

He shook his head with a rueful smile. 'You really do remind me of my ex.'

'And the compliments keep coming...'

'Please. It won't take long.'

'Five minutes,' Gaby said. 'I'm too busy today for your crap.'

'Five minutes is all I need.'

Gaby followed him up the steps to the terrace, hoping nobody would notice but certain somebody would. If there was gossip she'd have to deal with it – she was becoming quite an expert at that these days.

Lloyd unlocked the doors while Gaby scanned the crowds below, her gaze settling on the throng of children still gathered around the inshore lifeboat. Killian seemed engrossed in his task – at least that was something.

'We're in,' Lloyd said, and Gaby crossed the threshold, from blazing sun to instant cool shade. The interior of the restaurant had changed beyond recognition. What had been chintzy and comforting was now sharp and sleek, coloured in cool greys and chrome, with exposed pipes running the length of the ceiling and a wider serving hatch to display the shiny new kitchen. Betty's wooden counter was now glass and mirrors, and there were rows and rows of bottles containing various spirits arranged on shelves behind it.

'It looks done in here,' she said.

'Would you like a drink?'

'I don't think that's a good idea.'

'Would you like to sit for a moment then?'

'I'm fine where I am.'

Lloyd took a breath, seeming to be struggling with something. 'I owe you an apology,' he said finally.

'Wow...' Gaby fixed him with a cynical look. 'I get the feeling you don't do that very often.'

He gave her a half-smile. 'I don't, so enjoy it. I don't expect there'll be another one.'

'I'm sure. What's the apology actually for? Not that I don't appreciate it, but I'd like to know – is this a general all-purpose apology that I can apply to any of the shitty things you've done since you got here, or was it for something specific that you feel particularly bad about?'

'You don't make it easy, do you?'

'Why would I?'

'OK, you might have a point there.'

'So your apology means an end to all this stupidity?'

'What stupidity would that be? I said I was sorry, but I never said I was stupid.'

'Trying to sleep with me was pretty stupid.'

'Was it?'

Gaby's forehead creased into a deep frown.

'OK,' he said. 'I know a lost cause when I see one.'

'So no more of that? You know, it's quite insulting, and I think I ought to tell you that. It shows you don't have any respect for me, and if you're like that with all women then I can see why your wife left you.'

'Ouch...'

'Sorry, but you need to hear it.'

'Perhaps I do. But in truth... while we're being so honest, I'm starting to feel that what I wanted from you was perhaps a symptom of something, rather than the cure I'd hoped it would be.'

'A symptom of what?'

He gave a vague shrug. 'Perhaps Helen – my ex – hurt me more than I cared to admit. Actually, I know she did and I don't know why I'm pretending otherwise – at least to you. She did hurt me, and I think you can see that. She crushed me, and you were...'

'Yes, I know, I remind you of her. So I was what? A way to get revenge? If you hurt me, it might feel as if you'd hurt her?'

The irony wasn't lost on Gaby that in many ways, her flirtation with Lloyd was exactly the same – she'd done it to get back at Killian, and she understood that now. And she'd caused far more damage than Lloyd would ever have done, and she understood that too.

'Not so much that. But I suppose I might feel as if I had some agency after all. Of course, you're not her, and the cold light of day is a good place to see the truth of these things.'

'It is,' Gaby said. 'Well I'm sure this wasn't easy for you, so thank you. I appreciate your honesty. And I think, for the first time, you are actually being honest with me, aren't you?'

'You think I might live to regret it?'

Gaby shook her head. 'I think it might make life a bit easier for you from now on. And you don't need to worry – nobody will hear any of this from me.'

He dug into his pocket and pulled out a wallet. 'I also wanted to give you this.'

Gaby took the cheque from him.

'It was wrong of me to promise what I wasn't prepared to give,' he said. 'And I know you really need it.'

'The station does.' Gaby looked at the cheque. It was all there, the whole ten thousand pounds. For the first time in what felt like forever, a genuine smile pulled at her lips. Despite how she felt about him and what had happened between them, there was no denying that this money made her very happy. 'I don't know what to say.'

'I'm sorry it took so long. Despite appearances, ten thousand isn't so easy to just give away – at least it seemed so after a heated debate with my accountant.'

'I'm glad you won the argument. They'll be thrilled at the station – this will make a massive difference.'

'Even your husband?'

'Killian's not stupid. In fact, he's annoyingly practical – he'll have no problem separating what this means to the service from what happened...'

'Between us?'

'Nothing happened between us, did it?' Gaby said very deliberately.

He shrugged. 'But I felt like there was a connection. I didn't dream that – I've been honest with you, so I think it's fair you're honest with me.'

'Perhaps there was, but I don't think it came from a genuine place for either of us.'

'You're probably right. But it was fun while it lasted.'

'I'm afraid I'd have to disagree with you there.'

'Really?'

Gaby couldn't help but grin now. 'I should go; there's so much to do and I'm not going to get any of it done standing in here.'

'Of course. Don't let me keep you – I just wanted to give you that.'

She paused. Her next sentence might make things worse, but she decided to throw caution to the wind. Perhaps this apology and the donation had earned him that much. 'Will you come down and join in? If it's not beneath you, of course...'

'It's not, but I don't think so.'

'Well if you change your mind, you'll find we're a forgiving bunch. You'd be welcomed.'

'I'm not sure I believe you, but thanks. Perhaps another time – I have things to do in here.'

Gaby nodded. 'When do you open?'

'Next week, I hope.'

'Right, so I suppose there must be plenty to do. Good luck with it.'

He gave a brief, wan smile, and Gaby took that as her cue to leave.

The transition from cool shade to bright sunlight hit Gaby as soon as she stepped outside the restaurant, as did the noise and bustle and sense of anticipation. She looked at the cheque in her hand before slipping it into her shoulder bag. That was one development she hadn't seen coming today. But she'd done it. With this money and what she'd collect from today's event, surely she must smash her target, as she'd hoped. It felt like a good day's work, however fraught the path to it had been.

A single glance back showed her Lloyd locking the restaurant doors and pulling down the blinds. It saddened her to see him shutting out the world after what he'd just told her, but perhaps he was right about staying out of the way. Gaby believed the community of Port Promise was a welcoming and forgiving one – despite their love of gossip – but perhaps Lloyd had gone a step too far. Whatever had been eating him, it had caused him – and many others – to behave badly, and it felt like a lot of damage had been done; maybe too much to fix. She'd noticed a new distance – not just between her and Killian but between her and Ava, and so, by default, Harry too. Jill had tried to ignore that there was any tension, and poor Clara had clearly been horribly torn.

When she got back to the donation point outside the station, Killian had finished his demonstration and was waiting for her there.

'Where's Meredith?' Gaby asked.

'Gone to get ice cream,' Killian said tersely. He angled his head at the restaurant. 'What did he want?'

Gaby showed him the cheque.

'And what did you do to earn that?' Killian asked.

'If you're going to be childish about it—'

'I'm sorry – that was out of order.' Killian did look sorry, and Gaby's annoyance softened. 'But you have to understand, I can't...' He glanced around and lowered his voice. 'The thought of you and him...'

'I've told you a million times,' Gaby said. 'Nothing happened.'

'I know. I just have a hard time believing it.'

'You do realise how insulting that is to me? What is it with you two? I'm not a toy to be squabbled over by two nursery kids! I'm your wife; you should trust me when I tell you nothing happened.'

'I want to... I wish I could, but...'

'Go away, Killian! I can't deal with this right now.'

'I can't; I need to know once and for all.'

Gaby looked at him. She felt anger but also a desperate sadness. This was what they'd come to? After all they'd been through together, this was their end? She didn't want to believe it, but she didn't see what else she could believe. 'If this is about keeping secrets, then you've kept them too.'

'It's not the same.'

'I think it is. If we're talking about trust here, then I don't think there's any difference.' Gaby glanced around. The beach and promenade were packed with visitors. 'I really don't think this is the time.'

'I know that. Do you think I'd be asking this now if I felt it could wait?'

'OK, so let's talk,' she said. 'But not here. It's quieter down the far end of the beach.'

Gaby couldn't have known how their talk would end. Divorce wasn't even in her mind at this point. She couldn't have foreseen that in less than ten minutes her marriage would be over, and another twenty minutes after that, the man she was supposed to be divorcing and yet still loved desperately would be called out to a rescue, and that rescue would end in disaster. A shock, the kind of shock nobody could even begin to imagine, was about to hit Port Promise, and if Gaby had known, she would have chosen her words on the beach far more carefully.

CHAPTER TWENTY

Less than half an hour after the explosion, not even an hour since an argument with Killian that had ended with talk of divorce, Gaby was staring at the pillar of thick black smoke on the horizon, still spewing from the site at sea where the stricken boat and the lifeboat were entangled. Killian was on there, maybe even fighting for his life, thinking that she didn't love him. What if he didn't come back? What if that was the last conversation they had? What if her final words to him were to ask for a divorce? She pushed those unbearable thoughts aside – she couldn't dwell on any of that now when there was so much else going on. She had others to think of, people here who needed her too, and she had to keep it together for them.

The emergency services had acted quickly, and now there were two helicopters circling the bay, while another boat sped towards the stricken cargo vessel and the Port Promise lifeboat. Gaby thought she could see flames coming from one of them – or perhaps even both. It was hard to tell from this distance.

There was a faint murmur from the nearby crowd, people being shoved out of the way, and Meredith burst through and ran over to them. She was tearful, though she held it back as she looked for reassurance that Gaby just couldn't give. They were still so new to each other – any of the townspeople would have offered a hug to anyone, but it felt like nobody had worked out yet how to act around Killian's oldest daughter.

'What's happened?' Meredith panted. 'What was that? Did the lifeboat blow up? Was Dad on it?'

'I don't think it's the lifeboat,' Gaby said, but her face betrayed the lack of conviction in her words. Who was she kidding? There was every chance the lifeboat could be the vessel on fire. In vain, she peered into the distance again to see if she could make out what was happening, but it was too far to distinguish. What she wouldn't give for some binoculars, though she was too paralysed by shock to think further than that.

'What are those other boats?' Meredith asked. 'What about the helicopters? Will they get everyone out?'

'Looks like at least one navy boat,' Marina said.

The packed beach was eerily silent as everyone stared out to sea.

'What's that mean?' Meredith asked. She'd never been through this kind of situation before and there was probably so much she didn't understand about the way it worked. But then, neither had Gaby. She'd watched dozens of rescues in her time, maybe even hundreds, and yet this was on a whole different level. She could barely process her thunderous thoughts, let alone explain or reassure anyone else.

'There's another lifeboat coming too,' Clara added, her voice thick with unshed tears as she rocked a sleeping William in her arms, almost as if it were a nervous tic.

'Probably the Perthalenny one,' Gaby said in a dull tone. She was on autopilot, her arms around her children as they stood at each side of her. Fern was sobbing and Elijah was staring straight ahead, clearly wanting to cry but not allowing himself to.

'I can't bear it.' Jill's voice was both full of fear and resentful. 'I can't lose anyone else to that blasted service!'

'I'm sure it'll be fine,' Marina said, though her tone didn't match her words. Then she glanced up and seemed to be the only person able to recognise Meredith's distress. She did what Gaby had been unable to: she moved closer and put an arm around her shoulder. But there was no way even that would make Meredith feel better. Marina could say it would be fine, but at this moment, nobody could possibly think anything would be fine.

'Could we go and find out what's happening?' Clara asked.

Gaby shook her head slightly. 'Ordinarily I'd say yes, but I don't know this time... I'd rather they concentrate on getting everyone back safely than telling me what's going on.'

'I don't care,' Jill said. 'I can't just stand here waiting—'

'Mum, no.' Gaby reached out to pull her back. 'I think this time we have to wait.'

Marina pulled Meredith closer. 'She's right. Let's give the professionals time and space to do their jobs.'

'If that's a military boat,' Gaby said, craning to see better what was going on at sea, 'then what does that mean?'

'My money's on an unexploded mine or bomb,' Marina said.

'A bomb?' Meredith cried.

Gaby turned to Marina with a look of disbelief. Trust her to go for the most dramatic option – not to mention the most pessimistic. 'In Port Promise?'

'Why not? During the war they got everywhere. And we know for certain there are wrecks out there – both ships and planes. It only takes one of them to still have something aboard.'

Gaby shook her head. 'It doesn't make any sense. They'd be hundreds of feet down. And the shout was for a vessel that was stuck.'

'Well perhaps the anchor was caught up on a wreck. And when they tried to pull it free...'

'Mum!' Elijah looked close to losing it now. 'Has Dad been blown up by a bomb?'

'No,' Gaby said. 'He's fine.'

'Is Dad dead?' Fern sobbed.

'No!' Gaby said more firmly.

'So there wasn't a bomb?' Meredith asked.

'No... I don't know...' Gaby looked hopelessly out to sea again. That black smoke kept on billowing into the sky and it was hard to make out what was going on. An unexploded bomb? Could that really be it?

Gaby refused to believe it. Things like that simply didn't happen in places like Port Promise. And as far as she'd always been told, their village had been largely peaceful, even during the tumult of the Second World War. Sure, everyone knew there were wrecks further out – hobbyist diving clubs travelled from miles away to come and explore them – but they were in much further and deeper waters. Weren't they?

'No,' Gaby decided. 'If it was a bomb they'd be moving us all off the beach.'

'Not if they don't have the resources,' Marina said. 'Port Promise is off the beaten track – it would take a while to get people to us for an operation like that. Perhaps they're concentrating on what's going on at sea for now.'

Meredith started to cry. Gaby was full of pity but still too shocked herself to do anything about it. And so she was filled with a detached kind of shame to see Fern do what she couldn't – reach out and wrap her arms around the older girl's torso and pull her close.

'Dad will be all right,' Elijah said firmly, with all the conviction of a boy who will one day be a strong and confident man. 'He's brilliant.'

Fern twisted to look up at Gaby. 'He will, won't he, Mum? And the others? They'll be all right, won't they?'

'Yes,' Gaby said automatically, but as her gaze went back to the smoke pouring into an azure sky, she wished she could actually believe it.

As the time ticked by and the rescue operation continued, rumours started to work through the crowds. People were saying the same thing as Marina – that an unexploded bomb had gone off. Gaby still found it hard to believe, yet she had no explanation that made more sense. Part of her didn't care what had happened – she only cared that the crew was going to come back safely to them once it was all over. The one thing she could see now was that the Port Promise lifeboat was still afloat. At least that was something. If it had taken the full force of the blast then surely it would have sunk quickly. But that still didn't tell her about any casualties there might be. They watched as the helicopters winched some people away from the scene, but there was no way to tell who they'd taken.

Nobody moved from the beach – it was as if they didn't dare to. Everyone stood or sat on the sand and watched the drama out to sea, and everything was silent – the music of the carousel had ceased, the crowds were quiet and even the donkeys that had been tramping the beach seemed to have forgotten how to make a noise. Gaby felt as if everyone – local or visitor – was with her, praying and hoping with her that everyone would come back safely. In the midst of her anguish she was aware of a wall of solidarity like none she'd ever experienced before, and it filled her with a fortitude that she couldn't have mustered alone. She glanced up towards the restaurant and could see Lloyd standing at the window watching too. He caught her eye, gave her the briefest nod, and then his gaze went back out to sea.

The silence was suddenly pierced by the sound of Gaby's phone alerting her to a new message. She took it out of her bag and saw Clara and Jill reaching for theirs too. It was from Shari at the station and had been sent to all three of them.

All accounted for.

Jill burst into tears as she read the message, while Clara let out a breath and staggered back against the wall so violently that Marina leaped forward, perhaps fearful she might have to catch baby William falling from Clara's arms. Gaby didn't know how to feel, but she forced a smile for the children.

'Dad's OK,' she said.

While they all looked delighted, Gaby couldn't allow herself to relax. All accounted for could mean a lot of things. Nobody was dead – she was certain Shari wouldn't have sent such a message otherwise – but that didn't mean nobody was injured. It meant the fate of the crew was probably known to Shari, but it meant no such comfort for them, and if she'd sought to reassure them, it hadn't given much in the way of reassurance to Gaby. She wouldn't be happy until she'd seen them all for herself, safe and well.

While Jill sobbed with relief, it seemed Marina understood Gaby's reluctance to celebrate just yet. While Marina often seemed silly and carefree, that wasn't really the case. Sometimes there were flashes of common sense, even astuteness, and so Gaby wasn't surprised to see her sceptical look as she took Jill's phone and read the message.

'The Perthalenny lifeboat's leaving,' Clara said.

Gaby looked out to sea. The neighbouring town's lifeboat was speeding away from the operation. It set a course towards the headland of Promise Rocks and then disappeared from view behind it.

'Does that mean they're done?' Jill asked. 'Does that mean ours is coming back in?'

They watched, but the other lifeboat stayed where it was, alongside the stranded vessel and the military boat.

Gaby looked at her phone. 'Come on, Kill... just bloody text me; I can't stand this!'

'He can't—' Jill began.

'I know!' Gaby snapped. 'Sorry...' she added quickly. 'I know he can't; I know he's still out there, but I can't stand all this waiting. I just want to know what's going on.'

'But they're all right.'

'Are they? *All accounted for*, Mum. That doesn't mean all unharmed. Sorry,' Gaby apologised a second time as she noticed Clara's fresh look of alarm. 'But we have to be realistic here. You saw that explosion—'

'Why would you say that?' Clara asked. 'Why do you have to be so negative? Can't we have some hope?'

'We do have hope. I'm just saying—'

'Well don't!' Clara cried. 'Don't *just say*! They'll be all right – they have to be!'

'So they're not all right?' Meredith asked, her eyes wide and fearful again.

'Let's just wait,' Marina said. 'If the Perthalenny lifeboat has gone back then it must mean they're not needed now and the worst is passed.'

'Or there's another shout at their station and they're needed there,' Gaby said. 'End of the holiday season – they'll be as busy as we are keeping the visitors safe.'

'We don't know that,' Marina insisted. 'We don't know anything, so let's stop jumping to conclusions. All we can do is wait for news and try to stay positive.'

'Oh God...' Gaby nodded at a man racing down the hill towards the station.

'Sandy!' she called. 'Sandy!'

Harry's dad stopped and turned around. 'Do you know anything?' he asked, coming over to them. 'I was just going to see if—'

'All accounted for,' Marina said, repeating the text message sent to them. 'Didn't Shari message you?'

'Ruddy phone's broken; haven't got it with me.'

Sandy was agitated and breathless, and Marina gave him a patient smile. 'Watch yourself, Sandy. Don't forget your heart. Breathe, calm down – you're no good to Harry having a heart attack here while you wait for him.'

'Wait with us,' Gaby said. 'We've just seen the Perthalenny lifeboat go back, so we think there might be more news soon.'

'Isn't that Vas?' Clara asked, pointing to someone walking towards the inshore lifeboat. The bigger all-weather was still out at the scene of the explosion, but it looked as if they'd finally been given permission by the coastguard to take the other boat over. Perhaps the all-weather boat was damaged and out of action, so the smaller boat was going to its aid. Everything was guesswork at this point, and it frustrated Gaby not knowing exactly what was going on.

Within minutes the smaller boat had launched and was speeding towards the scene of the explosion. By now the smoke pouring into the sky seemed to be less than it had been at the start, but Gaby couldn't be sure of that either.

They watched, barely blinking, until Gaby felt as if her eyes would burn from staring so hard at the boats and the black smoke rising into the clear sky and the helicopter, which had now returned and was hovering above the scene. And then the helicopter winched another person up and flew them away. There was no way to tell whether it was a crew member from the cargo vessel or the lifeboat.

'Who's that they've just taken?' Sandy asked. 'Can someone text Harry for me?'

'I doubt he'll be able to answer,' Gaby said. 'If there was any very bad news, Shari would have told us when she sent us that message.'

'Would she?' Clara asked. 'She'd hardly give us the worst over a text.'

'Then she wouldn't have texted at all,' Gaby said. 'She said they were all accounted for.'

'And you said that didn't mean they were all safe...' Clara said, her voice rising to something like hysterical.

'Clara...' Jill stroked her arm. 'You're no good to William like this. I know it's hard but we all have to be calm and positive.'

'That's not what you said before!' Clara replied tearfully.

'I know, but—'

'The boat's coming back!' Fern yelped.

The inshore boat had turned and was heading back towards the station. Gaby wondered who was on it. The all-weather was still out at sea and wasn't showing any signs of moving, so perhaps it had been damaged in the blast after all. Gaby could have screamed in frustration. But she needed to keep it under control – if not for her own sake, then for everyone who was with her. If she lost it, who would help her mum and Clara through this terrifying time?

The smaller boat drew closer and eventually landed just beyond the beach to be hauled the rest of the way by the tractor. Maxine or Shari would be driving that, and so perhaps they'd get another status update soon. There were definitely more people on the boat coming back than there had been going, but from here Gaby couldn't tell who they were.

'Should we go down?' Clara asked.

Gaby shook her head. 'They'll need to clean down, so we won't be able to talk to them yet.'

'But we'll be able to see who's just come back,' Clara said. 'It definitely wasn't everyone...'

'I know,' Gaby said tersely. 'And I know we're all desperate to see our own back on dry land but I don't think it's helpful to go down there and—'

'Jesus, Gaby!' Clara snapped. 'How are you always so cold? Aren't you scared? Don't you want to know who's come back in?'

'I'm not cold!' Gaby said with as much patience as she could muster – which wasn't much, and her tone showed it.

'Girls,' Jill cut in. 'Clara, your sister is being practical. We can't just barge in there – that's not how it works and you know it.'

'I just want to know…' Clara sniffed back fresh tears as she cradled William a little closer.

'We all do.' Marina rubbed a hand across Clara's back and gave her a reassuring smile. 'And we'll know soon enough. I'm sure they're all fine – like Gaby said, Shari wouldn't have messaged us at all if there was bad news.'

Gaby had said it, sure, but she wished she believed it herself. Would Shari have told them if something bad had happened? Or not told them anything? Or would she have told a little white lie, just to give them hope, to keep them all calm while they waited?

Clara looked as doubtful as Gaby felt. While she allowed Marina to soothe her, Gaby could see in her body language that she was itching to rush to the station to see who'd come back in on the boat. The entire crew hadn't come back in with Vas as far as Gaby could tell. So who wasn't back and where were they? Were they still working on the rescue? Or had the casualties winched up to the helicopters included one of their own?

'There!' Elijah suddenly yelped and pointed. Before Gaby could issue a warning, he and Fern were both running down to the station. Gaby glanced at the others, and then they all took a collective, unspoken decision to follow.

Harry and Ava came out. They both looked exhausted and grim-faced, but were holding hands and appeared unharmed.

'My boy!' Sandy threw himself at Harry, and Jill did the same with Ava. Then Clara and Gaby took their turns to express their relief, but almost as soon as she'd let go, Clara cast around with new fear in her eyes.

'Cormac? Where's Cormac?'

'Don't worry,' Harry said, 'Vas is patching him up. The Perthalenny guys wanted to take him to the hospital to get checked over, but you know Cormac – said he'd had enough of hospitals and wouldn't go. If Vas thinks he needs to go, you might need to persuade him.'

Clara gave a small nod. 'Should I go in now?'

'I'd give it a minute,' Ava said. But then she sent a worried glance Gaby's way. 'The helicopter took Killian.'

Gaby felt her legs go from under her. She reached out and Marina caught her beneath the elbow. She'd spent so long trying to be strong and brave, but the effort was finally catching up with her.

'What's...?' she asked, her mouth dry.

'He took a direct hit from some shrapnel in the blast.'

'Oh my God!' Meredith cried.

'But I think...' Harry hesitated and glanced at Ava.

'He wasn't caught in the actual blast,' Ava said. 'Just got in the way of some of the debris.'

'Well...' The sky was spinning above Gaby as she tried to grab words from her numb brain. 'Is he... is he OK?'

'We're not sure. There was a lot of blood but... well, you know Killian; he's made of sterner stuff. He'll be at the hospital by now and I would imagine they're looking at him, so perhaps you'll hear soon.'

Gaby looked at her mum. It felt as if she wasn't driving her own body right now, as if someone else had taken over and she was watching from the sidelines. 'I have to go to him.'

Jill nodded. 'Go. I can look after things here – of course you need to be with him.'

Fern grabbed Gaby's hand. 'Can we come?'

Jill gently pulled her away. 'It's better if you stay here with me. I'm going to need your help anyway – who's going to look after all the stalls when your mum has gone?'

'But—'

'No,' Jill said, more firmly this time. 'Your mum needs to focus on your dad.'

'But I want to see—'

'Can I go?' Meredith asked.

Jill put a hand on her arm. 'I know this must be scary, but I think it's better if you wait here too. I doubt you'd be able to see him even if you did go to the hospital with Gaby.'

'The minute I have news I'll text,' Gaby said.

'But—' Meredith began, but Jill took her to one side and started to talk to her in soothing tones.

Gaby didn't wait to hear any more. She started to run for home, where she'd left her car that morning, a growing knot of fear in her stomach. She couldn't lose Killian, not now, not without telling him that she hadn't meant any of the things she'd said to him on the beach before the shout, not before she'd said sorry, not before she'd told him that she loved him desperately and would do until her last breath, no matter what life threw at their marriage, no matter where the path took them. It was now, with that fear stark and bare, that she finally saw it. She loved Killian more than she had words for, and she knew that they had always been destined for a shared life, and it didn't matter who had come before and what legacy they had left, nothing would ever change that.

There were crowds in her way, and she struggled to push through, and even as the frustration grew at her lack of progress, she heard, above the din of low, concerned conversation, her name being called.

'Gaby!'

She halted and turned to see Harry waving her back. He was pointing at a jeep that had just pulled up on the promenade. Gaby didn't recognise the car or the driver, but then she saw Killian getting out of the passenger side.

'Killian!' she breathed.

She raced back, but Elijah and Fern got there first,

Meredith in their wake. Killian winced as they all threw themselves at him. He cried out, and all three stepped back looking worried.

'Gently,' he said with a tired smile.

His face was smudged in soot and there were layers of tiny cuts across one cheek, his arm was strapped up and he appeared to be struggling for breath. Gaby's stomach lurched at the sight. But she threw her arms around him, even though he'd just told the children it caused him pain. She didn't care and he'd have to deal with it, because she'd never needed to feel him close like she did right now.

'I thought I'd lost you!' she said, her voice low and fierce in his ear as she fought back tears.

'You don't get rid of me that easily,' he said in a weary tone.

'What happened?'

'I got a bit blown up.'

'I can see that...' Gaby pulled away to look at him, still unable to shake the fear that things were worse than he'd have her believe. She was afraid that at any moment, despite him standing tall before her, he'd collapse in her arms, that she might yet lose him. 'It looks bad...' She put a gentle finger to his cheek and traced one of the cuts.

'It looks worse than it is,' he said, but then coughed so violently that Gaby knew he was lying.

'You should be in the hospital – why did they let you go?'

'It's only a bit of smoke in my lungs – nothing the sea air won't clear.'

'Doesn't seem like only a bit to me.'

'I'm fine, Gab.'

'You're not!'

He caught one of her tears on his thumb. 'I am. You don't need to fuss. Honestly... anyone would think you liked me.'

'You stupid sod! I thought you were dead!' She slapped him so hard on his arm that he cried out.

'I'm sorry,' he said, looking slightly bemused.

'You should be! What the hell happened out there? Why were you called out to something so dangerous? Why didn't the navy—?'

'We didn't know it was going to be that dangerous at first,' Harry cut in. 'Ship's anchor was stuck – that was all. Nobody could have known what it was stuck on, and by then it was too late.'

'Marina knew!' Gaby said. 'Marina knew straight away!'

Harry shrugged.

'It's not like we asked to go and play around with an unexploded bomb,' Ava said. 'Do you think we'd have gone out if we'd known what we were dealing with? We'd have waited for the military.'

'No you wouldn't,' Gaby said. 'There was a casualty and you all know damn well you'd have gone out, so don't give me that!'

As she caught sight of Killian, he was smiling faintly.

'And what's so funny?' Gaby slapped him again. 'That we were all scared half to death?'

'It's not funny,' he said, his smile fading now. 'It's just... I can't help being glad.'

'You're glad I was scared?'

'Glad because a bit of it was for me.' He lowered his voice. 'I thought...'

She threw her arms around him again. 'I never meant any of that,' she whispered. 'I could never be without you – you know that.'

'Do I?'

'God yes!'

He kissed her gently. 'I'm sorry for being such a dick. I just got so... The thought of you leaving me was...'

'Shut up,' she said, taking her turn to kiss him now.

He winced as she buried her head in his shoulder before encircling her with his good arm.

'I love you, Killian. Whatever we go through, that will never change. Whatever has been said, that much was always true.'

'I love you too,' he whispered, holding her closer.

She looked up at him, and the words were out before she could stop them, even though she knew that to speak them would be futile. 'Then prove it. Leave the lifeboats.'

His smile became a vague frown. 'You know I can't do that.'

'Why not?'

'Are you seriously asking me that?'

She shook her head, her eyes misting again. 'I don't suppose I am. At least promise me you won't scare me half to death again like you did today.'

'In fairness, I can't really promise you that either. But I can promise we'll talk more. I know I've shut you out, and I realise it's caused so many of our recent problems. I don't want to lose you.'

Gaby held him tight again. She was probably causing him considerable pain, but considering the fear she'd been in all afternoon and his refusal to leave the lifeboats for a life of safety, she figured he deserved it. And besides, she loved him so completely that she couldn't let go. She loved him despite his stubborn loyalty to his crewmates and the lifeboat service, his refusal to show weakness, his refusal to back away from danger, the way he stuck to his guns when he thought he was right and all the other things that she both admired and yet got incredibly frustrated by. He made her angrier than any other man she'd ever met, and yet she was consumed by her love for him in a way that she could never even begin to comprehend, let alone explain to someone else. Their relationship was often messy, confusing and infuriating, and yet it was also beautiful. In her eyes, no man – save her father – had ever lived up to him, and she was certain no man ever would. Killian made her a worse person as often as he made her better, but she knew that a life without him was barely worth imagining.

While Gaby had been saving her marriage, it seemed people on the beach had started to notice that some of the crew were back on shore. And when Cormac came out to join them, his cuts cleaned up, a round of applause began. It rippled politely out at first, but grew and grew until the entire beach was clapping and cheering so loudly it echoed around the bay.

Harry clung to Ava's hand, both of them looking embarrassed, while Sandy looked on with pride, and Clara beamed at Cormac's side as she cradled baby William. Elijah and Fern looked as if they might burst with excitement while Meredith openly wept, and Gaby held on to Killian as if she might never let him go.

Jill was clapping too. She smiled at Gaby through her tears. 'Your dad would have been so proud of the crew today.'

'He would,' Gaby said. And though she was relieved and happy beyond measure to have everyone she loved back safely from the sea this time, she was struck by a sudden note of melancholy. Her dad would have been proud, she was sure of that, but they'd never hear it from his lips.

CHAPTER TWENTY-ONE

Over the following autumn and winter, things in Port Promise had been thankfully quiet. Perhaps not that quiet, but since it involved no more unexploded bombs or threats to her marriage, Gaby would take it.

As Killian came in from the shower, towelling his hair, spring was in evidence beyond the bedroom window. Gaby could hear the chirrups of baby birds nesting in a nearby tree as she opened the window to let a breeze in.

'I don't know why we need to have all this fuss.' Killian dropped his towel to the bed, and Gaby frowned as she picked it up and tossed it into the laundry basket.

'It's not a fuss. You've earned today – just shut up and enjoy it.'

'I can't enjoy it – you know I hate stuff like this.'

'Then try to pretend to enjoy it for everyone else's sake. Clara's so excited I swear she'll go into early labour.'

'Clara can go and pick up my award for me then.'

Gaby threw a comb at him. 'Shut up and brush your hair. You're picking this medal up and that's that. If you don't want it, I do; I'm going to put it up in the living room.'

'You can have it for all I care.'

'I've bloody well earned it. Married to you, I ought to have a lifetime achievement award, let alone a bravery medal.'

'I'll mention it to the higher-ups. Someone might have some liquid paper – they can put your name on the certificate instead. For services rendered to the lifeboats by putting up with their crew members.'

'For bravery in the face of extreme sock washing...'

Killian grinned. 'Something like that,' he said, crossing the bedroom to catch her in his arms. 'I can think of a few other services that might call for extreme bravery...'

'Oh yeah? Come to think of it, me too.'

'How about we blow off this whole awards thing and you show me one of those services right now?'

'You're not getting out of it that easily.' Gaby laughed, but was soon left breathless by a passionate kiss. 'No, really...' she said as he pulled away, and he held her in a gaze so intense she felt she might combust. 'I know you have a good success rate, but that's not going to work on me this time. Besides, the kids are excited to see you get your medal – you wouldn't deprive them, surely?'

'I suppose not,' he said, letting her go. 'But it was worth a try, wasn't it?'

'Try again later – you might have more luck.'

'I'm going to hold you to that,' he said, going to the wardrobe. Gaby gave his bare torso a once-over. His broad chest was still damp from his shower, a towel tied so low on his toned waist there was very little left to imagine. Even the scar now at his shoulder from the day of the explosion was strangely sexy on him this morning.

'I'm counting on it,' she said in a tone that barely hid her lust.

Their marriage hadn't magically fixed itself, even after that terrible day the previous summer where Gaby had feared him dead, but they'd both worked at it, and that was the difference. They'd both recognised their own faults, both acknowledged that they had to toil together to save it and, in doing so, had found new joy in the effort. It was almost as if the act of pulling together to save it had brought them closer in a way they could never have been before. While it had been easy they'd both taken what they'd had for granted – now they both recognised what they had and they both wanted it to last.

'I'm glad Meredith could come,' Gaby said.

He turned and smiled at her. 'I knew she'd win you over eventually.'

'All right, I'll admit she's sweet. Nicer than you – must be Vicky's influence.'

'Must be.' Killian's smile turned into a broad grin. 'It's a shame she can't stay for long, though.'

'We can pop up to Bristol if you'd like. Maybe next week, if we can get the time.'

'Let's play it by ear... but thanks. I know this hasn't been easy for you and it means a lot to me that you're trying.'

'Mum!' Fern's voice came from down the landing. 'Mum! Eli says he's going to get a milkshake!'

'Not in that suit he's not!' Gaby yelled back, exchanging an exasperated grin with Killian.

'I think you might have more pressing matters than checking to see I get dressed,' he said.

'I think I might – though I do quite enjoy watching you get dressed and I'm quite aggrieved that I won't be able to on this occasion.'

He laughed. 'I love it when you talk all properly. I might let you watch me get undressed later if you give me a bit more.'

'You'll have to wait,' she said, going to the bedroom door. 'Now stop trying to put this thing off and get ready.'

. . .

At many other stations, award ceremonies were low-key affairs, mostly involving crew and families. But this was Port Promise and there would be no such half measures here. Marina and Jill had led the way, insisting that it would take place outside, in full view of any villager who wanted to attend, and that there would be seating and speeches and decorations, followed by celebrations. It wasn't every day their crew received bravery commendations, and everyone wanted to be a part of the occasion. It held a special significance for Jill too, because her husband Jack had received one posthumously for his actions the night he'd been lost at sea, and that time had been one of a great bittersweet sadness. This time, she could enjoy the moment and give thanks, knowing that the people she loved had all made it back safe and victorious. Thanks to their courage and skill (and some heaven-sent luck) not a single person had been lost the day the bomb had gone off in the bay. Nobody wanted to think about how close things had come to ending in a different way.

Chairs were arranged in rows on the promenade overlooking the station. There was more space here than inside and Vas had said he was expecting a good turnout. The forecast had been kind too, and why not make the most of the spring sun as it gently warmed the cobbles and sparkled on white-tipped waves as they rolled onto the beach? Though it was early in the season, there were still enough curious visitors to give the event an unofficial audience too, but onlookers were something the lifeboat station of Port Promise was used to by now. In fact, Harry and Ava had expressed the notion that it was a good thing, even though sometimes they got in the way. It meant that people were interested in what they did, and if watching them inspired one young person to join up then that had to be a good thing for the future of the service.

Today was a little different, however. While people watching them launch was one thing, the crew seemed less keen on being the main attraction for this event. It was all a little bit mortifying for every one of them; they simply loved doing their job and had never looked for praise.

Gaby joined Clara, Jill and Harry's parents on a row of seats at the front, while Elijah and Fern sat across the makeshift aisle next to Meredith and Vas's husband, prodding and goading each other, as they had been all morning. But it would take more than their misbehaving to put Gaby in a bad mood today. She sent a warning glare their way, but as she turned back to Clara her face instantly transformed into a smile.

'You look really well today; better than when I last saw you.'

Clara was bouncing a red-cheeked William on her knee. Her second pregnancy was just beginning to show beneath her floral dress. 'Hopefully I'm over the worst of it,' she said. 'At least I'm keeping my breakfast down now and I've got a bit more energy. I wasn't sick at all with William; I don't know how I've been so ill this time.'

Clara's ex-colleague at the caravan park, Tanika, was sitting behind them, and she leaned in. 'Probably having a girl. Girls are always more trouble – I'm right, aren't I, Gaby?'

'I wasn't sick with any of my girls,' Jill cut in.

Tanika shrugged and sat back.

'All pregnancies are different,' Gaby said.

Clara stroked a hand over her bump. 'It's lucky I didn't have this one first; I might not have wanted to do it again.'

'You had a pretty terrible time with William at the end, as I recall,' Jill said, 'and yet, here you are, doing it again. We're programmed to forget how awful being pregnant is. If we remembered each time, women would stop getting pregnant.'

Clara kissed William on the head as he rammed a fist into his mouth and began to chew on it. 'That's true enough.'

'Oh, Marina and Bob are here!'

Jill waved to the couple as they took a seat behind Elijah and Fern. Meredith offered a shy greeting and then turned back to the front. Though she'd visited Port Promise a handful of times since she'd first come into their lives, she was still more reserved with the other adult residents than she was with Killian and Gaby. Gaby supposed it would take time for her to feel completely comfortable here, but that was one thing they had plenty of. But for all Gaby's initial resentment, Meredith was now a proper member of her family, and she even looked forward to her visits. Meredith was good for Killian and good for Elijah and Fern, and even Ava, Clara and Jill had become fond of her. What would happen should the worst fate befall her mum, nobody could say, but perhaps Gaby wasn't quite so opposed to the idea of her living with them in Port Promise as she'd once been.

Fern immediately swivelled round and began a long chat with Marina. Gaby didn't catch much of it, but she loved that her daughter was still at the age where she was interested in everyone, no matter how much older they were. Elijah was more sullen these days and found everything deeply embarrassing. He'd get over it, but his new attitude made Gaby realise that her little boy was turning into a teenager, and if she blinked for long enough, she'd open her eyes again to find him a man. She looked at Clara's growing bump with a sudden pang of envy. Perhaps it was time to add to their family – one last go before she was past it. Now that her marriage was in a much better place, maybe this was the right time. She allowed herself a little kick of excitement and resolved to put it to Killian later.

As she smiled to herself, she glanced up and noticed Lloyd standing on the terrace of the restaurant, smoking a cigarette as he watched everyone arrive for the ceremony.

'He's still keeping his distance,' Clara said in a low voice, her gaze following Gaby's. 'He knows he doesn't have to, right?'

'I think he just likes it better that way,' Gaby said.

'He's a strange one.'

'He is that. Still, it was nice of him to open up the restaurant to us later.'

'Do you think that means we're thawing him out then?'

'Maybe, though I wouldn't bank on it. At least we're all getting along; I don't think we can ask for more than that.'

Lloyd caught sight of Gaby and gave a nod of recognition. She smiled uncertainly in return. She had many regrets about how she'd handled things with him, but perhaps regrets weren't much good to anyone. How they went forward – that was what really mattered, and she didn't want what had happened to cast a shadow over that either. Lloyd wasn't in Port Promise all that often, but she hoped for a time when he'd drop in and feel at home. Gaby hated the thought of him feeling like an outsider, especially now that she knew of a secret pain he hid so well he'd made himself almost unlovable.

'He's probably thinking about all the money he'll make out of us later,' Tanika said from behind them.

Gaby turned to her. 'You do know he's not charging anything?'

'He's not?' Tanika frowned.

'No, he's putting on food as a thank you to the lifeboat volunteers.'

'Oh. Well nobody told me that. Maybe I'll swing by later after all. Still...' Tanika sniffed as she looked at Clara. 'I expect he's doing it because he feels guilty about putting Cormac's fish shack out of business.'

'He hasn't exactly done that,' Clara said with a patience Gaby couldn't help but admire – it was certainly more than she'd have with Tanika, who'd always struck Gaby as someone determined to see the worst in everyone. 'It was Cormac's choice to reopen as a grill and he's more than happy with the move. To be honest, on busy beach days there's far more call for his chargrilled chicken wraps than there ever was for crab salad, so if anything it's turned out to be a good move.'

'Well you always were a glass-half-full girl, weren't you?' Tanika said.

'It's not like that at all,' Clara said. 'They were never really in competition anyway – totally different clientele.'

'You're not still thinking you might work for him when your maternity leave is finished?' Tanika asked.

Clara shrugged. 'Right now I'm not ruling anything out. I'm concentrating on getting through this pregnancy and William cutting these pesky teeth so he'll stop slobbering over absolutely everything.' Just to make her point, she wiped a line of dribble from her dress.

'There's no rush, right?' Gaby said. 'You've got all the time in the world to figure out what you want to do next, and at least you have Cormac, who is way more supportive than...'

Gaby stopped short of mentioning Logan, but Tanika did it for her.

'Oh, how is little Lord Fauntleroy?' she asked. 'Have you heard from him?'

'He's good,' Clara said in a carefully neutral tone. 'He's actually due to visit soon.'

'That's something to look forward to,' Tanika said in a tone dripping with sarcasm.

'Sandy...' Gaby called to Harry's dad in a bid to change the subject. 'Still set on retiring?'

'I am,' Sandy said. 'Harry thinks it will be retirement in name only, but I've told him, the business will be his to run as he sees fit and I won't interfere.'

Harry's mum, Cynthia, gave a sceptical look that made everyone laugh. It was good to see her out – she was naturally shy and didn't do socialising very often.

'I might offer advice every now and again,' Sandy said sheepishly. 'But it will be Harry's business once I hand it over. It's time I slowed down – even I can see that. Besides, Harry needs to build his future now – I've had my time; it's his turn. And we can't wait to have Ava move into the new house he's building next to the brewery. She's been so good for Harry – and we love her like she's our own.'

'Here's Robin with his boys,' Jill said, angling her head at the new arrival. Robin took a seat across the aisle and nodded to acknowledge them.

'Looking as cheery as always,' Tanika said.

'It's his way – nothing wrong with it,' Jill returned, the barest edge of haughtiness to her voice. 'We can't all be the life and soul of the party, and poor Robin's suffered more than most.'

'Not more than you,' Tanika said, undeterred by Jill's tone. 'After all, if it wasn't for him, your Jack—'

'Oh, look!' Clara said with more animation than was necessary. 'The higher-ups have arrived!'

'Looks like we'll be starting any moment then,' Gaby said, throwing Tanika a look she hoped would communicate that she ought to shut up. Today wasn't a day for dredging up old heartache or portioning blame. Today was a day for celebration and recognition of the very best and bravest of them, and Gaby was damned if she was going to let Tanika's thoughtless comments ruin it.

Over the next few minutes the rest of the seats filled up. Almost everyone was there – even Nigel from Salty's, who rarely turned up to anything because he simply didn't want to have to close his fish and chip shop. Gaby glanced up towards the restaurant terrace to see that Lloyd was still watching from his vantage point. She tried to signal to him that he ought to come and join them on the seating, but as he didn't move, she wasn't sure if he'd understood her intention or not.

But there was no time to worry about it, because the crew started to file out from the station and make their way up to the seating area. Fern let out a little squeal of excitement and began to wave madly. Gaby would have assumed it was for Killian, but knowing Fern's soft spot, it might well have been for Harry. Elijah watched with obvious awe in his expression, and at that very moment, Gaby knew for sure she'd lost the fight over whether he'd one day volunteer for the crew himself. Jill started to cry as she smiled with intense love and pride in Ava's direction, while Clara wiped away her own tears – not only for her sister but for Cormac too. Gaby's heart was so full for Killian she felt it might burst. While she'd often shown her disapproval of his choice to risk his life week after week, and sometimes she'd been downright resentful, she couldn't deny that he was an amazing man who gave the very best of himself to others, and she loved him for it.

As they arrived on the promenade, the assembled crowd stood to give them an ovation. Every one of the crew looked partly pleased and partly mortified at the attention, and all smiled awkwardly as the applause continued for a good minute.

After a brief speech by one of the higher-ups, every member of the crew who'd been on duty the day of the explosion was awarded a certificate and sincere thanks, and then it was all over, so quickly Gaby wondered if it had really happened at all.

As everyone poured to the front to catch them all and offer congratulations and pats on the back, Killian looked across the crowd and caught Gaby's eye with a smile so full of love she was afraid she barely deserved it. But she felt it too. In fact, as her gaze travelled the faces of Port Promise's heroes, she felt so much love for them all her heart could barely contain it.

Marina handed out glasses of champagne and everyone shared a toast, before those who weren't staying for the food at Lloyd's restaurant began to move away.

Elijah went to look at Killian's medal. 'Wow...' he breathed.

'Pretty cool, huh?' Killian smiled.

Elijah nodded. 'I hope I get one when I join up.'

'I don't,' Gaby said. 'It means you had to do something terrifying first.'

Killian laughed. 'I certainly hope you don't get blown up

when you join the boats. On that your mum and I definitely agree.'

'Let me see yours,' Fern said to Ava, who was coming over to say hello after chatting to Harry's parents.

Ava held out her medal.

'It's the same as Dad's,' Fern said, examining it. 'Meredith...' she called her half-sister over. 'Come and see...'

'I think so.' Ava nodded as Meredith joined them, and Ava held it up to her. 'Though I think your dad should have got a way shinier one than this – he did more than I did to deserve it.'

'I disagree,' Killian said. 'For my annoying little sister-in-law, you didn't do half bad out there.'

Ava laughed. 'Thanks.'

'Lloyd's opening his doors.' Clara held Cormac's hand as they joined them. 'Ready to go for food?'

Killian shot Gaby a glance edged with the merest doubt. She could understand why. Even though she'd reassured him hundreds of times since the yacht incident, it was hard for him to accept that Lloyd posed no threat – and that was all Gaby's fault. They were both working hard on their marriage, but she recognised she had extra to do to regain his trust.

'He wants to be friends,' Gaby said. 'He's making an effort, so the least we can do is have the grace to accept.'

'I know.' Killian reached for her hand. 'Forget it – I'm being an idiot.'

'No you're not.' She lowered her voice. 'And, remember, we're meant to be talking. If something is bothering you, talk to me. I can't do anything to help if I don't know about it.'

'It's just...' He took her in his arms and brushed her hair behind her ears. 'When I see him, it reminds me of how close I came to losing you. My own stupid fault, but still... Gab... nothing in my life, not the lifeboat service, not my job or anything else, none of it means anything without you. If I didn't have you I'd—'

'You wouldn't,' she said, kissing him tenderly. 'And even if that were true, you don't have to worry. I'm not going anywhere.'

'I'd like to go and see your father's plaque before we eat,' Jill said. 'If nobody minds.'

'Me too,' Ava replied.

Everyone nodded agreement and they began to walk the path to the harbour, where the small bronze plaque commemorating Jack Morrow's life was set into the wall.

Jill buffed it with her sleeve as they all looked at it together – the Morrows and the people they loved best in the world.

'He was an incredible man,' Killian said.

'He had an incredible family too,' Cormac added. 'I wish I could have met him. I'd have liked him for sure.'

'Me too,' Meredith said. 'I mean, I know he's not really my grandad, but I think he would have been cool.'

'He'd have loved you,' Clara said, looking at Cormac and then Meredith. 'He'd have loved both of you.'

'Wasn't so keen on me at first,' Killian said with a chuckle.

'You certainly tested him.' Jill shot Killian a wry smile, but there was great affection in it, despite their ups and downs.

'I hope he would have been proud of us all,' Ava said.

'Of course he would.' Harry smiled down at her. 'Especially you.'

'You think?'

'Are you kidding? Look at what you've achieved!'

'I know I am,' Jill said. 'So I know your dad would have been too.'

They spent a few moments more in silent contemplation, with the sounds of the sea and children playing on the beach as their accompaniment and the sun warming their backs.

'Are we going to get some food?' Clara asked finally. 'Lloyd will think we're not coming.'

'Oh, right.' Gaby laughed. 'That's the reason you want to get up there, is it? Nothing to do with you being hungry?'

'I *am* eating for two,' Clara replied with mock affront.

'That's right. So that bit's the same as your first pregnancy. I seem to recall you eating for two that time as well.'

'I have hungry babies, OK?'

Cormac wrapped an arm around her and pulled her close. They made such a perfect couple, Gaby could barely imagine Clara without him now, and yet her sister had come so close to a very different life. And there was Ava, standing side by side with Harry, both of them in their uniforms – how different things might have been there too.

As they all began to walk back to Lloyd's restaurant to continue their celebrations, passing through the village where the curve of beach was bathed in golden light, the distant cliffs were speckled in yellow broom, where crooked streets of coloured houses crowded together like old gossiping friends, where the harbour was full of boats bobbing on a millpond sea, Gaby took a moment to count her blessings. There had been turmoil and heartache enough to last a thousand years, but, together, they'd come through it.

She turned her gaze to the steps that led to the restaurant. It seemed so long since it had been Betty's cafe, and yet, at the same time, it felt like yesterday.

Jill, Marina and Bob were the first up, followed by Harry, Ava and Harry's parents. Then Clara and Cormac with baby William and another on the way. And lastly, Gaby, with Killian's hand wrapped around hers and Elijah and Fern and Meredith ahead. She looked up at him, her brave, principled, sometimes stubborn and frustrating husband. They'd had good times and they'd had very bad times, but for his love, she'd take the worst of times, no matter how many she had to face. For his love, for her remarkable family, for the slice of heaven that was life in Port Promise, she could face anything.

A LETTER FROM TILLY

I want to say a huge thank you for choosing to read *A Secret for the Lifeboat Sisters*. If you did enjoy it, and want to keep up to date with all my latest releases, just sign up at the following link. Your email address will never be shared and you can unsubscribe at any time.

www.bookouture.com/tilly-tennant

I'm so excited to share this book with you. I can't stress enough how writing it gave me new insight into how incredible the RNLI is and how lucky we are to have it.

I hope you enjoyed *A Secret for the Lifeboat Sisters,* and if you did I would be very grateful if you could write a review. I'd love to hear what you think, and it makes such a difference helping new readers to discover one of my books for the first time.

I love hearing from my readers – you can get in touch on my Facebook page, through Twitter, Goodreads or my website.

Thank you!

Tilly

KEEP IN TOUCH WITH TILLY

https://tillytennant.com

 facebook.com/TillyTennant
twitter.com/TillyTenWriter

ACKNOWLEDGEMENTS

I say this every time I come to write acknowledgements for a new book, but it's true: the list of people who have offered help and encouragement on my writing journey so far really is endless and it would take a novel in itself to mention them all. I'd try to list everyone here regardless, but I know that I'd fail miserably and miss out someone who is really very important. I just want to say that my heartfelt gratitude goes out to each and every one of you, whose involvement, whether small or large, has been invaluable and appreciated more than I can express.

When the idea to write about a family serving on the lifeboats was first discussed with my editor, I admit that I knew very little about the RNLI. I'd seen the stations of course, during holidays up and down the coast, and being from Dorset, I knew there was a training centre there which I've driven past many times. I'd donated on occasion too, stuffing a few pounds into a bucket, like many of us, but that was the extent of my involvement.

But then I started to write this series and everything changed. I began to talk to people who volunteered in the service; I watched videos and read accounts of real-life rescues, and through that research I began to understand what truly unique and incredible people those who serve are. They are selfless, unflinching, dedicated, brave and generous. Most answer 'the shout' whether it's day or night, summer or winter, during Christmas lunches or family weddings, whatever they're doing, in all kinds of weathers and sea conditions. There is no question and no complaint – they just run for the station. Almost all do it without pay or reward, juggling their commitment to the lifeboats with other jobs and their family lives. And yet, they venture out where most of us would turn and run. I can't think of any other organisation quite like it. There is no funding for the service other than charitable donations, and yet, somehow, they keep going.

I'd like to thank the RNLI for their help in writing this book. In particular, the folks at Lytham St Annes, Poole and Aldeburgh. And a very special thanks goes out to Caron Hill at Aldeburgh lifeboat station, who gave so generously of her time and patiently answered all my questions (so many of them!) about life in the service.

If you would like to donate to keep this vital service going, you can go to www.rnli.org and do so there. Not only can you donate, but you can also find out more about what they do and just how important it is.

I also want to mention the many good friends I have made and since kept at Staffordshire University. It's been ten years since I graduated with a degree in English and creative writing, but hardly a day goes by when I don't think fondly of my time there.

Nowadays, I have to thank the remarkable team at Bookouture for their continued support, patience and amazing publishing flair, particularly Lydia Vassar-Smith – my incredible and long-suffering editor – Kim Nash, Noelle Holten, Sarah Hardy, Peta Nightingale and Jessie Botterill. I know I'll have forgotten others at Bookouture who I ought to be thanking, but I hope they'll forgive me. Their belief, able assistance and encouragement mean the world to me. I truly believe I have the best team an author could ask for.

My friend, Kath Hickton, always gets an honourable

mention for putting up with me since primary school, and Louise Coquio deserves a medal for getting me through university and suffering me ever since; likewise her lovely family. I also have to thank Mel Sherratt, who is as generous with her time and advice as she is talented, someone who is always there to cheer on her fellow authors. She did so much to help me in the early days of my career that I don't think I'll ever be able to thank her as much as she deserves.

My fellow Bookouture authors are all incredible, of course, unfailing and generous in their support of colleagues – life would be a lot duller without the gang! I'd also like to give a special shout out to Jaimie Admans, who is not only a brilliant author but is a brilliant friend.

I have to thank all the incredible and dedicated book bloggers (there are so many of you, but you know who you are!) and readers, and anyone else who has championed my work, reviewed it, shared it or simply told me that they liked it. Every one of those actions is priceless and you are all very special people. Some of you I am even proud to call friends now – and I'm looking at you in particular, Kerry Ann Parsons and Steph Lawrence!

Last but not least, I'd like to give a special mention to my lovely agent Hannah Todd and the incredible team at the Madeleine Milburn Literary, TV & Film Agency, especially Madeleine herself, Liv Maidment and Rachel Yeoh, who always have my back.

I have to admit I have a love-hate relationship with my writing. It can be frustrating at times, isolating and thankless, but at the same time I feel like the luckiest woman alive to be doing what I do, and I can't imagine earning my living any other way. It also goes without saying that my family and friends understand better than anyone how much I need space to write and they love me enough to enable it, even when it puts them out. I have no words to express fully how grateful and blessed that makes me feel.

And before I go, thank you, dear reader. Without you, I wouldn't be writing this, and you have no idea how happy it makes me that I am.

Printed in Great Britain
by Amazon